Blackgang 1835

KEITH DYER

Blackgang 1835

G2 rights ltd

G2 rights ltd

Blackgang 1835
Copyright © Keith Dyer 2012

First edition published in the UK in August 2012
© G2 Rights Limited 2012
www.G2rights.co.uk

Print Edition ISBN : 978-1-909040-62-5

G2 Rights Ltd, Unit 9 Whiffens Farm, Clement Street, Hextable, Kent, BR8 7PG

This book is dedicated to my wife Jane, and to Georgia, Steven, Tim and Fran, together my pride and joy.

Also it is dedicated to my brother Peter, the memory of my parents, and a marvellous childhood on the Island.

AUTHOR'S NOTE

This book is based on fact. The main events actually happened, but here they are put in the context of the lives of local personalities and situations, without changing the timing of their sequence. All of the named people existed, but I have had to imbue them with life and characters they might not have had.

There is no record of John Wheeler being a smuggler. However, there is a strong likelihood, given his occupation as a fisherman, and the time, that he would have been. He certainly was a local hero for his rescues from shipwrecks. There is no record of his father being jailed. As there are so many Wheelers in the area, their relationships are not clear. Additionally, there is no record of Frances being related to Andrew Gothen, who was the vicar of Chale. These are inventions to embellish the story.

Lieutenants Josiah Dornford and John Bulley were well known Coastguard Chief Officers, and their heroic exploits are locally notorious. I have not been able to obtain the original records of the Court of Inquiry, but have adapted the account by A.G. Cole in his book 'Yarmouth, Isle of Wight', as well as contemporary newspaper reports. There are discrepancies between these sources which I have used writer's licence to resolve. I am grateful to the Curatorial Officer of the Naval

Historical Branch (Iain Mackenzie) regarding the procedures for Courts of Inquiry, and for bringing to my attention the anonymous letters to the Naval and Military Gazette regarding the difficulties with the Revenue Service.

For the wreck of the Clarendon I have used the books by F. Mew 'Back of the Wight', and J.C. Medland 'Shipwrecks of the Wight', as well as contemporary newspaper reports, enlivened by my own memories of wrecks on the Back of the Wight.

I have also borrowed several smuggling yarns from the book 'Back of the Wight', as they are appropriate to the date of this story.

Additionally, I am grateful to Dr. Steven Smith for carrying out research in the National Archives, and a number of other people for tit-bits of useful information. However, any errors or misunderstandings remain my fault.

SOURCES

George Brannon, Views of the Isle of Wight. 1824.
Republished 1972. EP Publishing Ltd, Wakefield.

A.G. Cole, Yarmouth Isle of Wight. Some records of an ancient town.
1951. IOW County Press.

J.C. Cox, County Churches, Isle of Wight. 1911. George Allen, London.

R.F.W. Dowling, Smuggling on Wight Island. 1978. Grosvenor Press. Shanklin.

Tony Gale, Coastguards of the Isle of Wight 1809-present. 2005.
Coach House Publications Ltd. Freshwater.

Anthony Heckstall-Smith, Sacred Cowes, or cream of yachting society.
1955. Allan Wingate, London.

R.J. Hutchings. Smugglers of the Isle of Wight. 1972. G.G. Saunders Ltd, Shanklin.

R.J. Hutchings (Ed). Isle of Wight Dictionary. 1984. IOW County Press.

J.C. Medland. Shipwrecks of the Wight. 1986. West Island Printers, Freshwater.

F. Mew, Back of the Wight. 1965. IOW County Press.

M.W. Norman. 1887. Geological Guide to the Isle of Wight. Knight. Ventnor.

Rev. E. Venables. The Isle of Wight. 1860. Edward Stanford. London.

Ian Williams. Monumental Folies of the Isle of Wight. 2008.
Rockpool Publications, Sandown.

Christopher J. Willis and Edward H. Roberts. 1986.
The Lifeboats of Brighstone Bay. IOW County Press.

Chale Church records.

Hampshire Telegraph and Sussex Chronicle.

Isle of Wight County Press.

Times Archives.

Various websites, including: Ancestry.co.uk and www.members.lycos.co.uk/s0uthbury/

Blackgang Chine

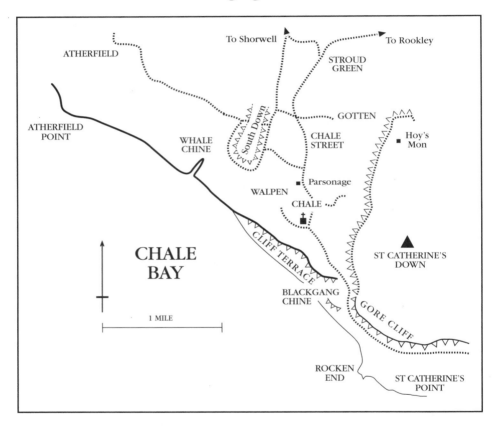

Chapter 1

John Wheeler was an Islander, a fisherman and a smuggler. He was an Islander because he was born and brought up on the Isle of Wight, just like his father and grandfather before him. He was a fisherman, because his father, his uncles and his cousins were all part of a fishing tradition. He was a smuggler because it was the only way of ensuring his family had enough to live on. John was one of a long line of smugglers. Normally, having to compete with the weather and sea as a fisherman was a big enough challenge, without the extra problem of trying to outwit the Revenue. But hunger is a powerful stimulus for lawbreaking, and times were often hard on the Isle of Wight. For many people living near the coast it was their only way of obtaining a living in the winter when fishing was poor, when there were no crops on the land, and no other source of employment.

Smuggling must have gone on for centuries; certainly John Wheeler can remember his grandfather telling exciting tales from his exploits in the late 1700s. When the duties imposed on imported goods are too high; on goods that might be essential, such as corn, or just desirable, such as spirits, then evasion will be rife. In the nineteenth century excise duty was the main way the government raised money; it provided much more than taxes on wealth or income. Whereas income tax affected only the rich, excise duty hit the poorer relatively harder. Therein lies the iniquity, particularly for the poorer people like John; what they paid saved the wealthy from having to become poor. Smuggling of spirits, and items such as tobacco and lace, which had high value, were the easiest for the poorer people to carry, provided they had the wealthy to invest the finance.

It has been reliably estimated that one way or another eight out of ten Islanders took part in smuggling in the nineteenth century. This reveals the extent of hypocrisy and calumny. Many a parson would be preaching from the pulpit on a Sunday about sin and retribution, and then go home and enjoy a glass of smuggled brandy after his dinner, knowing full well how it was obtained. It is also quite possible that he might have provided the initial finance, and stood to gain most from its success. Even the judge who sentenced smugglers to jail, or worse, may have financed the smuggling runs on which they were caught. Quite probably smuggling provided the gold for Napoleon to prolong his wars, thereby desolating the whole of Europe. Considering the intensity of the regular, illegal traffic across the Channel, that conjecture is quite plausible.

John had just heard of a run of contraband cargo carried out in the East Wight that had been intercepted by the Coastguard. They had been tipped off by an informer, who would have claimed a large reward for betraying his friends. The smugglers involved, some of whom John knew fairly well, and had worked with at one time or another, had been arrested, and tried at the assizes in Winchester. Some had been fined, and others, who had offended before on the same charges, were jailed. But it was only occasionally that a tip-off from an informer led to arrests. Those who did inform were ostracised by the community, had a hard time making a living, and ended up having to move away. Much more often false information was purposely fed to the Coastguard, but this can only have been done occasionally to distract them away from the real location of the main activity.

John turned the story over in his mind, as he trudged to his mother's cottage, wondering how long it would be before he too was caught, to languish in jail alongside his father. Earlier in the year his father, confusingly also named John, but commonly known as Jack, had been arrested with a tub of brandy, part of a consignment he and a gang had landed at Whale Chine. There was no evidence that an informer was involved that time, though there were suspicions. The rest of the gang had dropped their tubs and escaped. But John's father had been arraigned before a very unsympathetic magistrate at Newport. Normally possession of smuggled spirits would have attracted a fine, or a period in the bridewell at Newport, but he was sent to the assizes at Winchester, because he had refused to implicate any of the rest of the gang. There the judge had been equally unsympathetic, and he had been sentenced to a year in Winchester jail; he had strong principles, one of which was he wouldn't betray his friends. He had served some months of the sentence already, and was due to be released the following April. Because of the distance, neither John, his mother, nor his brother had been able to visit him; for an active fisherman the confinement must have been terrible. They had to rely on letters to keep his spirits up, and the two younger men had to comfort and provide for their mother, Hannah, in her loneliness. She had still not fully recovered from the shock, and had aged noticeably over the weeks. So at every opportunity they would call in, do necessary jobs, cheer her up, and keep her company.

It had been blowing a near gale most of that Friday morning in October 1835. That's why John was glad to have returned during the night from fishing, having read in the sky the signs of the approaching storm. He had woken late to find his wife, Frances, had taken their two girls out, to give him some peace and quiet. Once he had risen and taken a quick breakfast he decided to pay his mother an unexpected visit. Leaving a scribbled note on the table he left the cottage and walked the few hundred yards through Chale village, past the inviting prospect of the White Mouse Inn, and turned right at the church along the muddy lane towards Walpen Farm. His little terrier, Brandy, trotted happily by his side, occasionally pausing to root in the hedges, or scampering on his short legs around the deeper puddles. The lane followed parallel to the cliff, but being set back by about half a mile from it meant there was some protection from the worst of the south-westerly wind. Nevertheless, it was still very windy, with heavy, rain-filled gusts frequently buffeting them. So John kept his collar turned up and his head down most of the time, with his hands in his pockets turning over the sixpence that he aimed to give his mother. Once, looking up, he saw Robert Draper, a labourer at the farm, who was clearing ditches, a sack over his shoulders as some protection from the elements. John waved, and thought that he didn't envy him his poorly paid, solitary hardship.

Beyond the farm the track led on round the end of South Down, a remarkable, elongated hill with steep sides and a sharp summit, resembling an upturned boat, set broadside on to the wind. On the windy western side of the hill, tucked close into the foot of the slope was a line of small cottages, together known as Under South Down. Here lived his mother, his twin brother Robert with his family, and several other people, including one of the reviled Coastguards. Each cottage, set in its own small garden, was made of the local greensand stone, generally covered with ivy, and roughly thatched with straw off the fields, or reed from the marshes. Because of the wind, the windows were tiny and the roofs had weighted ropes over them to help keep the thatch on. Even so, the local thatcher had to make frequent visits to repair the ravages of winter storms and busy, nesting sparrows. A line of stunted trees on the other side of the track gave some protection from the wind, but one of the things that John remembered best from his childhood was the almost incessant moaning of the wind round the house and the rattling of the shutters. As it was only a couple of hundred yards to Whale Chine, the nearby access to the beach was of much greater importance for men whose livelihood was fishing.

Only a few yards further brought him to the front door of his mother's cottage, where he had been born and brought up. He paused to look at the garden in its autumn dilapidation, thinking he would have to come and wield a spade at it soon. But he needed to shake himself out of his mournful mood, as he knew his mother would need cheering up, even though she had solace from frequent visits and unstinting help from the comrades his father had protected in court. Despite the wind, a robin sang merrily from somewhere in the trees opposite, lightening his mood somewhat. John was struck by the thought that it might be a descendant of those that used to nest in the ivy beneath his bedroom window when he was young.

Unconsciously he took off his cap before he knocked twice and walked in, ducking his head beneath the low lintel. Hannah Wheeler came out of the kitchen, her heels clicking on the stone flags. She wiped her hands on a cloth, and met him in the narrow hallway. As she only came up to his shoulder, he had to bend down while she put her arms round him, squeezed him and kissed him on the cheek, her eyes shining with delight. She was in middle age, little, but neat and perky like the sparrows in the roof. As usual, she was dressed in a black skirt that reached almost to the floor, a check pinafore, and a white blouse with a cream lace jabot. Black laced ankle boots peeped from beneath her skirt as she moved. She smelt of lavender and camphor. The aroma of fresh bread came from the kitchen behind her, making John's mouth water, as he was again hungry and hadn't yet had any lunch. He anticipated a customary offering of fresh bread, cheese and an onion.

'Come in John, my lad. It's so good to see you. And hullo, Brandy,' Hannah said, stooping down to fondle his ears. 'I was half expecting you. Frances said yesterday it was likely you'd be home today from your last fishing trip. Sit you down. I expect you will be hungry, as usual.' She always spoilt him, right from when he was very young.

'You're looking very well, Ma,' he answered, thinking how

she never seemed to change, always the same, never aging; though he was forced to admit that she had slowed down considerably, and gained many more grey hairs and wrinkles since his father had been in jail. But he was glad that Frances had called in, as she frequently did, despite the distance and the difficulty of coping with the girls. His mother needed help to survive until Father returned, so it was lucky that Robert lived just up the row; he called in every day, and John did whenever he could.

'I could do with a snack, now you come to say it,' John said thankfully. Brandy settled down on the scrap rug in front of the range, his head on his paws, but eyes watching every move. John took off his jacket and sat in one of the old, wooden upright chairs at the table, its top scrubbed and white. Both chair and table had been made by his father from timbers recovered from one of the numerous shipwrecks, perhaps it was even the *Carn Brae Castle*, wrecked half a dozen years before.

An old blackened timber, now seasoned by the sea and the heat to be as hard as iron, had been set into the chimney breast as a beam above the fireplace. The old cast iron kitchen range was well alight, glowing and radiating welcome warmth; Ma took great pride in blacking it every week. It made the kitchen and most of the rest of the small house warm and snug, despite the wind moaning in the chimney. Rough wooden shelves on either side carried the everyday crockery, chipped and stained – much of which came from wrecks; each had its story. Copper pans, beaten from the anti-fouling cladding of an East Indiaman, hung on the wall, glowing with reflected light, sending bright lights around the room to contrast with the colours of the old floral wallpaper. The small window looking out to the west was steamed up and gave only a poor light into the room. From there you couldn't see the sea, but on a good day the view was for many miles across the Back of the Wight to the downs. John knew well that his mother, whenever she had the time, would sit knitting in the old chair with the broken arm, thinking over her memories, anticipating her husband's return, and watching the shadows of the clouds chase each other across the landscape.

'Here you are then, lad.' She always called John lad, or my lad, even though he was fully grown, tall, broad and strong, and in his late twenties. His twin brother, Robert, was always called boy, an appropriate distinction for the younger one. She put a large platter with the anticipated victuals in front of him. 'Now tell me all the news.' Frances must have already told her all the new things the girls were able to do, as they were developing quickly, but she would relish hearing it again. 'Have you any news from your father?' She knew that fishermen had a long chain of contacts which passed information very quickly.

'No, Ma. I have heard nothing since last time.' The last time was the week before when a man from Yarmouth, who had been to visit his son, also in prison for smuggling, had brought back a message saying that his father was well, but suffering from inactivity, and the monotonous diet of potatoes, bread and watery soup.

John cut a wedge of cheese and put it onto a chunk of the soft, warm bread. He was just about to take a mouthful when he heard a shout outside. 'Ship in the Bay! Ship in the Bay!'

This was the universal warning of a sailing ship being stuck on the lee shore with the possibility of being driven aground and wrecked. It was the call for all able-bodied men to assemble in case assistance was needed to rescue the unfortunates.

'Please excuse me, Ma. If there is a ship in the offing I must go and see whether there is anything that I can do.'

'It's alright, I understand John,' she said, clasping her hands to her chest. 'Your father is just the same, always ready to help; and your grandfather was too, in his day. Go and do what you can, but make sure you come in and tell me about it later. I might even come out and take a look myself, providing the rain holds off.'

'Do you mind if I borrow Father's spyglass, so that I can see better what is happening?'

'Of course you may. He would be pleased it is still being used. Just be sure you bring it back.'

He put his reefer jacket back on, put the glass in a pocket and took the bread and cheese in his hand to eat as he went along. Brandy jumped up with his stump of a tail wagging furiously, ready as always for further exercise and excitement. After giving Hannah a quick kiss on the cheek, they left the house and turned towards the sea. It was about half a mile to the cliff, and every step took them further from the shelter of the other houses, the walls, hedges and trees. John munched on the bread and cheese, and the gnawing feeling in his stomach immediately lessened to be replaced by one of anticipation, of the excitement and possible risks to come.

The wind felt stronger now even though they could not yet see the sea. The noise of the wind increased as it thrashed round the trees and through the hedges, stripping off the dead leaves and whirling them away. Several other men were walking quickly along in front, their heads down and their shoulders hunched against the wind. They all had oilskins or reefer jackets on, stout leather or rubber boots, and the traditional navy blue caps. John recognised them one-by-one by their familiar gait; being such a small community everyone knew everyone, and everyone was related to almost everyone else too. They turned and acknowledged him when Brandy ran up beside them.

Nearer the cliff the sea was clearly visible. It was very rough, sullen and grey with angry white waves rolling in, their crests blown out by the wind into sheets of spume and spray that ascended the cliffs like a salty fog. The clouds overhead were rushing past, coloured in various shades of dark and lighter grey, and ominous purple, with occasional gaps through which a watery sun appeared, casting patches of brightness onto the tumult.

At the cliff edge the lane ended at the broad footpath worn along the cliff by frequent use. John stopped, with the familiar vista open before him. He had to straddle his legs and lean into the wind to stay upright while he looked along the beach and out to sea. To keep his cap from blowing off he crammed it firmly onto his head, and his trousers thrashed coldly against his legs. With eyes half closed he peered against the chill wind that blew tears across his cheeks. Brandy squatted down behind a tuft of grass awaiting developments.

John knew the coast well, both from land and the sea. It was bleak, and treeless. Stunted trees only grew further back, away from the worst of the wind and spray, but even then they were sculpted by the wind; fresh green shoots in the spring were quickly seared by the salt. The turf was short and yellowed, and few flowers could tolerate the salty moisture. Even in summer there was a bare solitude about the harshness of the landscape. Below them the cliff was about 200 feet high, dropping almost vertically to the shingle of the beach, where a host of seagulls lined up, faces to the wind, waiting to search the stranded flotsam for food.

To the right the deep cleft of Whale Chine cut back into the cliffs for about a quarter of a mile; it was named because of the huge sea creature once washed up there, to the astonishment and awe of both locals and visitors. A path led down the chine to the beach through the steep sided canyon of red and ochre sandstone. The hardest layers had been fretted by the wind and rain into patterns of cavities where the doves and jackdaws nested; a real test for clambering boys trying to collect their eggs. The stream in the bottom of the chine tumbled over fallen blocks and round stunted willow trees to disappear in a pool of rank water at the back of the beach, at present a haven for a flock of gulls. Fishermen used the path which followed the stream to reach their huts and their boats, now pulled well above the high tide line out of the reach of the waves. It was a good landing place in reasonable weather, but when the wind was in the west the waves rolled in to break thunderously with a ship-wrecking roar. That was the time for mending the nets and pots.

Beyond the chine the cliffs curved round to the headland of Atherfield Point, where the local Coastguard lookout stood, and where a line of cottages was being built to house them.

Further west the brown and red cliffs continued for another six miles past Brook and Compton, until the white chalk cliffs appeared towards Freshwater. There the downs that formed the spine of the Island were exposed, reaching out with 400-foot-high cliffs to end at the stacks of the Needles. Normally, the lighthouse overlooking the Needles was visible, constructed at the end of the last century to warn ships of the dangers below. But today it was lost in veils of rain and the drifting haze of spray blowing inland from the sea.

To the left there was a further, smaller chine, Walpen Chine, and a ledge of rocks started near the top of the cliffs, getting wider and lower as it approached Blackgang Chine. This formed Cliff Terrace, patterned with small trees and clumps of bushes, and marshy patches where the water issued from clayey layers in the cliffs above. But there were occasional small cottages and fishermen's huts scattered on the drier areas, most made from wreckage timber, rudimentary but adequate.

Further along, the terrace sloped gradually downwards, but narrowing to end as a thick ledge of hard sandstone over which the stream of Blackgang Chine poured as a waterfall. The cliffs behind increased in height until they towered as a steep irregular slope about 300 feet high, almost devoid of vegetation, being blasted either by salt spray, rain or baking sun. The harder sandstone beds created a succession of small, brown and yellow cliffs, with loosened blocks sliding and tumbling down onto the intervening flatter areas where clayey bands created wet, muddy marshes; the cliffs there were frequently unstable, moving and sliding towards the sea.

At Blackgang Chine the small stream had cut a ravine deep

into the cliffs and the land behind. The small hamlet of Blackgang which had developed at the top of the chine was becoming an attraction for visitors who came to wonder at the majesty and bleakness of nature. As a consequence, the steep zigzag path had been improved to give better access to the beach and the few huts and store-sheds the fishermen had constructed.

Behind Blackgang towered Gore Cliff, another menacing couple of hundred feet of greensand rocks, which the wind and rain had weathered yellow and grey, and etched into a horizontal pile of ledges where the seagulls, doves and falcons nested. Many times, John, as a boy, had risked everything on the bare rock close to the edge at the top of the cliff, searching for flattened snail-like fossil shells which the geologists now came avidly to collect, draw and name as ammonites. Behind Gore Cliff stretched the bleached turf of St. Catherine's Down, eventually reaching up to almost 800 feet high, but often hidden in low clouds.

In the wooded area at the base of Gore Cliff ran a narrow road passing eastwards over the massive landslip that occurred in 1799, when 100 acres of land had fallen from above and slipped into the sea to form Rocken End, the start of the notorious headland of St. Catherine's Point. Beyond the landslip, round the aptly named Windy Corner, was the Undercliff, stretching many miles to the east, and formed from many other past landslips. There, many of the gentry and aristocracy were building summer retreats in the verdant and picturesque wilderness protected from the wind, and blessed by winters made mild by the nearby sea.

It was a magnificent, bleak, awe-inspiring scene, one that John frequently stood to marvel at. The huge bay, generally known as the 'Back of the Wight', stretched about fourteen miles from the cliffs of the Needles to those of St. Catherine's Point, throughout backed by narrow beaches, which were only accessible at a few places, and by steep cliffs. In truth there were three bays, separated by the ledges that reached far seawards from Brook Point and Atherfield Point. The whole coast faced into the prevailing south-westerly wind, forming a dreaded lee shore within which ships could become embayed and wrecked. But it was the two ledges that were the greatest danger, many ships running onto them just when they thought they were clear.

From the sea the whole frightening vista of high and jagged cliffs fringed by the foaming white line of the breaking surf was horrifying, sending shivers of fear through even the most hardened seamen. Ships sailing in the murk with the wind up the Channel, and not knowing their longitude, could run down towards that shore and be confronted by the immense cliffs stretching before them, and find that they couldn't get across the wind in time to clear St. Catherine's Point. Many was the vessel forced to beat backwards and forwards within the bay, unable to make headway against the wind, only to be gradually pushed onto the beach and be lost, the frightened crew and passengers either drowned, or never to be seen again. It was the worst end that a seaman could envisage. Only the lucky few were rescued by the efforts of the local men, or the Coastguard. Once wrecked, the ship would be stripped of every useable item.

Yet in calm weather when the seas broke gently against the shingle, and the sunlight sparkled off the blue sea, it could not have been a better place to gain one's living. John loved those days when it was a joy to be hauling nets or pots, and counting Neptune's bountiful produce into the creels. But those days were not that plentiful, as often their labours were unproductive, despite the balmy conditions, the fish not always being there to be caught.

This day the sea just off where John stood was seething, with waves marching regularly in towards the beach. It was close to low water, and the waves were breaking well out over the reef of Atherfield Ledge. He could see from the movement of the water in the wave troughs that the tide was beginning to flood strongly towards the east. At least the worst of the sea would now diminish, the waves travelling with the current rather than against it. The waves were approaching the beach obliquely, breaking progressively from the far western end towards him, indicating a more westerly direction in the wind driving them, giving hope that the vessel might be able to weather Rocken End.

Nevertheless, the waves must have been at least eight feet high, and were breaking hugely, curling over within yards of the steep shingle of the narrow beach, each crest falling down onto the downwash of the preceding wave with a roar, throwing spray, shingle and foam high into the air. Then, as the wave began surging up the beach, carrying sand and stones with it, the air trapped within the wave burst upwards through the back of the wave throwing up even more spray. The surge of the wave pushed shingle up the beach with a clattering roar, until the water percolated into the stones, and the momentum was lost. As the water started retreating, it left a fringe of dirty, yellow frothy foam behind which the wind immediately picked up and blew further ashore. Then came the backwash, and water flowing back out of the stones combed down the beach, taking the stones back seawards with another clattering, rattling roar. The sound was almost continuous and deafening.

'There she is! Just about in line with the Needles. She must be about two miles off Brook Point.' One of the men to John's right pointed.

John took out the spyglass, and after a little focusing had the ship in view. It was difficult to hold still, the wind constantly buffeting and shaking him. He crouched down to rest a steadying arm on his knee; he could see better that way, but the wind still whistled and drummed in his ears. 'She's a brig,' he called out. 'And she's English, must be about two hundred tons or so.'

Between the squalls he could clearly see the two masts with square rigging. All of the square sails were furled or off the spars, and the fore-and-aft sails were reefed hard. The fore staysail had blown out and the tattered remnants were flapping before the foremast. The gaff-mainsail was tan coloured but bleached almost white by sun and salt, probably a replacement for a damaged better one. She was on the starboard tack and pointing so that John could see obliquely her port bow. The force of the wind heeled her over, and each wave that struck took her almost broadside on, increasing her list and sending sheets of water and spray cascading across her mid-ships. He could see two men at the wheel fighting to keep her pointed as close to the wind as they could. It must have been an exhausting and terrifying job, and they must have been lashed to the wheel to give them purchase in struggling to hold the ship steady. It was just the situation that would lead to broken fingers.

Despite being on dry land John could imagine the heave and lurch of the deck under his feet, and hear the wind roar through the rigging, setting the ropes thrumming and vibrating; the creaking and groaning of the ship's timbers as she flexed and moved with the strain; the pounding roar of the waves, and the crash of the impact as they hit the hull and exploded into sheets of spray; the sharp crack of the sails flapping, and the beat of the spray on the sails. He did not envy them their plight; they would be cursing the wind and the waves, and when not cursing they would be muttering prayers for salvation. Even though she was moving forwards, each wave and gust of the wind forced the ship sideways towards the land almost as fast.

A shaft of sunlight pierced the clouds, briefly turning the watery tumult to a bright, shining pattern of white, silver, and grey. The sunlight raced across the surface faster than the waves were travelling, emphasising their height and the turbulence by the reflections and shadows. It also picked out a few seagulls that were struggling to make headway against the wind, but they finally gave up and turned for the shore.

In the brightness of the sunlight John could pick out through the spyglass several men on the poop deck tied by lifelines to the weather rail, scanning the sails and peering landwards. Behind the patch of sun he could see a gust of wind racing across the waves, whipping even more spray off the surface. The gust hit the ship and it heeled further over, with the lee gunwales underwater. The helmsmen struggled to point the ship further into the wind, gaining an extra few yards upwind before the leach of the foresail started shaking and they had to ease off. The patch of sunlight passed on, racing towards the shore. Though the ship was making headway along the land, it was gradually converging with the shore. It was going to be touch and go whether it cleared the land. John could feel himself becoming tense as he willed the ship on through every gust.

To the west the clouds were darker, ominous with the possibility of further more continuous rain. Several showers were already rapidly approaching, obscuring both the sea and the sky with a continuous grey curtain of falling folds of moving rain. However, this gave John some hope for the ship and its crew, because with rain it was possible that the wind might lessen; it was often true that the worst wind appeared before the rain came, and once the rain started then the wind quieted down.

He judged from the distance the ship was offshore and the set of the tidal currents, that she was much more likely to come ashore east of where he stood, further towards Blackgang. Calling Brandy, he started to walk slowly eastwards along the cliff edge, past the white posts the Coastguard had put in to guide them in their vigil on dark nights. But he kept on looking back over his shoulder to check on the ship's progress.

Along the top of the cliff knots of people were gathering, waiting. If the ship was to come ashore there would be many men rushing to the beach, John included, willing to risk their lives in the surf, trying to help rescue those from the ship. After that, they would become wreckers, collecting all the flotsam and jetsam spewing from the stricken ship as it broke up, and plundering all they could to supplement their meagre livings, or to sell for extra income. Even the ship's timbers, being well seasoned and tar soaked, would eventually be used to repair cottages and houses, or build new sheds or fishermen's huts.

A couple of boys ran past, their hobnailed boots striking sparks on the stones; Schoolmaster Grapes must have let them out from the Charity School to see the excitement, knowing full well that they would never pay attention to his lessons if he kept them in. They were chattering and calling excitedly.

A crowd now lined the cliff top near Blackgang. Not surprisingly they were separated into groups related to their class, or position in society. John naturally moved to join a group that comprised almost exclusively native villagers, to which the schoolboys became loosely attached, though even they kept somewhat apart, out of the reach of their fathers or relations. John immediately became involved in conversation with his friends, though he kept a close eye on proceedings.

Further along there was a group of middle-class owners, those who had come to live in the neighbourhood from the mainland. John could see Jane Newnham of Blackgang House, who was talking to her neighbour Jane Rose, the proprietor of the Blackgang Hotel, and to Caroline Paterson and her husband Captain Charles Paterson of nearby Five Rock Cottage, who styled himself a 'captain of army horse'. They all lived in the hamlet becoming separately known as Blackgang, increasingly nowadays a focus for upper class visitors wanting to marvel at the rural and coastal beauty; sometimes for the sake of their health they were even persuaded to drink the foul tasting water of the nearby Chalybeate spring. Though the visitors were bringing welcome money into the poor villages, they were gradually changing the pace of life and the moral outlook of the local people, who were often upset by the visitors' sarcastic and patronising superiority, and their loose religious attitudes.

The word had spread and several pony traps and chases had brought visitors along the lane from Chale to Cliff Terrace to view the excitement. Some were locally hired and some obviously privately owned and driven by servants. A few of the richly clothed men had descended and walked out to the cliff edge, holding their top hats firmly on their heads against the wind, their thick coats flapping behind them, and leaning against their canes to brace themselves. If the ladies had ventured forth, it was only briefly, as they were easily deterred by the wind that swept their crinolines round their legs and threatened to blow them over; they would watch from the safety of their cabs, which even so rocked alarmingly in the wind.

Further along from them, John could see the Coastguard Chief Officer, Lieutenant Josiah Dornford R.N., seated on his favourite grey mare. His officer's cap was pulled firmly on his head, his beard stuck stubbornly into the wind, and the brass buttons shone brightly on his serge uniform jacket. He was alone, being someone the villagers tended to avoid, because his job was to try to prevent smuggling and the looting of wrecks. As almost the whole population were involved in one way or another with smuggling and wrecking, the local people were wary of him and his snooping and spying. Nevertheless, despite his gruff manner he was friendly enough, and seemed to enjoy the games of hide-and-seek that went on between his men and the Islanders. Though it hadn't been widely discussed, John was very aware of the general feeling that he was more on the Islanders' side than on the government's. In particular, he was highly respected because of his bravery in rescuing the crew and passengers from the *Carn Brae Castle* when it was wrecked on Brook Ledge half a dozen years before. There were always rumours that he might have been in league with some of the smugglers at one time, but John had never heard any firm information to support that contention.

John was surprised to see him as he was in charge of the Coastguard at Freshwater Gate Station, about ten miles away, though he was well known for always travelling widely. He had come far outside his normal territory, across that of Lieutenant William Gould, now the Chief Officer at Brook, and into that of Lieutenant John Bulley, at Atherfield Station, who had responsibility for the Chale and Blackgang section of coast. Perhaps he wasn't on duty, but just out for a good ride. On the other hand, he may have been given some inspecting duties at the request of his superior, as he was very experienced, being almost fifty years old.

Dornford's horse didn't like the wind, and was stamping her hooves, with her mane and tail blowing behind her. He had to fight to keep her under control. John knew him fairly well because they had served on the same ship at one time, and despite the difference in age and in rank, they had become well acquainted, as he was not a particularly strict disciplinarian. Since he had been stationed on the Island, he had become well acquainted with John's brother-in-law, the vicar of Chale, and his wife Elizabeth had become friendly with John's mother and sister-in-law; he had even attended John's wedding. John acknowledged him, and moved up towards the officer, hoping to obtain news of his family, as the two of them hadn't met for many months.

'Hullo Wheeler! Do you think they'll make it?' Dornford said, his gruff voice lightened by the twinkle in his eye.

Most people would avoid looking directly at a law enforcer, feeling intimidated by his presence. But John looked him directly in the eye as he replied. 'Good afternoon, Lieutenant. I'm surprised to see you so far from your home territory, on a day such as this.' He looked again at the struggling ship, judging its progress using both professional and local knowledge. He shrugged his shoulders, as he put out a hand to calm the horse. 'I think it's still touch and go, Lieutenant. But the tide is now setting fast, and should help them clear.'

It was true. The flooding current pushed by the wind was speeding up, as well as the flow accelerating as it converged towards Rocken End. This was helping to reduce the leeway the ship was making, so that it was now travelling more parallel to the shore.

Looking into the wind, John added, 'Also it seems to me that the wind is veering. It was south-westerly earlier, and now it is a point north of west. Each minute they can hang on could help them, if the shift continues.'

The Lieutenant nodded his agreement, and looked down to where a group of men were struggling along the beach, making the seagulls take off and move further along. 'It looks as if the Coastguard from Atherfield are bringing along the rocket-throwing apparatus in case the ship comes ashore near here,' he said with approval.

Below them were six men, who had carried the rocket apparatus from their station two or three miles along the beach, anticipating the ship's fate. They were obviously worn out, trudging over the shifting shingle carrying the heavy and awkward load in the wind. Leading them was their Chief Officer, Lieutenant Bulley.

John scowled down at Lieutenant Bulley with a feeling of bitterness and distaste, as he had a real grudge against the officer. It was he who had arrested John's father and had him taken to court for smuggling. Admittedly John's father had made the situation worse by choosing to protect his friends, but it was that man who was responsible. There was scarcely a day went by without John mentally cursing the man as an unprincipled bully.

But there were other reasons that John used to help him justify his feelings. He just didn't like the Lieutenant. He gave the appearance of being extraordinarily bumptious and belligerent, swaggering, speaking loudly and gesturing widely, as if trying to impress the world. Yet the men under his command seemed to respect him, though they were often afraid of his quick temper and change of moods. The Lieutenant wasn't a small or insignificant man. He was as big as John, though not as tall. They were both about the same age, but there was a contrast in their upbringing and education; so there was a distinct class divide between them. But that difference was not important in many other relationships that John had. You might think John was being unfair, as the Lieutenant was only doing his job, and you might be right. But, John tried hard to be Christian about it, and not let the feelings warp his mind. Nevertheless, maybe they did.

'But the ship has yet to clear Atherfield Ledge, and, as you know well, that runs quite a way out to sea,' John responded. 'If it does strike there, I suppose the wreckage would still come ashore near here. May the Lord protect her,' John prayed, as Lieutenant Dornford pulled his own spyglass out of a pocket in his jacket and clapped it to his eyes.

Through his spyglass John could see the beleaguered ship rapidly approaching the notorious ledge. The ship plunged towards them, digging its bowsprit into each trough, as its stern was hit by a wave, only to rise shrugging the water off as the bow lifted, corkscrewing. Though under water, the ledge made itself apparent as an area of white water created by a series of huge breaking waves, continuously forming in the same place and then sweeping in succession landwards. The ship was hit by the first of the waves and reeled from the blow. It canted so far over John thought she was going to roll onto her beam ends, and she would have done had the next wave struck quickly, but luckily she recovered; she had time to come sufficiently upright for the excess weight of water to pour out of the drainage ports on her lee side, before being pushed over again. But by then she was through the worst of the maelstrom.

'Thank the Lord, she's through. She hasn't struck, but there's a heavy squall approaching.' To seaward of the ship the water surface was obscured by a furious blast of wind and rain, rapidly scudding down on the ship. 'Thank goodness that it didn't hit them a moment ago,' John said. 'It would have done for them, surely.'

Half a minute later the ship disappeared into the curtain of heavy rain that had raced down onto her. Above, the writhing cloud was dark grey, almost black, and the rain descended from it in visible torrents, flattening the waves when it hit them, and turning the tumultuous sea into a foaming white sheet. The squall rapidly swept on, approaching the shore where they stood. Seeing it, the crowds on the cliff ran back to find shelter where they could, or turned their backs, pulled up their coat collars, and squatted down to brave it out. John was quite amused to see the smartly dressed gentry running for the shelter of their carriages; not their usual poised and sedate habit.

Seeing what was coming, Lieutenant Dornford dismounted, and stood beside his horse, holding her bridle so she faced away from the wind, and letting her take the brunt of the rain. He gestured John to join him in the small protection she afforded.

With a noise that could be heard over the wind as an approaching roar, the rain swept toward them. Then it hit, almost like the slap of a huge, punishing hand, rain mixed with hail. Immediately, nothing could be heard but the beating of the large raindrops and hailstones that struck in immense gusts. The hail bounced about a foot high off the ground, and the rain almost immediately penetrated through anything but the thickest oilskins. John could feel the cold water trickling down his neck, and his sweater quickly became wet against his back. They had to stand and suffer, but it was nothing like the punishment the poor seamen had to put up with, as the cold rain and vicious hail added to the sea water, spray and spume. John knew the feeling well, and could sympathise with them.

CHAPTER ONE

With the noise of the wind and the rain, further conversation was impossible, but after a couple of minutes the rain eased, and John turned to see how the ship had fared.

She was doing well. She seemed to have even gained distance off shore during the squall, and he realised that the wind had veered by another half a point. Also, she was being swept along at an increasing speed parallel to the shore by the tidal currents. She was now just about straight off where they stood and about quarter of a mile out. John looked at the Lieutenant with a grin as they both realised it was obvious she was going to make it; she would weather Rocken End and St. Catherine's Point, and would survive to fight another day. Like old conspirators they smiled and nodded to each other in satisfaction and relief.

A cheer went up from the watchers as it became obvious to them too. Everyone waved and shouted; the boys were jumping up and down with excitement, screaming with joy. Despite regretting the fact that there wasn't going to be a wreck to plunder, there was jubilation that the ship and the crew had escaped the jaws of death. It was unlikely the cheering could be heard on the ship, but through the newly wiped glass John could see the helmsmen waving in reply. A lone figure struggled along the still heaving deck to the shrouds where he unlashed the flag halyards and dipped the ensign in recognition of the visible joy. They too must have been saying prayers of thanksgiving in their relief at being spared.

Now that they were clear, the helmsman, with a look at the sails, eased the wheel a point or two, the head of the ship came off the wind, and its motion eased. Though she still bucked and reared, no longer were the seas washing over the mid-ships, and the list had lessened, the ship sailing more upright. Then she entered the confused seas off Rocken End, and within a couple of minutes disappeared round the point. There was now a certainty that she would survive into the calmer water south of the Island where the huge cliffs and the high downs would give her a good lee, and shelter from the worst of the wind. They could now anticipate reaching their destination, and undoubtedly a bit of well-earned shore leave.

The soaked crowd turned away and chattered together, sharing the excitement and the thrills of what they had just seen. They started wending their way back home in the gathering gloom of the autumn afternoon.

Lieutenant Dornford looked at John with a calm face, as if what they had seen was a commonplace thing. He pulled out a handkerchief and wiped the rain off his face. 'They were fortunate to escape today. The change of wind came just at the right time.' Then, with a sigh of relief, he muttered, 'At least it saves me having to supervise any rescues, or salvage.' Despite his long experience he had never, ever enjoyed having to deal with the dead bodies, or guarding valuables or cargo against pilfering by the people he knew and lived with; he never liked considering the consequences of denying them the means of alleviating their poor conditions, if only briefly. Then, changing the subject, he asked, 'Tell me, is your father well? I hope that he is surviving Winchester with his customary fortitude.'

'As far as we know he is well, and luckily we manage to get money to him regularly enough for him to be reasonably nourished and comfortable. He has completed half his sentence and should be home in April. My mother will be mightily relieved when he does return, for she worries so.'

The Lieutenant looked pleased to hear that news, and took a glance at the watch which he took from his pocket. 'Are you going home now? If you are, I will come and pass my wife's respects to your mother. That is if she is at home. I hope she is well.'

'Yes, she is very well, and I was with her before I came out here. I haven't seen her appear on the cliff, so I expect she'll still be at home. I will have to call back there before I go to my home, despite it now being out of my way.'

The Lieutenant looked pleased. 'In that case, I will call in on my way back to Freshwater. But I will have to go on ahead otherwise it will be dark before I am home. Goodbye Wheeler!' He clapped John on the shoulder with a comradely gesture, straightened his cap, mounted, gathered up his reins and trotted off down along the cliff edge, raising his cap as he went past several people he knew. John followed, but stopped to talk to several of his friends on the way. By the time he returned to his mother's cottage, the Lieutenant had gone.

At the cottage John stood for some time before the fire, talking to his mother. Apparently the Lieutenant had commiserated for her husband's sentence, and had brought his wife's heartfelt condolences. Hannah was really touched by that kindness, and John was grateful there was humanity in some of the Coastguards, and not all of them were unfeeling and brutal. When he had warmed up and dried out somewhat he headed back home, in the fading light, to his cottage and his waiting family.

As he tipped the latch on the gate, Frances appeared at the cottage door, having seen him coming along the lane. The wind blowing along the road etched her figure into sharp relief, blowing her skirt close against her long slim legs, and her blouse tight against her bosom. John's heart leapt in appreciation, and he thanked the gracious Lord for such a lovely wife and companion. Even though they were open to anyone's view, she threw her arms round him and tipped her face back for him to reach down and kiss her; as he was over six feet tall, and she was almost a foot shorter, her head barely came up to his shoulders. He shut the door to keep out the prying eyes of inquisitive neighbours.

Frances was a striking woman in an age when hard work and perpetual child-bearing prematurely aged even the strongest females. She was eight years younger than John and only in her low twenties, so the years hadn't yet taken their toll. Her lustrous brown curly hair framed an oval face, with attractive dark brown eyes and dark eyebrows set within strong cheekbones and a small pointed nose. Her lightly freckled skin was still healthily and unfashionably tanned from the summer sun. When she smiled her lips curved open to reveal even white teeth, a dimple formed in her cheek, and a bewitching sparkle appeared in her eyes. Though she would never be called a beauty, she always attracted men's gaze, being what many men would reckon an ideal of grace and femininity. Despite having had two children, she had a figure any woman would be jealous of, and any man would crave for. When she snuggled up to John at night beneath the goose down overlay she could rouse him readily.

She led him by the hand into the kitchen where it was warm, and heavy with the smell of cooking. She helped him off with his still damp reefer and boots, which she put in front of the range. 'The children are already fed and in bed,' she said, having always had the country philosophy of early to bed and early to rise. 'You had better go and say good night to them if they are not asleep. Then you can tell me what you've been up to, to get so wet, and whether you found your mother well.'

John crept upstairs in his stockinged feet, went into the girls' room and kissed them gently in their sleep. Then he told Frances about the excitement over the brig in the bay, and his meeting Lieutenant Dornford.

'Thank the Lord they are safe,' she said. 'I'm glad that you didn't have to risk yourself in trying to rescue anyone today.' She knew, and had had to accept that John felt it his Christian duty to do what he could to help anyone in peril. What she didn't say, ever, was that it was that trait that had swayed her brother into accepting John into his family as a brother-in-law, despite John's lowly background.

Later, as they were almost asleep she whispered in John's ear, 'John! I forgot to tell you. My brother called, and said that he would like us to dine with him after church on Sunday. Apparently he has a proposition that he wants to put to you. But he wouldn't tell me what it is.'

John had to wait two days to find out what Frances' brother, Andrew, planned.

Chapter 2

It is important to the story that at this stage something is revealed of the life and upbringing of John Wheeler, and the social framework of his life. In 1835 he was twenty-nine years old, and born and bred in the Chale area of the Back of the Wight. He, and his twin brother Robert, came from a long line of local families who had extensively intermarried over the years. Consequently they were related to many of the locals: the Whites, the Cottons, the Rayners and more. The twins were born in 1806, the year after the Battle of Trafalgar; it is even probable that they were conceived during the exuberant celebrations that followed news of that momentous battle.

Growing up on the Island meant that they had the inevitable choice that most young men of the area had, to become either farm labourers or fishermen. Being born into a family that had been fishermen for many generations, fishermen, and at times smugglers and wreckers, the choice was inevitable. But their parents were adamant that they should attend school, and learn to read and write, before they had to start seriously earning their keep from the sea; though they would be expected to help with the fishing at times. At least they would then have enough education to take up a different career if there was the opportunity. Their parents

31

were hoping that they might be able to move up into a situation where they could have an easier life than the hard, relentless toil they had been forced to endure.

Robert was a smaller version of John, not as tall, slighter in build, not as dark in colouring, but less intelligent and less good at bookwork. John enjoyed school, and proved more adept at learning than his twin, who preferred to be out fishing with his father whenever he could. Mind you, John enjoyed the open air and revelled in the hard work, but he could happily settle down with a book from the penny library, or a newspaper, and let it take him away into another world, of imagination, information, and experience. John would not easily admit that he had developed into a strong, able and intelligent lad, with a yearning for travel and excitement, and the desire to see a bit of the world outside the confines of the Isle of Wight. Despite being capable and deserving, he was a young man of a low social class, and opportunities to escape were few; his speech was broad and his manners coarse. The only way open to him was to join the Navy.

As he didn't have the money or breeding to buy preferment it meant that he had to enter as a lowly seaman. But the fleet had been reduced to less than a half in the few years after Napoleon's defeat at Waterloo, many of the older ships became hulks, or were broken up, and their complements discharged. That put many very able seamen and officers back on land. Despite that, his youth and experience of fishing was valuable and he served for several years in a number of first or second rate ships around the Channel, the North Sea and as far as Gibraltar. It made a man of him at a very young age, and gave him confidence and self-reliance. He had endured and survived battles, hunger, cold and many other privations, including the notorious cat-of-nine-tails. Discipline on many ships was harsh, and the officers malevolent.

Following one voyage when his ship was badly damaged in a very severe storm, and was declared not worth repairing, he was paid off. He had the choice of re-enlisting or returning home to fishing with his father and brother, the news having reached him that they needed help at home. He chose the latter. But he still did some professional sailing on a yacht called the *Falcon*, owned by Lord Yarborough. The noble Lord, head of the ancient local family, the Worsley family, had large estates on the Island and a big mansion just over the downs at Appuldurcombe. As he kept his yacht in Cowes and raced it regularly against his friends, he hired local crews to man it for him, and John had been enlisted. The discipline was, if anything, harsher than in the Navy, but the pay was much better and each man achieved huge status as a consequence of frequently being in the winning crew.

Though only an occasional summertime occupation, it gave John an enviable reputation and welcome extra money. But it also made him unhappy with his situation. He had to rub shoulders with the gentry, and he took pains to closely observe their manners, the way they behaved towards others, and tried to understand their motivation. Having seen the advantages that money and breeding could buy, it made him ambitious to better himself, and his speech and manners improved. This brought out a conflict in him that made him uncomfortable. Poor families were always envious of the wealthy, and the luxury and freedom money gave them, but they gained much comfort in their religion, and the support of their families, friends and neighbours in their communities. This could provide bonds as strong, or stronger, than those of ancestry or money. John was aware that money endowed arrogance, a coolness and disdain that twisted the Christian principles of those who put money above God and humanity, so that they lost their humility and respect for their fellows. All that seemed to be important to them was their status. He did not want that to happen to him; it offended against the standards he was brought up to respect. As will become apparent, the problem had been acceptably resolved for him by the way his life subsequently developed.

Since he had returned to live and work at home and try to make a living at fishing, and smuggling, the young daughter of the widowed local squire at Billingham Manor, had caught his eye. The attraction was mutual, and often they happened to meet when casually walking, or when she was out riding. At first their meetings were by chance, but later John would try to plan to be where he anticipated she would be. And it transpired that Frances was doing the same. Their attraction developed, and later turned into affection and love. Frances was young, wayward and determined, to the extent that she was not considered a match for the sons of the local gentry; she could not bring a big enough dowry to attract a good social marriage, as her father lived well above his means. But the squire died before John could formally ask to court his daughter, and his only son, Andrew, had had to sell the estate to settle the debts, leaving Frances virtually destitute, and dependant on her brother.

CHAPTER TWO

Andrew Gothen had attended Oxford University and gained a Master of Arts degree and had accepted the living at St. Andrew's Church in Chale, from Keble College, who had the advowsen. So he was the local vicar. Whilst a student Andrew had become a Radical, believing that reorganisation of the social structure and political framework of the country was essential to cope with the changes that the French Revolution, and the Industrial Revolution, had thrust upon the world; changes that had been developing for many years, but that had been successfully suppressed in England despite much unrest. Though his undergraduate beliefs had moderated somewhat, he was still a Whig, and felt he had a greater affinity with the common people than with the aristocracy. In this he had much in common with the principles of the rector of nearby Brighstone, Samuel Wilberforce, with whom he became very friendly. Samuel was the son of the famous anti-slavery campaigner, William.

As Frances had not been left enough money to set up her own house, Andrew offered her the choice of living with him and his wife, or trying to find a post as a governess for another family. But, typically, she proposed her own solution. She said she wanted to marry John, and become the wife of a poor, but honourable fisherman.

Andrew was taken aback initially, and refused to even think about the possibility. He worried about how it would be viewed by his peers, and whether he would end up having to support John's family as well as his own. But, being fair-minded, he set out to really get to know John, so that he could make a decision based on facts rather than prejudices. After a period of mutual reticence their relationship developed and they had many long discussions about religion, science, politics, trade, and rural poverty. They found that on many issues their views coincided. In truth, John was able to bring a wider and a more basic experience of life to the discussions, to compare with Andrew's more elevated horizons and book learning, and they came to respect and like each other and appreciate each other's moral standards. Eventually Andrew agreed to the wedding, and welcomed John as a brother-in-law; he may have seen it as a way of applying his radical principles, and passing on the potential domestic problem of a difficult sister.

Understandably, John had had his own trepidations about marrying into a family with the better manners, breeding, and expectations than he could offer. John's parents had also been very worried that he would be out of his depth in such a situation, and that they would too. But there was a necessary delay for a period of mourning for Frances' father, and for his estate to be settled, during which they got to know Frances, and her family, and came to accept the situation.

After about a year's engagement Andrew officiated when Frances and John married, to restrained jubilation in the village, and scepticism, or even outright disapproval, of some of the local gentry. They thought Frances to be considerably above John in breeding and status, and that she was dishonouring her class by marrying him. However, John was widely known and respected as an upright and Christian man, tolerant, but principled and forthright. Though he was inferior by birth, he could show that he was their equal in spirit and intelligence, and was respected in the local community, being in many ways one of their leaders, so that he felt he didn't have to be overly deferential in dealing with Frances' family friends, and could withstand their scorn.

Nevertheless, the months after they were married were a difficult time for Frances, as she missed the comparative luxury in which she had lived before, and felt the other village women resented her and her birthright. But she soon made it plain she wasn't a snob, and her sympathetic manner and calm assurance settled their prejudices. She was then generally considered one of the village folk, rather than the gentry. One of her greatest difficulties was coming to terms with cooking, as this was a new skill she had to learn. Though she had done some simple things in the kitchens as a girl, it was very much under the eye of the cook, and the results were treated condescendingly as experiments. Now she had to cope with complete meals, and John's serious appetite. But she was a feisty and supportive wife, and accepted guidance from John's mother who helped her master the essentials to become a reasonable plain cook. Though she accepted it as part of her role, she would never say that she enjoyed it, and there were still the occasional disasters. But she gained satisfaction from the contentment in John's eyes when they looked at each other across the dining table.

In fact, Frances and John were very happy. She had taught him to ride, and they often rode together on two of Andrew's horses. You might think it a little unusual for a fisherman to ride a horse, and John did feel very uncomfortable to start with; he felt that he would be considered by the villagers to be getting above himself. But many of the country people could ride. It was the only way of getting about, apart from walking. All of the farmers and many of the farm labourers clambered onto a horse almost as soon as they could walk, though they were carthorses and ponies rather than high spirited stallions. It didn't take John long to realise the enjoyment and freedom of spirit that a good gallop could give. When he was not fishing or tending the little garden they had, they found they had a common interest in nature and the countryside, as well as trying to help others in the community not as lucky as they were. After a couple of years they had a lovely daughter, Charlotte, fondly nicknamed Lottie, who was two years old when a second, Emily, was born; she was six months old when our story unfolds. John was hoping the second would be a boy, but that wasn't to be; maybe in the future?

Fishing meant that it was a hard and poor life, but Andrew had been generous in allowing Frances a small annuity from the residue of the estate, a dowry that their father would have found difficult to manage. John was loath to touch any of it, and Frances had to persuade him to use some to make them a bit more comfortable than the normal villagers were; John's conscience was recently helped by having to support his mother after his father went to jail, and prevent her from having to go on the parish poor relief. Nevertheless, John felt he had to take other opportunities to earn some money wherever and whenever they arose, such as the sail racing, and, of course, smuggling.

What were the alternatives, though? Farming on the Back of the Wight was difficult. Much of the land around Chale was owned by Michael Hoy, who had made his money trading with Russia, but the rents were as high as anywhere else. It wouldn't have been too bad if one owned a farm; the farmers did not have to do the majority of the work, and they took the profits, leaving a pittance for the labourers. For them it was ploughing in the spring, harvest in the summer, threshing and ditching in the winter. Nevertheless, the farmers would complain; the land was poor, badly drained, and scoured by salt-laden winds for most of the year. Whenever there was a good growing spring, gales in the summer bleached and stunted the shoots and flattened the crops. It's seldom that it can be said there was a good harvest, and many wondered whether it was worth the effort put in to the unyielding land. The only thing that did reasonably well was the cattle, but even they had to be hardy, able to withstand the rain, the wind and the poor forage. To be able to get a living from the land was very wearing, and the labourers died young, worn out by hard work. John would do almost anything else to avoid that.

Throughout the whole country agriculture was in ferment. The Corn Laws, passed in 1815, kept taxes on imported corn high, and this maintained the price of home grown corn, to the benefit of the large farmers. As a consequence bread was expensive. The wages of the labourers that produced the corn were kept low, so that large profits were made by the larger farmers in areas where corn growing was easier. The smaller farmers that depended on crop rotation to maintain fertility, and had small fields, did not fare so well, because the high price of bread meant that few could afford to buy their other produce; butter, meat, cheese and eggs. The labourers agitated for higher wages, as they only earned ten or twelve shillings a week, but so many men had been released from the army back to the land after the defeat of Napoleon, that the farmers could just sack the agitators, and employ someone else. Many farm workers were so poor that they had to have poor relief in order to live. This situation was of major concern to the Radicals, who were putting pressure on parliament for repeal of the Corn Law, saying that cheaper corn would benefit the great majority and get rid of hardship.

But, the general response to the unrest and the pressure was to increase control, and harden the punishments meted out by magistrates. Only a year before, in 1834, a group of agricultural labourers at Tolpuddle in Dorset tried to form a union, and withdraw their labour until the wages increased, but this was met by martyrdom. The ringleaders were hanged and the rest sentenced to deportation. But not only was this discontent occurring in agriculture, but also in the new industries of the north of England and the cities, where wages were low, and living and working conditions harsh.

The basic problem was the fact that the government did not represent all the people of the country, but only the upper classes. Therefore, only the views of a minority were considered, and that minority had all the wealth, and influence, and they protected their own interests. The Radicals, after much political manoeuvring, got a Reform Bill passed in 1832. Admittedly that went some way to improving representation, by widening the range of those allowed to vote, and rearranging the election boundaries of members of parliament. This effectively got rid of 'rotten boroughs'; previously,

Newtown, a little hamlet on the north side of the Island, sent two Members to Parliament, even though the population was only a couple of hundred. However, not only did it affect parliamentary elections, but it affected the boroughs as well. In Newport, their two members of parliament were previously elected by the town corporation. After the Reform Bill the Mayor, Aldermen, and Chief Burgesses were to go out of office at the end of the year, but the election under the new rules returned nine Tories and nine Radicals, and they could not agree who would be Mayor. Without his casting vote they, therefore, could not agree on who should be elected for Parliament. Presumably the Town Clerk, William Hearn, carried on the rest of the business as well as he could. Obviously further amendment of the Act was necessary, and there was much heated debate and agitation.

It was calculated that this Bill would increase by fifty per cent the number of men eligible to vote, and decrease the influence of the wealthy in formulating the laws. But even so it was still only those who owned fairly expensive property that were entitled to vote, not everyone, and most of those would be in the increasingly wealthy industrial areas in the North Country. Consequently, it was the upper middle class who could newly vote, not the common man – John Wheeler most certainly wouldn't. It took many more years before the wider needs were recognised and these injustices rectified.

As you may appreciate, in those days it was the big landowners and the wealthy aristocrats that dispensed justice, as they were the Justices of the Peace, and they could be very harsh and self-serving. In London there was a police force, the 'peelers' or 'bobbies', started by Sir Robert Peel, which ensured discipline and tried to control crime. Also some parishes had parish constables or wardens, but they were few and far between as not all parishes could afford them. So in most rural areas it was the people themselves, as well as the employees of the landowners, who kept the peace, and any offenders were either deterred by their fellows, or by the stringency of the punishments meted out by the Justices. There were over 200 different offences which merited the death penalty, though merited is the wrong word, for stealing a crown piece from a shop does not merit being hanged. But the death penalty was not always applied; many sentences were commuted into transportation for life, or a long term, though this could be as good as death, as many did not survive the ordeal.

Though local laws were set by the parish, it was generally the landowners that formulated them; even the poaching of a rabbit could lead to transportation, though at least the setting of gin traps was outlawed. Any widespread law-breaking normally resulted in the army being called out, as happened some years before at Peterloo, when eleven people were killed and over four hundred wounded when the army were sent in to a crowd to try to arrest a radical orator, who was thought to be creating trouble.

You can be assured that there were great pressures within the population for improvement in the way the lower classes were treated, as well as in removing the great inequalities in the way that justice was meted out. There was a widespread fear that an uprising similar to the French Revolution would break out, and this drove the desire for regulation. However, the Island had no large towns, had no developing industry, and was far distant from the centres of power. Consequently, the Islanders' concerns were of little import in the greater scheme of things. The communities were largely peaceful, within reason law-abiding, and relatively healthy, despite being poor. The only way that many people managed to survive was by free-trading; in other words smuggling, about which more later.

On the Island the only real alternative to agriculture was fishing, and fishing had a slightly higher status than agricultural labouring, at least the fisherman was his own master, except when he was at the mercy of the sea. But fishing is not something that can be done by oneself. It has long been a family occupation. The coast around Chale and Blackgang is very exposed; to launch a boat from the beach, often through rough seas, and row out to the best grounds takes several strong men. So boats were owned, maintained and manned by families, fathers, sons and even grandfathers all helping. John normally fished with his brother, Robert, and Uncle James, in a boat jointly owned with his father, Jack. During calm weather the catches could sometimes be good, but there were long periods when the boats could not put to sea, the crab and lobster pots were swept away, and the nets had to be mended because of snagging on the rocks. Mind you, the fishermen generally knew where the rocks were, and how to avoid them.

If storms suddenly arose, and squalls swept down on them, they might not be able to beach the boat safely. Then they would raise a jury sail and run for the nearest shelter. For the

Wheelers that would be either running eastwards, rounding St. Catherine's Point and making for Puckaster Cove, or Binnel Bay, or sailing west for the Needles and into the West Solent. Either could be very hazardous, and many local men had been lost in the attempt. If they did get a good catch, they had to carry it to market in Newport, a good ten-mile walk with a heavy load, and even then the price would be low if others had good catches too. Many is the time the Wheeler brothers had been out early lifting crabs and lobsters, then cooked them, either rowed or sailed to Portsmouth or Cowes to sell them, and returned to lift the pots again. It was a hard life. They all developed strong backs and arms from the rowing and hauling nets and pots, and leathery skins and hard hands from the sun, the salt, and the oars.

During the summer season the mackerel came into the bay in large shoals. A watcher would be sent to the cliff to look for the ripples and small waves the fish make as they break surface, and for the fins of the porpoises that chase them. He would direct the boats to cast nets around the shoal, and on good days the boats could be filled within minutes. Those fish that couldn't be taken to market, the womenfolk then had to salt to preserve them; but it was generally considered nothing was better than a salted mackerel or herring for tea in the winter.

Other days, when the fish came close inshore and the sea was calm, would be the time for seine netting, and then the whole village would help. One end of a long net would be held on the beach, while the other end would be rowed in a long arc round, and back to the beach a little further along. Both ends were then hauled in until the centre, with luck, came ashore full of flapping fish of all sorts: bass, mackerel, cod, flatfish, gurnard, bream, and even sometimes the solitary salmon. Back-breaking work, I assure you, all to bring in a shared few shillings and a nutritious meal.

When fishermen earn their living from the sea they run the risk of losing their lives every time they set off, and John had friends and relations that were drowned at sea. Surely they deserved some compensation, some return from the sea.

So you can see why it is not surprising that the coastal villagers, the fishermen and the farm workers, had to take part in wrecking and free-trading; it was the only way they could keep body and soul together. John was a wrecker, but only under the right circumstances. He would never be involved setting lights to lure ships onto the rocks, or deliberately leading ships into situations where they would become wrecked; he had not seen that happen, nor had he heard of it being done around the Island. God have mercy on those involved and save their souls from the devil, if it's true. What he did was the retrieving and recovery of the remains of a wreck that occurred from force of nature; in other words, salvage. The Islanders worked on the principle that the seas take away and the seas deliver. Occasionally Spanish dollars minted in 1701 coming from Armada wrecks could be found in the beach sand at Blackgang; who would give those in to the Customs?

In return for this harvest they did their utmost to rescue the passengers and crews of the ships when they broke up in the surf. John had friends and relations lose their lives doing that, without having taken a second thought about the risks. If lives were at stake, they did it, even though their compensation may have been in Heaven. The belongings, the cargo, the ships' timbers and fittings would all be broken, lost and destroyed if they were not there to save them. There can be nothing wrong with using the salvaged items to benefit their families and children ultimately with food, warmth and shelter that they otherwise would not have. Would the cargos of sugar, cheese and other perishable goods have been of any use to anyone but those who pulled it out of the sea?

The churchyard of St. Andrews in Chale attests to the numbers of bodies that have been brought ashore and given a good Christian burial, all by the hands of the wreckers; and there are many more that can only be listed as 'lost at sea'. However, in some places it had been reported that rings and other belongings had been taken directly from the drowned and broken bodies, even from their very fingers. May God have mercy upon them, if that is true. In olden days it was common that the children would be taught the wrecker's prayer:

'God bless Daddy, God bless Mummy,
Come wind, come storm,
Ship ashore before the morn.'

However, John would not tolerate even the thought of instilling such desires in his children.

Just imagine wading through the raging surf with a rope around your waist, being pounded by the breaking waves and half drowned, to reach a ship hard ashore and being broken up. And they can be broken up by only a few waves; half a dozen of the waves on Blackgang beach can be the finish of a ship. After a fight through the surf a survivor can be dragged to the beach in the rescuers arms by those on the other end of the rope. On the way there is the vicious undertow to overcome; the breaking waves producing a current sucking along the bed. It drags people under and takes them out to sea, holding them under until they drown. Drowning must be a horrible way to die. But those who work with the sea have to come to terms with dying in that way, with the cold seawater in their throat and lungs, and a blackness descending over them. Many who attempt to rescue those on wrecked ships from the beach have experienced these awful feelings; only to have the rope thankfully pull them ashore where they could retch, breathe and recover.

When the breakers are not too bad they help man a boat to row out through the surf to helpless ships. Getting through the waves needs courage and skill. If timing is bad, the boat can be swamped, broach-to, and overturn. Then the crew would be in the water, needing rescuing as well, and the boat becoming splintered timber. Admittedly the boats were fishing boats, and built for hard work, but they were not built for such treatment, and their loss could mean the end of a family's livelihood, with no compensation.

But times were changing. Lighthouses were being built to help show the ships' captains where the headlands and shoals were, so that they could take avoiding action long before it was too late. However, their locations were not always ideal. Many were constructed on the tops of the headlands in order for their lights to be seen far out to sea, but much of the time they would be hidden in cloud or fog. The light above the

Needles was fairly new, being built in 1786, but it was over 450 feet above the sea and could not be seen in bad weather. That on St. Catherine's Down must have been at least 700 feet above the sea, but it was then abandoned half-built at huge expense. They should have known by experience what the problems would be. Though it was very close to a hermitage-cum-lighthouse built many centuries before as a penance by a local lord, it was not very effective; if only they had consulted the local people they needn't have repeated the mistake. However, at the time of our story there were plans to relocate it lower down, actually on St. Catherine's Point.

Another development that might help save seafarers' lives was a new way of getting a lifeline from the shore onto a wreck. It was invented by a man from Carisbrooke, a Mr. John Dennett, at one time an ensign in the Newport Loyal Volunteers. He used a heavy rocket, like a huge firework, weighing over a stone, with a light rope attached to it. It was fired from a long, iron tube, to carry the rope, hopefully, across the ship. It was successfully used in an October gale in 1832, when a ship, the *Bainbridge*, was cast ashore on Atherfield Ledge, but couldn't be reached by boat. Using the rocket, the Coastguard rocket crew rescued all nineteen men from the vessel, and two of the crew, Boatmen Thomas and Stubbs, received silver medals from the Lifesaving Institute in thanks. As a consequence of this success three of these rockets had been stationed at Freshwater, Atherfield, and St. Lawrence, so that the whole coast could be reached. It was considered that, with experience, many more lives could be saved. Though the rockets were often unreliable, and didn't always work well, they were better than standing helplessly watching people drown. It was one of these devices that John had seen being carried along the beach that stormy day.

Also, there was muttering that designs of special lifeboats were being considered, to be stationed on the coast where access and the topography were likely to allow easy launching. They would need crews of ten or a dozen men. But, of course, it would be the fishermen, and longshoremen, and the Coastguard, who would have to man them. Though the risks, hopefully, would be lower in a specially constructed boat, who would look after the families if the menfolk were drowned or injured in a rescue?

Free trading is a euphemism for smuggling, but this doesn't mean that it is any the less illegal an offence. At that time excise duty was charged on spirits, especially brandy and rum, and on tobacco, lace, and even such things as salt and calicos. But no one wanted to have to pay such exorbitant amounts if it could be obtained more cheaply. Nevertheless, despite the men in general being deeply religious, there were few problems of conscience troubling those involved in trying to evade the duty.

Smuggling was not something that could be done by an individual. It required quite a large team of like-minded people to carry it out successfully, as well as careful planning. First of all the finance would have to be put in place, so that the cargo could be bought, and a boat and the men to man it organised, with their cut or fee accepted; a large landing party was needed to unload the cargo and hide it for eventual distribution; and all of this had to be done without a whisper of the run reaching the Coastguard. The fewer in the know the better, as informers could always drop a hint and obtain a reward.

In the runs John had been involved in, the cargo had always been brandy, and most of those involved had some interest in drinking a little of the liquor themselves, in lieu of payment; therefore not all of the cargo reached third parties. Brandy was comparatively cheap in France and easily bought on the other side of the Channel. The liquor cost about fourteen shillings per tub, and a tub was a half-anker barrel, or cask, holding five gallons. The charge for carrying a tub across the Channel was generally three shillings, with a comparable sum to pay for the landing party. As the value of a pound sterling was slightly higher in France, each tub cost about one pound on the beach. The brandy was colourless and was of very high proof. Since it was virtually undrinkable in its neat form; it had to be diluted before consumption, but the wholesaler would expect to receive it undiluted. Normally for home consumption dilution was done by the womenfolk, using the same quantity of water with some burnt sugar added to provide an attractive colour.

If sold to the customer at half a crown a bottle, each tub would be worth fifty shillings. Since the government duty was thirty-two shillings a gallon, each bottle was less than half the normal price, and the operation made a profit of at least 100 per cent; the profits being shared with those who put up the money in the first place. One tub in twenty was normally allowed as the boat's share. So, if a boat were to load 100 tubs of brandy in Barfleur or Cherbourg, the outlay would have to be at least one hundred pounds, and this would be needed in gold sovereigns. Also the boat and crew would need something on account to ensure their interest, cooperation and silence; they might even be asked to provide a share. You can see that we are talking about significant sums of money to be risked, but also large sums to be made.

What were the risks of being caught, you might ask? This is a difficult question to answer, because of the many factors that have to be considered, mainly relating to the efficiency of the Coastguard and the state of the weather. Obviously, if the run was unsuccessful, a large amount of money was forfeit.

The Coastguard had the responsibility for ensuring that the laws were upheld and those breaking the law were apprehended. The force was formed in 1822, by bringing together three separate organisations: the Revenue Service, the Preventive Water Guard and the Riding Officers. All then came under the control of the Board of Customs. The Revenue Service, previously the responsibility of the Admiralty, was still manned by them, and they had a fleet of fast cutters, often called cruisers, that tried to intercept smuggling vessels off shore. The Preventives used to man small boats to patrol the coastline and intercept suspected smugglers; they were on duty sixteen hours a day, mostly at sea, all for three shillings a day, plus a share of any prize money. The Riding Officers patrolled on land to catch smugglers; they operated mainly at night, and were paid seventy-five pounds per year, but had to pay for their own horse and its keep. Obviously there were many operational conflicts between them and clashes of status and seniority which led to inefficiency.

After amalgamation the Coastguard had to do both the small boat and the land patrols. Their remit was to catch smugglers and prevent smuggling; they were not officially supposed to help save lives until much later. The Coastguard force was organised into stations located at convenient intervals along the coast. The Chief Officer of each station would normally be a Naval Lieutenant, in charge of about eight Boatmen. The Boatmen were still paid only three shillings a day plus a share of any prize money, and so could often be bribed by the smugglers. Partly to prevent this, the Boatmen were not recruited near their birthplace, and they frequently moved station to ensure independence.

Because of their chequered history, the Coastguard were often still called the Revenue, the Excise, or the Preventives, and more often they were nicknamed 'gobbies', to rhyme with 'bobbies'. They were armed with pistols and cutlasses, so clashes with the smugglers could be bloody, especially as the punishments were heavy if smugglers were caught, and proven guilty. Even so, many free traders were not convicted, because it was difficult to obtain evidence, and witnesses were not very forthcoming. Also the punishments could sometimes be light, if the magistrate was sympathetic; that is why many of the cases coming from the Isle of Wight were tried at Winchester.

Because of the profits to be made, the punishments for being caught were large. The punishments received would depend on the social class and circumstances of the accused; the higher social classes were often thought to be morally incapable of smuggling, or being involved in it. But punishments ranged from confiscation or destruction of the boat, a one-hundred-pound fine, or imprisonment for a year, to transportation, or a period of service in the Navy for persistent offenders. If a Coastguard was killed it would definitely be the death penalty. The poorer were of course much more harshly treated than others. Ironically, it was possible for a confiscated boat to be used by the Coastguard to try to prevent more smuggling by its previous owners. Though the magistrate in the court may well have drunk some of the cargo with his dinner after the case was heard, it doesn't necessarily appear to have had much influence on the penalties imposed.

It is clear that in general no ill will was borne against the Coastguards, though they were shunned and disliked. It was accepted they were only trying to do their duty, and their pay was not great, considering the conditions they had to work in – all hours in all weathers. However, if they did not play the game fairly, the free traders could be hard task-masters in making them aware of what they considered the rules should be. Conversely, the gobbies were not averse to turning a blind eye, or a deaf ear, some of the time. Nevertheless, accidents did happen. Poor John Hillier, a Coastguard at Atherfield, was killed when he fell over the cliff in 1834; his tombstone is in Chale churchyard today. It is not clear whether this was a genuine accident or not; it is always possible that someone had a grudge against him. Nevertheless, in most circumstances there must have been a certain amount of grudging respect between the two sides; they could both be at the mercy of the sea, which could easily make any wives into widows, and children into orphans. Also their essential humanity must have prevailed, as they did work together during shipwrecks to save lives.

There were several ways in which a run was carried out. Sometimes a rowing boat with a small lug sail and four or six valiant oarsmen would slip across the Channel in calm weather and bring back a cargo of forty or fifty tubs. John had done this, and he can testify that it was hard on the back and the hands rowing for twelve hours or more in each direction. There was a risk of being caught by a Revenue cutter far from shore, or that the weather could blow up, preventing landing the load on a secluded beach. In those cases the load would be slipped over the side somewhere where it could be relocated from shore marks, and the boat would run for the nearest harbour. The tubs were ready made up onto weighted lines, because they were buoyant and floated unless weighted. If a Revenue cutter should chance upon them, they could insist they were innocently fishing, having also had nets or pots prepared on deck. When the coast was clear the load would be grappled for and raised. Mind you, the Coastguard were quite adept at grappling for the tubs too, if they thought that's what had happened.

The other way was to take a fast cutter across the Channel, and they could load anything up to 200 tubs. It was known for these cutters to be so fast they could outrun the Revenue, but that just made them suspicious and determined enough to use their guns to force the cutter to stop, and then board and search. It was much safer to approach the shore at night and complete the landing in the dark, providing the coast was clear. John had a good, trim little fishing smack that was moored in one of the creeks at Newtown right under the eyes of the Coastguard station. As he used it for fishing when he was not working in the boat from the shore, it was legitimate! It had been bought from the profit of free trading, and John looked upon it as a sound investment.

The tubs were difficult to handle when wet and slippery. It was easier if two were roped together. In some places they could be bought already roped together. Otherwise the crew roped them like that on the way back across the Channel. Then the tubs were slung over a shoulder, one hanging forwards and the other astern. A good man could carry them like that for miles. On several occasions a load was landed on the rocks right beneath High Down, between the Needles and Freshwater Gate. There, the cliffs must be all of 500 feet high, and the path to the top was steep, narrow, crumbling and treacherous. The tubs were carried, in the dark, up to the top and down the other side to the High Down Inn where they were hidden. Think about it, the pair of tubs would weigh the best part of a hundredweight. It would need a strong back and legs, and an even stronger head for heights. But they did it in the dark, and undetected. On one occasion a man who stumbled on the way up, lost his footing, and though he stopped himself falling, his load went down the cliff to smash on the rocks below. For several days there was an overpowering smell of brandy in the air, which could be detected for a long way. Luckily, no notice appeared to be taken of it by the Revenue.

As well as buying the smack, the free trading gave John occasional gold sovereigns in his pocket, as well as a small house in the village, Fulford Cottage. His parents already had a small cottage bought in the same way. But times were changing. The Coastguard were becoming more effective in catching the smugglers or forcing them to become better organised in bigger gangs. Unfortunately, this resulted in much more violence, because there was so much more to lose. In his more philosophical moments John wondered how long he could go on running cargos. He didn't want to get caught, and Frances worried that she might be left alone to cope with the children and John's mother by herself, without any money coming in. Perhaps two or three more runs and John would call it a day.

Many are the other tales of skirmishes of the smugglers with the Coastguard during landings. If the reader stays a while, some of those will come out.

Chapter 3

By Sunday the weather had changed, and it was a brighter and milder day; very pleasant for late October. The church bells were pealing merrily as John and his family walked down the road, having set off in plenty of time to allow for Lottie's slow walking. On the way they had been overtaken by many neighbours who were all in their best church-going clothes. The men would doff their hats, or bow in greeting before they hurried on to be sure of getting good seats.

They arrived at the church porch just as the minute bell commenced ringing, showing the service was still some way from starting. John's brother Robert, his wife Charlotte and their son, James, had coincidently arrived at the same time. They greeted each other in their usual jovial way, smiling and shaking hands, while they stood in the sun. John wanted to talk with Robert about plans he had for a family celebration of their mother's birthday, which would come soon. But they could do no more, for just at that moment Lieutenant Bulley and his wife, Sarah, came through the gate and up the path. The Lieutenant was in his best uniform, with white trousers, a white shirt and black tie, and a double breasted blue jacket, cut low around the hips for warmth. His peaked cap was firmly on his head, and white gloves in his hand. Sarah looked very serene in a high-waisted dark grey dress, a short black coat and a frothy white hat. Brandy started to bark at them. The Lieutenant frowned and pursed his lips.

John cursed inwardly, and glanced at Robert, who was obviously also feeling annoyed at the close presence of their mutual enemy. There was no time to avoid a confrontation by entering the church; they still had to round up the children and make sure Brandy was safely out of harm's way.

Both brothers had no choice but to acknowledge the Bulleys, which they did rigidly with a curt bow of their heads, and they received the same gesture in return from him. He took his hat off preparatory to entering the church and acknowledged the ladies with a bow of the head. The ladies returned his gesture demurely with small curtseys, as custom required. Robert and his family quickly preceded them into the church, leaving Frances trying to collect Lottie, who had wandered off to investigate the tombstones. John and the Lieutenant awkwardly faced each other, both trying to manoeuvre through the narrow porch, and failing miserably because of an old woman who was in the way. She was also trying to enter, having decided to get up from one of the porch seats where she had been resting. The two men were left eying each other with more than a little embarrassment.

In other circumstances John and the Lieutenant might have had a great deal in common. They were the same age, with not too dissimilar backgrounds and experience. The Lieutenant had been born at Dittisham, close to the sea in Devon, and had also grown up with salt water in his veins, but his upbringing would have been different; his parents' wealth or connections had started him on a different rung on the naval ladder than John. As an officer the Lieutenant should have been respected, as he was a conscientious law enforcer with the mission of apprehending smugglers, and did a thorough job in difficult circumstances. But John didn't trust him, and the memory of his father's apprehension by him would always be a barrier to fellow feeling. John was sure that, in turn, the Lieutenant was wary of him as a lowly fisherman and suspected lawbreaker. However, they had a common battle against the eternal enemy of the sea, which caused them to both be brave seamen and courageous in spirit.

'Good morning, Lieutenant and Mrs. Bulley,' John mumbled, feeling awkward, and anxious to cover up the embarrassment that was making the ladies uncomfortable. Once he started speaking, he felt obliged to carry on. 'I hope the builders are progressing well with the new cottages. I am sure that you and your men are looking forward to being able to move in, and be together, rather than spread out round the village in lodgings.'

'Unfortunately, no,' the Lieutenant replied, relaxing slightly as he still couldn't move away. 'The weather has been against us, and we fear that it may be late spring before we can get occupation. But, to be honest, it is a very bleak and exposed place, and there is no protection from the wind, which whistles round most of the time. I fear my wife will find it rather tedious in the winter.' He looked at his wife for confirmation, and solicitously inclined his head towards her. She sadly nodded in agreement, and felt obliged to join in the stilted conversation.

CHAPTER THREE

'I am afraid that with my husband's occupation, I will find it even more difficult to become involved in village life, and I hope that we don't become outcasts as a consequence,' she added, as she felt distinctly ostracised and was upset at being considered an outsider from the tight village community. They had no children, and time probably hung heavy on her hands. Also being the Chief Officer's wife she had the daunting prospect of not even being able to become friendly with the wives of her husband's men, the Boatmen, who would soon be living as neighbours in the same row of cottages.

'I think that will be rather inevitable, my dear,' the Lieutenant said stiffly, as he guided her into the church, the way now having become clear. It sounded as if this might have been subject of a long-running discussion about their family life, and source of friction between them. Frances looked at her with understanding and sympathy, as to some extent she had gone through the same problems after she had married. She told John later that despite the tension between the two men, she would call on the young lady to try and help her overcome her difficulties. John was not happy with the idea, but knew that he would have a fight on his hands if he tried to persuade Frances not to do something that she felt was her Christian duty.

John and his family also passed into the gloom of the church, an eye-straining contrast to the relative brightness outside. They crossed the flagstones of the Manor Chapel on tiptoe, and through the archways into the main nave, to find their seats in the family box pew, crushed in next to Robert's family and Hannah Wheeler, who had arrived much earlier. The church was lit by a few small windows, all filled with coloured glass, which gave a delightfully patterned but sparse and sombre light. The light from the altar candles did little to improve the natural light, hidden as they were behind the rood screen. Above them the tie-beam roof was dark with age and draped with cobwebs. The air was full of the smell of soap and damp clothing which combined with that of damp wood and the mildewed stone walls. The bell ringers had finished their tolling and were standing in the gallery tunelessly preparing their instruments for the hymn singing, the violins trying to match the pitch of the flutes and trumpets.

Frances' brother, the Reverend Andrew Gothen, appeared from the vestry and standing beneath the rood screen, began the service. He was eight years older than Frances, and that made him much the same age as John, but he was very different in physique and in temperament, being impetuous and excitable. He was fairly short, and as he had a large appetite, and did very little exercise, he was becoming rather portly. He was popular with the parishioners, having grown up locally at Billingham Manor, so he knew most of them and their families well, having grown up with them from childhood. Now he lived with his wife, Anne, in the parsonage just along the road, he could keep an even more fatherly eye on them. As they had no children, in many ways they looked upon the children of his flock as being their children, taking a close interest in them. John could see his sister-in-law, Anne, sitting in the front row, recognising her bonnet sticking up above those around.

The vicar stood looking out at the pews full of the congregation, his normally ruddy face shining. Some of the congregation were already absorbed in devout holiness. Others were there mainly because it was expected of them. But they were all in their Sunday best; the men in their black or navy suits, smelling distinctly of camphor, white shirts with wing collars, their bowler hats or caps on their laps, covering their hard, calloused hands and broken fingernails. Most of them wore beards or moustaches, as was the custom, but they were freshly combed, trimmed and neat. Their hair was well brushed and slicked down with pomade or macassar. Their boots were all shining brightly with new polish. The older wives were wearing dark skirts, lacy white blouses, shawls around their shoulders, bonnets on their heads and gloves on their hands. The younger ones, as well as the children, were more adventurous and up-to-date, when they could afford it, wearing more colourful Empire-line dresses, with high waistlines in pastel colours, and frilly bonnets.

John had his best navy serge suit on and had tried to flatten his unruly hair into some measure of tidiness. Frances sat demurely beside him, holding the sleeping Emily in her arms, and stroking her cheek with her fine gloves. She was wearing the light grey dress with a stylish design that John had bought her after the last successful run. The square cut and the high waist emphasised her bosoms, only partly obscured by a cut-away jacket with puffed sleeves and lace trimming. The whole effect was very attractive, and she gave the impression she felt very elegant and aristocratic when she wore it, and she certainly acted differently, treating everything with an air of condescension and approval. It made John smile inwardly to see her so contented. Lottie was fidgeting, but sitting quietly between them, playing at turning over the pages of a prayer book.

During the hymns the band in the gallery at the back played energetically, but badly. Their bows scraped on the fiddles and the trumpets and flutes were often discordant, being a beat or two apart. Nevertheless, everyone knew the tunes and sang heartily, perhaps endeavouring to cover up the noise of the band.

The vicar led the prayers, during which some gazed with rapture at the cross on the altar, carried away by their intense religious devotions. Others kept their eyes fixed purposefully on the floor and thought about their forthcoming dinner, hoping that they would be forgiven for being diverted by hunger. When the vicar ascended into the pulpit to present his sermon the congregation settled back as comfortably as possible on the hard pews, and tried to focus their minds to receive his thought-provoking words. The sermon was about duty; duty to God, to family and friends, and respect, which John thought was rather appropriate. The Reverend Andrew contended that it was duty and respect that were the glue that kept the village folk together, made the younger ones look after their elders in their old age, and kept families together under the strains of hard work, deprivation and illness. He was quiet about duty to the government, and respect for the law enforcers because he understood that most of those there had no qualms about breaking the law by running contraband and avoiding paying taxes, in order to make their lives less hard. Despite being good Christians, it would be agreed by most present that their first duty was to their Lord, and after that to their families and friends.

At last his sermon drew to a close, and the congregation could stretch their legs by standing for the closing hymn, easing their backsides from sitting so still for so long on the hard pews; not that they had had to endure anything like the hour-long sermons that some priests felt empowered to give. Andrew Gothen was a realist, setting himself a limit of a quarter of an hour, or twenty minutes, accepting that a short message was best and a bad, short sermon was better than a long, good one; a trait that helped endear him to those other than the most fervent.

A few minutes later the vicar stood at the door shaking hands with the departing men, bowing to the ladies and patting the heads of the children. A quick word here and there also helped him to judge where his ministrations might be needed during the coming week, where there might be sick to be visited, or poor to be helped. He spent a little longer with unfamiliar faces and visitors, finding out where they were from, and impressing them with the qualities of a rural parish; rural they might be, but not necessarily backward in Christian spirit, or lacking in sophistication.

Frances and John hung back, waiting for Andrew to finish so that they could walk with him to the parsonage, while Robert and his family took their mother off to dine with them. Lottie went and ran round the gravestones chasing Brandy, until she fell over, grazed her knee, and started wailing for sympathy. Frances rushed to pick her up and cuddle her, to stop her tears, and sat her on one of the flat-topped tombstones to tie a handkerchief round the knee, more as consolation, rather than from necessity.

Just then Lieutenant Bulley walked stiffly past without a glance, putting his cap back on his head. But his wife hesitated beside Frances, and appeared about to say something, before she was called to come on quickly and not to dawdle. The Wheelers walked slowly towards the gate, while the Lieutenant and his wife disappeared along the road towards Atherfield. John gazed after them pondering on the possible problems that had been exposed of their awkward life together, and comparing it with his satisfying and fulfilling family life. Then Andrew and Anne caught up with them, he full of news about his parishioners, information that they most probably knew anyway.

Being childless, Andrew had been able to develop unchecked a singular fussiness and absentmindedness that his flock treated with amused tolerance. But it was all a façade, and underneath he was a clever and astute man; after all he had been to university and was proud possessor of a degree. He indulged in the common activities of the educated and those of independent means, collecting butterflies, birds' eggs and fossils, and studying science and nature. These interests were not only tolerated, but largely shared by his wife, who was able to carry on with her own activities unencumbered by domestic needs, for they were both adequately served by the determined and forthright Mrs. Shepard, who acted as their housekeeper, cook, and general domestic. She was only known as Mrs. Shepard, and no one could remember her ever being called by a Christian name, even by her husband, Alfred. He acted as groom and gardener, as well as being sexton of the church. Together they ensured a very comfortable life for their employers, looking after their every whim. In return they also had comfortable lives. As a consequence, with little domestic affairs to concern her, Anne was able to spend her time sewing, reading, and studying nature in the parsonage grounds and the countryside around. She shared Andrew's passion as a keen amateur naturalist and observer of all that went on around her, and kept prodigious diaries of interesting trivia. She was a good complement to the vicar, as she was small, neat, slight and dark haired, but with large, intense black eyes. Her demure manner covered a very forceful personality.

The group strolled at a leisurely pace down the road to the parsonage, which was about half a mile towards Chale Street. Andrew insisted on carrying Emily, who had woken and was thinking about demanding lunch, and Lottie walked hand in hand with Anne and Frances. Brandy trotted happily along just in front of them, to show them the way. The parsonage was on the left, set back from the road along a short gravel drive behind a line of fir trees. It had an imposing but very plain elevation, quite old but much altered. Four gables faced eastwards towards the road, with steep pitched slate roofs. The middle two sections were the oldest part of the building, and contained the main rooms, the left-hand one having a deep porch to shelter the door from cold winds. Unusually the building had three stories, the rooms having small, narrow, rectangular windows with leaded lights, set in pairs, or fours, with thick mullions between them.

To the left-hand side of the house were low stables and a coach-house, which contained several horses, and a pony and trap. By far the most interesting side of the house was the back, which faced south-west, and had larger windows to let in the afternoon and evening sun, with extensive views over the fields toward the distant downs, and attractive lawns and rose-beds, which were Anne's pride and joy. Obviously, it was much too big a house for Andrew and Anne, having been built for families with many children and servants.

At the door Frances took the baby from Andrew who was hesitating, wanting to take his coat off, and Anne rushed in to ensure that the dinner preparations were progressing satisfactorily. In actual fact Mrs. Shepard was relieved that her mistress had been out of her way, rather than fussing around all the morning. Anne returned mollified, and she and Frances went to feed the two girls. Brandy went too, certain that Alfred would find him some titbits.

Leaving the ladies to their pleasurable tasks, Andrew gestured that John should follow him into the library where he offered him a glass of sherry. Though it was not John's preferred drink, he accepted.

The library was dark and gloomy at this time of the year, when it seldom received any sunlight, but it had the appearance of being well used and loved. The walls were lined with bookcases full of leather bound books with embossed spines. Some were about religion, but most were about nature and travel in foreign lands, subjects that intrigued both Andrew and Anne. In the middle of the room stood a large desk where Andrew composed his sermons, with a comfortable arm chair beside it in which he snoozed and gained inspiration. A fire burned brightly in the grate, and the vicar went across to stand in front of it with his sherry glass in one hand and the other behind him extended to the warmth. He was a shorter man than John, with a luxuriant brown moustache and side whiskers. He looked at John speculatively.

CHAPTER THREE

'I hear the fishing has not been particularly good this autumn, John. Have you been able to put enough by during the summer to last you and Frances over the long winter?' he asked. He was always considerate of his sister's wellbeing, and was unusual in having settled money on her after their father's estate had been wound up. Their father had always exhorted him to ensure their bequest to him, as only son, was used to also benefit his sister, and he had faithfully honoured the obligation.

John sipped at the sherry. 'That's right, Andrew. The fishing was good during the early summer, but the mackerel shoals were very poor, and we haven't seen any cod yet. But I am sure we will survive, despite the necessity of supporting Father.' He referred to the fact that they had to pay the prison warders to ensure the prisoner had reasonable food and some comfort; the normal gruel and stale bread, wet cells and damp blankets were not good for the older man's health. But John wondered what this was leading up to. Why was Andrew interested in the state of the fishing? It was normally far from his thoughts. Maybe it was the prelude to an offer of further money; something that always embarrassed John and made him feel he was being asked to accept charity.

'Let me get to the point,' Andrew said. Thank goodness for that, John thought, for he was not normally one for beating about the bush. 'While Frances is busy with the children, I think I'd better put before you the proposal I've had in mind for a while. You might, or might not find it reasonable.

'I know your father is in jail as the result of being involved with smuggling, and I know you are a smuggler too. You don't think I know, and I know you don't think I know, but I do,' he said with a smile. He went over to the desk, opened a drawer, and took out a bag which he put down on the desk with a chinking sound. 'In there are a hundred sovereigns. I want to invest them in a cargo of brandy, and I would like you to arrange it for me.'

John was astonished, because the topic had never come up before, and Frances and he had been very careful as far as Andrew was concerned to avoid any mention or implication of involvement in the business. However, on one occasion, Alfred, in his role as sexton, had opened up a grave in the churchyard for them several days before a funeral was due, and John had used it as a temporary hide for a dozen tubs. He thought that the vicar had not known about it, but obviously he may have done, though not necessarily of John's part in it.

Andrew went on, 'I have heard from several quarters that you have the skill, judgement and contacts to do it, and have done it many times before. I am not sure whether it is good practice to be involved with others so close to home, but I wouldn't know who else to ask. It will need you to get together a crew, as well as organise the boat, and the landing party. A few of them may want to put some of their own money into the venture and become additional shareholders; you may even want to put up a share yourself. I can certainly suggest a few others who might be interested in taking some of the cargo. What do you think? Are you interested?'

John was taken aback. He never thought that Andrew would ever contemplate such a risky undertaking, and an illegal one at that. He turned away with a thoughtful frown, and took a gulp of the sherry. He walked over to the window and looked out, while he collected his thoughts. He had heard whispers of a big run that was being planned in the West Wight before Christmas, either into Totland Bay or Colwell Bay. There would hardly be time to organise a run before that, and the success of a second one would depend crucially on how the first went; the first might alert the Coastguard and spoil the chances of bringing another one off undetected. On the other hand, the Coastguard might not expect two runs close together, and provided the liquor didn't flood the market all at once, the confusion might aid success.

A possible solution came to him. How about a run on Christmas Day? The Revenue Officers and the Coastguard would not want to be out and about at that time; their thoughts and their energies would be diverted by the seasonal celebrations.

'Let's put it this way, Andrew. I'll see whether it can be done. I will have to talk to one or two others first. No promises at the moment, but I always think the winter is the best time, because the nights are long, and the cold keeps the Coastguard near their fires. The one big problem of course will be the weather, but that will always be a problem no matter the time of the year,' he shrugged. 'I must talk it over with Frances first, but we will need to work quickly, because it takes time to set up the supply in France. I presume that it is just brandy you want, and nothing else?'

'Yes, John. That would do well.'

Nodding, John continued. 'There seems to be no problem, at the moment, about selling a cargo locally without having to take any to the mainland. There are so many wealthy gentry living or visiting the Island these days, there's always a ready market for the after-dinner drink, or something to purify the water.' Then, thinking more of the immediate practicalities John added, 'We will need to use some of the money for advances to the boat's crew and the landing party, to ensure their cooperation and silence. If I were to take fifty pounds now, I can always come back for the rest later when we need it for the actual cargo.'

The vicar nodded his agreement, and poured out the shining gold sovereigns onto the desk, roughly divided them in half, and put the two halves in separate bags. He handed one to John.

'Thank you, Andrew. If I can't get a crew together, I'll let you have this back. It's been some months since a run has been landed here, so I expect enough men will be willing to join in, especially as this winter will be a hard time for most of them.'

At that moment there was a knock on the door, and Anne came in to call them for lunch. Frances had finished feeding the girls, and Mrs. Shepard would look after them while the adults ate. Together Andrew and John went into the dining room, where their wives were already sitting on either side of the long mahogany table. A carpenter living just up the road at Stroud Green had made the table from wood saved from a wreck, and he had also panelled the room with timber obtained from another wreck, giving it a warm and homely feeling. A fire in the grate and four long candles glowing on the table sent flickering shadows playing over the rich brown wood, and over the moulding on the ceiling, making the cherubs on the coping appear to be talking. Frances' hair caught the light and it formed a lustrous frame to her face, healthy with rosy cheeks and ruby lips. She smiled at John and gave a lift to his heart, as she was looking so calm and beautiful.

The men took the chairs at the ends of the table, and sat down. Mrs. Shepard brought in the soup, and after a quick blessing on the food by the vicar, Anne started serving it out. Andrew tucked a napkin into his waistcoat, with an anticipatory smile, saying, 'After the communion and a sermon to give me spiritual nourishment, I am ready for some physical nourishment.' He was well known as a good trencherman, and it reflected in his waistline. Between each mouthful he asked Frances about the children, a topic she could talk on for hours, and she and Anne chattered away happily, as the ladies were wont to do.

John was quiet as he sipped his soup, thinking over the prospect of another run, and the risks involved. If he were to be honest, he enjoyed the thrill of the competition, the contest against the weather and the authorities. There was excitement and satisfaction in the teamwork with friends, and a great sense of exhilaration and achievement when the run was complete; it was rather like a game of chess, in the planning, the build up of moves, the overcoming of setbacks, and the final outwitting of the opponent. As far as he was concerned it wasn't just the money. When he started becoming involved in smuggling it gave his life an extra excitement and purpose; something to look forward to that was different from the daily round. The sail racing gave him the same lift in spirits. However, since being married and having a family dependent on him, his feelings had started changing. What if he were caught and separated from his family, as his father had been? How would they manage if he were imprisoned? It had got to the stage where he found it difficult to say yes to a proposed run, especially as it was no longer essential, thanks to the security that Frances' annuity gave them. But it was still difficult to step aside and not help his friends.

To decrease the risk of being caught he was always very careful with whom he associated. There were some smugglers who were not worried by being quite brutal to those who got in their way, particularly the Coastguard. Injuries and even deaths had been caused by some of the gangs; when confronted with Coastguards armed with guns and swords it was only to be expected. Of course there would be very heavy penalties if they were caught, probably the worst being transportation, after which the convicts would seldom be heard from again. John was careful to avoid conflict. As far as he was concerned the money was a bonus, and it was the enjoyment and the satisfaction that made the risk worthwhile. Consequently, if there was any risk of failure, he would prefer to walk away from a run, rather than carry on regardless. On this occasion, as he would be in total charge of the run, he could manage and control the risks properly. He could pick and choose those he worked with, rather than being one of many he didn't necessarily know or trust. Because of this he came to the conclusion that he was reasonably happy about the idea. But he needed to have Frances' agreement, as she would be the one to suffer any consequences.

The soup plates were cleared away, the meat course brought in, and some freshly brewed beer for the men and cordial for the ladies. Andrew stood to carve the mutton joint, licking the ends of his moustaches as he did so. While he was concentrating, John turned to Frances, assuming that Anne already knew of the proposal, and said, 'Your brother has made me a proposition for...'

Andrew immediately looked up, and waved the carving knife. 'No John. It was my proposal, let me tell it. Then if she doesn't agree with it, the onus will be on me, the fault will be mine.' Then, while he carved and handed out the plates, he launched into a repeat of what he had said to John.

Frances paled and her mouth became compressed into a firm line as she listened to the plan. Anne looked at her with concern, anticipating the possibility of a family argument. It was obvious Frances was not entirely happy, but whether it was because of John's or her brother's involvement, wasn't clear. Of course, before they were married she had found out about John's trading activities and that had been part of his glamour. She had accepted it as being part of their life, though now she took a more realistic attitude, and hadn't been exactly encouraging. But she could see the benefits accruing to herself and the children with a better life than they could otherwise afford. She had also realised that John actually enjoyed the thrill of outwitting the authorities without any harm being done. In fact, in the end, a lot of good was done to their little village community, with less poverty, and healthier children. John felt sure she would come around to accepting it with time and further discussion.

Because of the local implications, smuggling had never before been spoken of when sitting at Andrew's table; by tacit agreement it had been avoided. But, while they ate, John felt that if he related a story of some of his experiences, it might make the whole concept sound less like a criminal activity and more like an acceptable game.

John had in mind one story that he hadn't even told Frances before. He explained how he had come to hear it from a visitor that he had found clambering around the cliffs. The man was a geologist and he had taken lodgings locally while he mapped the rocks and the strata, and looked for fossils. He was called Joshua Haygarth, and John had met him several times on the cliffs as he worked. On one occasion they sheltered in the fishing hut by the beach during a rain storm, and he'd told John the story then. While they tucked into some preserves for dessert, John repeated the story.

'At one time Haygarth had been looking for lodgings in Freshwater while he did some geological investigations there. He had asked several men where he could find accommodation, and after receiving evasive answers, and having the doors of several houses slammed in his face, he came across a labourer somewhat gone in his cups, having had too much to drink. This man was more talkative, and directed my friend to a farmhouse called Woodbine Farm, owned by a man called Priddle. The farmhouse was a low, grey stone, thatched building, tucked beneath Freshwater Down. It had a square patch of flowers in front and a rickyard and farm buildings behind. As he was about to walk up the path, he noticed a paper attached to a tree in the hedge. It was an auctioneer's notice stating that the farm, buildings, stock and furniture would be sold three weeks later, by order of the court.

'While being undecided whether to ask for accommodation, or not, a young man came up behind my friend, saw the notice, cursed, tore it down and accused him of posting it. This accusation upset my friend, but the man's manner changed when Haygarth said he was merely looking for lodgings. He was welcomed in, and offered a room by the man's mother, even though the farmer was away.' John paused and drank some beer to ease his dry throat, unused to talking so much.

He continued after taking a mouthful of fruit. 'That night Mr. Haygarth was disturbed by footsteps, as someone left the house. As he peeped out he saw a man with a lantern moving about in the farm buildings behind the house. This happened for several nights. He was also puzzled by the fact that Fred, for this was the young man's name, spent more time on his boat than overseeing the farm labourers, and that his father was still unaccountably absent.' Frances looked intrigued and shared puzzled smiles with Anne.

'Eventually, Fred confided in my friend, because he wanted his help. Apparently, the Priddles were free traders, as everyone was thereabouts. The father had got into debt because of a succession of bad harvests and by an unlucky run, when all of the cargo had been seized by the Preventive Officers. Mr. Priddle was away at that time trying to recoup his fortunes in another run, but, because of the activities of a new Coastguard officer from Yarmouth, they hadn't been able to land the cargo; the officer's suspicions having been raised by

Mr. Priddle's absence. Fred had had to warn the boat off every night, because of the presence of the Coastguard, who were closely watching the farm. That was why there was so much night-time activity.

'Fred was at a loss for what to do, but had a plan, which depended on my friend being willing to cooperate. Haygarth said he would help, but he wouldn't tell any lies. He was assured that he would not have to do so, so he agreed. The following night at the stroke of midnight Mr. Haygarth left his room as he was asked, went out of the front door and down the lane to the junction. Suddenly a man leapt out of the hedge, accosted him and shone a light in his eyes. It was the Coastguard officer and his men. They were disappointed to find he was the visitor staying at the farm and not one of the smugglers. But he told them the reason he'd come out at that time was to find some help, because there had been noises, lights and activity at the back of the farm, and he thought there might be smuggling going on. Immediately they told him to come with them while they investigated. They all went round the back of the farmhouse and after a search, found obvious signs of activity in one of the barns; partly hidden beneath a wagon, they found the earth on the floor had been disturbed.

'The jubilant Coastguards grabbed picks and shovels that had been left conveniently nearby, and started digging, reckoning there would be tubs of liquor hidden beneath. They dug for hours and it was almost light when they revealed fifteen tubs at the bottom of the now large hole. Gleefully they loaded them on the wagon and went off, thinking they had proof enough to arrest the farmer.' Andrew broke in, asking how the smugglers could be so careless. John laughed and told him to wait and see.

'After the Coastguards left, Mr. Priddle appeared and, laughing, shook Haygarth by the hand, having heard from his son of his cooperation. He then revealed that the tubs were actually full of sea water. While the Coastguards were busy in the barn, they had been able to land the real cargo, bring it in by the front door of the farm, and hide the tubs in a cellar beneath the kitchen. The result was the farmer paid off his debts, the auction was cancelled, and thereafter the new Preventive Officer was much less zealous in his work. The ultimate irony is that the farmer insisted that the Coastguards returned and filled in the hole they had left in the barn floor.'

The others round the table were much amused at the story. Andrew slapped the table as he laughed, wiping his eyes with his napkin. 'That's a good one,' he said. 'I'll have to remember to tell it when I next meet the squire for dinner, but I will need to change the names and the location, won't I?' He moved over to the sideboard and poured glasses of brandy for all of them, and toasted a successful run. Frances only sipped her glass because she was still feeding Emily.

John explained to them about the idea of Christmas as a quiet time when it might be safe to run a cargo, but he was concerned that Andrew might object that it was not ethical, and mightn't accept it. But John was relieved and a bit surprised when he said that it would be up to John to set the schedule, and that if the Lord did not want it at that time, the weather would be bad as a consequence and defeat them.

John also had an idea as to how the Coastguard could be distracted when the time came. One of the Coastguards, a Charles Heath, lived near to Robert, and it would be easy for him to drop little pieces of misinformation that would get reported to the Chief Officer, and ensure the Coastguard were out of the way on the day, without anything actually being disclosed. This would be easy if Robert were in charge of the landing party, and had the responsibility for giving the boat the all clear signal. John was sure, also, that he would have to involve Alf Shepard, who had probably been listening outside the door to their conversation. But John knew he was trustworthy, for they had worked together before.

From her reaction John could see that Frances was much happier about the whole scheme, now the details became clearer, and she could see the risks weren't too daunting. She was more relaxed, and John could see in her smile the challenge appealing to her sense of fun. He felt much better about the whole thing then. In particular, he was glad to have become much closer to his brother-in-law, having been much in awe of him previously, because of his knowledge and his learning. Perhaps, after all, they were kindred spirits beneath the skin.

About a month later, after a lot of careful and clandestine discussion and bargaining, John felt happy that all seemed to be in place for the run. Between him and Robert they had managed to put together the whole party from relatives, friends and old accomplices from the village and the near neighbourhood. They were all known to be trustworthy and John was particularly pleased that they all had confidence in and respected each other; this ought to ensure that there was little chance of anyone failing in what they had agreed to do, or of information leaking out.

He had managed to get a message via a local wool factor, John Parker, to a contact in France, with whom they had worked before, with instructions to organise a load of brandy to be ready two days or so before Christmas at the small sheltered port of Barfleur. The factor was a boyhood friend from the village and he was still based there. He bought wool across the Island, and even into Hampshire, and sold it in the north of England, as well as exporting it to northern France. He had an aptitude for languages and for commercial dealing, and frequently he legitimately crossed the Channel to trade.

Consequently he was well known to the Coastguard, and though they always kept a close eye on his activities, they had never been able to connect him with any smuggling. He knew the town and the traders in Barfleur, spoke the language and could ensure that the bargain would be honoured. An added bonus was that the factor could arrange to be in Barfleur before Christmas, and, as none of the rest of them spoke French, and there was always a risk that something might go wrong, he would be there to help. Once this was settled John felt much more confident about the prospects of success, especially as no one but he knew about this contact.

Robert had organised the landing party, and recruited his next-door neighbour, Robert Stead, as his assistant. They had reckoned that a group of a dozen men, strong both in body and in mind, would be needed, men who could be trusted to keep their mouths shut both before the event and afterwards. They picked men who also possessed a number of different skills that were essential for success.

Two of them were carriers, or carters, David Cheverton and William Moorman. They were essential to help take the heavy barrels to their eventual destinations. Because they were always travelling around the Island carrying loads of all sorts, ranging from vegetables to market or grain to the mill, and coal in return, movement of their carts would raise no suspicions at almost any time of day or night. Initially they would take the cargo to the temporary hiding places. After that, they could easily hide a few tubs at a time amongst other loads, and take the tubs on to customers elsewhere.

A blacksmith, Benjamin Linnington, and a carpenter, Jeremiah Newnham, were also included. Their skills would be useful in making hides for the tubs, or coping with any emergency repairs. If necessary, both of them could hide a few tubs around their working premises. To complete the party a number of farm labourers would provide strength for handling and carrying the tubs, and knowledge of where they could be hidden around farmyards, outbuildings and fields. Two of them, George Walsh and Thomas Dove, both worked for William Jacobs at Chale Abbey Farm; appropriately he had been brought in as one of the shareholders financing the run.

Most of the landing party had managed to scrape together a sovereign or so each, either for a tub for themselves or for a part share in one. On completion of the run they would then all get a share of the profits. If any of the cargo were seized by the Coastguard, or lost, everyone's share would be reduced. But in the event of the entire load being lost it was agreed that the vicar and the other financers would be the losers, and the landing party would get their money back.

John had decided to use his smack to fetch the load, since the weather would probably not be good enough to use anything smaller. It was a handy craft and would cope with all but the most extreme conditions. Naturally he would captain the boat, and had alerted a crew of four, which included his uncle as mate, and his cousin, Charles, a 19-year-old always up for a bit of fun and adventure.

John reckoned that five men would be needed to handle the boat in all weathers, as well as the tubs, and had chosen another fisherman they were used to working with, an experienced man called John Richards. He lived with his wife, Sarah, and young family in a boathouse on the lower cliff, and had a very useful hut nearby which could be used as a temporary hide, admirably close to the likely landing site. He was keen to help, because fishing had not been good for him recently, and he was desperate for extra money to tide the family over during the winter. Another local fisherman, John Rayner, completed the crew. Even though the smack could be quite easily handled by four, or even three experienced men, the extra hands would be needed to load the tubs, and prepare them for the landing. Each of the crew had already been paid an advance of ten pounds which would not have to be repaid should the trip be aborted for any reason. They were the ones who were to bear the greatest risk of punishment at the hands of the Revenue, and potentially had the worst hardships to endure at sea.

* * * * * *

During the time all this was being organised Frances did something that, in the long run, turned out to be particularly momentous for the Wheelers. She insisted to John that she was going to visit Mrs. Bulley, to talk with her, hold out the hand of friendship, and try to alleviate her distress by involving her more in the village life. John was still not happy about associating further with the man who imprisoned his father, but decided not to make an issue of it; it would make life much more harmonious to let her make what he thought would be a mistake on her own. So one day she borrowed the pony trap from Andrew so that she could take the children and Brandy too, as she thought they would help to ease the surprise of an unsolicited impromptu visit, give Frances an excuse to depart quickly, if necessary, and give them something to talk about to break the ice.

When John arrived home from the day spent organising the run, she was much more interested in telling him about the visit she had made, than in hearing what he had achieved. She set out anticipating arriving at the Bulleys' cottage while the Lieutenant was on duty, having presumed rightly that he would be out during the morning. In fact John remembered having seen him in the distance riding along the cliff edge at that time, gazing at the beach.

However, when she found their lodgings at Atherfield, she had to knock several times on the door before it was answered; she had persisted because she knew that Sarah Bulley was bound to be in. Eventually, when Sarah peeped through the window and realised it was Frances, she welcomed her and the children in, and put the kettle on the range to make a cup of tea. She had been reluctant to answer the door because of the state she was in. She had been crying, her eyes were red and puffy, tears streaking her cheeks, and she kept her face averted to try and hide the fact from Frances. But, once she sat down at the table she again burst into floods of tears, and began to unburden herself of her pent up feelings.

Through her sobs Frances found out that Sarah was very lonely and depressed. Her husband, John, was on duty virtually all the time and they had little time together. When they did he was exhausted and they seemed to argue continually.

Sarah said that they had both been very excited when he had been offered the Chief Officer position, and saw it as an escape from the long periods he had had to spend away at sea. But as he settled into it he became dissatisfied with the way it had developed, and saw little future in it. He thought he could end up doing the same arduous job the rest of his life, with little prospect of advancement. They had paid out the required large premium to obtain the post in the first place, and she believed he now regretted it.

Sarah revealed that his pay was less than he would have been receiving had he remained in the Navy, and that pay was stopped if he was ill, or if they wanted a day off. Try as much as he could, he felt that he couldn't do the best for his men because of the inefficiency of the service, the amount of paperwork that had to be filled in, and the fact that his statements and opinions were not trusted by the administrators who appeared to control everything he did. These revelations came as a surprise to Frances, though she had suspected there must have been some underlying problem. She was amazed to find it was this bad. It was as much a revelation to John, when she told him; he had believed that John Bulley was zealous in his work, and thought he must get a great deal of satisfaction from it, particularly as he would have received extra monetary rewards for catching and imprisoning smugglers, such as Jack Wheeler. It just goes to show how wrong one could be about people.

Frances found that Sarah had her own problems too. She felt that she couldn't make friends with the wives of the other Coastguards, or confide in them, because of her husband's position as their superior. Also to avoid the men becoming too involved with local people, and becoming open to coercion or bribery, one of the conditions of the service was that the families were expected to move frequently. This took away any incentive for them to try to become part of the village life, and led to social as well as physical isolation. At least the other wives had each other to talk to and share problems with, but Sarah felt she was on her own, in a class above them. With Frances she at last thought she had the consolation of being able to talk to someone of her own breeding and background; even though Frances was a fisherman's wife, she was the daughter of a local landowner and sister of a clergyman, and was undeniably her equal.

As they talked Sarah had gradually relaxed and cheered up, seeming to be relieved by unburdening herself of her worries. She enjoyed holding Emily, who cooed happily in her arms, grasping her fingers in a small hand, and sucking at one of them. She looked at the baby with pleasure and envy. Then it came out that Sarah was longing to have a baby of her own. She wanted to start the family that all of her contemporaries were having, and her parents expected. She was envious of those who had families, and though the Bulleys had been trying for some time, it just hadn't happened.

Frances thought that this might be the root cause of the Bulleys' problems, but she could do no more than just listen, and try to help Sarah realise that their failure could have been a combination of the tensions in her husband's work, their lack of a social life, as well as her extreme desire to have a baby. If they could only relax, spend more time together, and have a holiday, perhaps visiting their parents, it might happen. It could have been they were trying too hard and were too worried about it.

By the time Frances had to leave, as Lottie was getting sleepy and needed her midday nap, Sarah was smiling and was much happier. The two women vowed that they would meet again, and Frances was thankful that she'd taken the initiative in making the visit. She liked Sarah, and felt she too had gained much from their exchange of confidences.

That evening when Frances described to John the result of her visit, his first reaction was to say, serve them right, and what did they expect. But it made Frances angry that he could be so short-sighted. He soon realised, when they discussed it, that all was not so clearly black and white; the more contented the Bulleys' felt, the more likely it was that the smugglers and the Coastguard could co-exist without dangerous friction between them. John, despite his underlying concern, agreed that Frances was right to try and help Sarah, and that she could visit again, at some stage, to give the poor lady further friendship and advice.

One major problem they agreed on seemed to be the Lieutenant's obsession with his duty. With his experience of the Navy John could see why such an obsession would develop in a Navy officer subject to tight regulations and discipline, but he thought the Coastguard needed a different standard. They weren't isolated in the way that a ship's company was, they had to work with and interact with the general public in a totally different way. He wondered what could be done to change John Bulley's attitude and make him more balanced in his interpretation of his duty. Even after a long discussion neither Frances nor he had any idea how to go about it. The irony was that at that moment John was doing entirely the opposite, and planning things that could make the Bulleys' situation worse rather than better. Unless, that is, he were to catch them smuggling. In which case the Lieutenant would feel his attitude vindicated by results.

* * * * * *

One day at the beginning of December John borrowed one of Andrew's mares to go to Newtown to check over the smack, and make sure it was seaworthy enough for a Channel crossing. It had been several weeks since he had used it for fishing, and he had noticed then that the main sheet was getting rather frayed, and the rigging in one or two places needed renewing. Also they would need new fresh water on board, and some extra rope for handling the tubs. So John took a coil of rope from their supplies in the hut on the beach, which he could carry behind the saddle. He was careful to make it appear that this visit and the preparations were simply getting ready for a normal fishing trip, so he also took with him some twine to mend some of the nets, and withies to mend some of the crab pots that were on board.

On a nice day John always enjoyed the ride to Newtown, a distance of about ten miles each way. He crept out of bed while it was still dark, leaving Frances warm and comfortable, snoring gently, and quietly peeped in at the children, who were peaceful too. It turned out to be one of those good days, a perfect, late autumn day with a gentle, cool westerly wind and small, fleecy clouds evenly spread and quickly scudding across the blue sky. He hoped that the run would be on a day like this. But the Revenue cruisers would be more likely to be out on such a day, and it would be easier for them to sight a small boat, something he could do without.

He took the road through Stroud Green, which was still largely sleeping, though there was a light in the bakery, and the smell of fresh baked bread in the air made his mouth water. He reached Shorwell as dawn was breaking, and then he took the road towards Carisbrooke, going up the hill known as Shorwell Shute, where the trees hung low over the narrow, wooded lane, almost meeting in the middle. The fallen leaves were blowing up the lane, and the horse seemed to enjoy brushing her hooves through them, making a crisp rustling noise. The stirring released the sharp tangy smell that was so redolent of autumn; in spring, the scent of the ransoms flowering in the woods would be as strong, almost enough to clear the nostrils with one deep breath.

On the way up the hill he passed the entrance to North Court, a large estate with an imposing Jacobean mansion tucked away in the trees. John remembered with pleasure having once had the honour of meeting Mrs. Bennet, the owner. She was much revered in the village, a very genteel lady, and gracious even to a simple fisherman, though he was delivering a tub of brandy at the time.

Breasting the top of the rise John turned the mare left onto the open downs where he spurred her into a canter, the coil of rope banging behind him urging the horse on. The mare snorted with delight, normally not being allowed to extend herself in such a way, and the thundering hooves quickly ate up the miles. They cantered effortlessly over Renham Down, Limerston Down, and Brixton Down, past many tumuli marking ancient burial sites and primitive dwellings. John always wondered how the occupants' lives would have been all those centuries ago, up here on the windy, exposed and bleak hills; much harder and uncertain than his, he was sure.

On the crest of New Barn Down John reined in and stopped to look down on the village of Calbourne, nestling in the bottom of the valley. He dismounted to give the horse a rest, and himself a welcome stretch of the legs. On the other side of the valley he could see the elm tree-lined avenue winding from the bridge over the stream up to Westover, a large and elegantly designed house surrounded by a handsome stone colonnade, and backed by a sheltering grove of huge trees. Formerly the house had been the seat of Sir Leonard Worsley Holmes, a distant relation of Lord Yarborough, for whom John sailed. Sir Leonard had died ten years before at the early age of thirty-three, but the house was still occupied by his wife, Lady Anne, who was the daughter of John Delgano, a merchant in Newport. John knew that the Holmes family had been very important in Yarmouth in the past. John had never had the opportunity of looking over the house while the owner was away, as was the custom, though Frances had. She frequently said it was magnificent, and had been impressed with the most attractive flower gardens and views towards the north-east. However, as far as John was concerned, if he couldn't eat what was in the gardens, it wasn't worth the effort.

From the saddlebag John took out a hunk of bread and cheese, and a bottle of water, and sat on the soft turf to eat. In the distance he could see the bright silver strip of sea which was the Solent, separating the Island from the mainland. About two miles wide it stretched from the Needles, far away to the west, eastwards to the Spithead, where, off Portsmouth, there was bound to be a large number of Navy ships moored and the continual activity of preparation for sea, or disembarkation on return.

Newtown Creek, John's destination, was on the north shore of the Island, and hardly visible, as it was surrounded by woods right to the water's edge. Just off the creek he could see sailing vessels of various sizes, and a large, fully rigged ship was bowling eastwards under full sail before the westerly breeze. It was a fine sailing day, and he looked forward to the exhilaration of a good, fast sail across the Channel in a couple of weeks' time.

Less than an hour later he crossed the causeway across an arm of the creek, trotted up the hill to the old town hall of Newtown, built to justify the village being able to elect two members of parliament, but now virtually derelict. Newtown itself was a small village that had not recovered from being raided and burned by the French in the fourteenth century, and it still could only boast nine or ten humble cottages. Turning left they carried on past the church and down to the hard. Here John dismounted with aching back and muscles. After a good stretch he unloaded and unsaddled the horse and turned her out into a small paddock owned by an old friend. The saddle he left quite safely in a shelter in the corner. The whole journey had taken just under three hours.

John had left the little rowing boat that he used as a tender in a shed down by the high tide line. The oars were still standing in a corner, put there to dry after last being used. He dragged the boat to the edge of the hard, and as the tide was high, was able to lower it directly into the water, and threw in the coil of rope and the other supplies. He had to be very careful climbing in as the boat was very unstable; on one occasion in a high wind it had shot away and left him floundering in the water. The last thing he wanted was to ride home wet and cold.

The other side of the creek he could see the *Sweet Frances* safely moored, with no visible change to when he had last seen her. When he clambered on board his nostrils were assailed by the smell of old fish, salt water and seaweed, a familiar and emotive smell. There were about five hours of daylight left to finish his preparations before darkness would force him to set out for home. If possible he would like to be under way before then; either that or he would have to sleep the night on the boat. He had warned Frances of that prospect if he couldn't get all the work done before dark.

The *Sweet Frances* was a small clinker-built smack, about twenty-five feet long, not including an eight-foot-long running bowsprit. She was half-decked, meaning that she had a small, separate forepeak, and a large hold taking up the majority of the hull space. Access to the forepeak was by narrow hatchway and a ladder, protected by a low cuddy, just before the mast. There was only about five-foot headroom in the forepeak, not enough for John to stand fully upright, but it was dry, and he had constructed a pipecot on either side. This meant that two of the crew could get their heads down when not on watch. Normally the sails would also be stored there in the dry. She was a trim boat and could out-point most others when tacking, and run fast before the wind, when her hull was clean.

Most of the deck aft of the mast was taken up with a hatchway above the comparatively spacious hold, which was partly planked on top of the mainframe timbers. The hatch too was planked and covered with a tarpaulin to keep the rain or the spray out. Normally the hold would be full of fishing nets or crab pots, and smelt pungently of stale fish. But it would take nearly a hundred tubs stacked and lashed so that they would not shift in heavy weather. Enough space was left at the stern for the helmsman to stand while at the tiller.

John was annoyed to see the deck was covered in seagull and cormorant droppings that had dried and curled up in the sun and wind. He always tried to follow his Naval training, being used to the principle of a clean and well holystoned deck; it avoided the risk of slipping on the deck when it was wet. However, the mess was the sign of a working boat, and he was careful to leave his standards to one side in the light of the camouflage it provided when one's objectives were not totally honest. Nevertheless, he lowered a bucket over the side and sloshed water over the deck to help swell the deck timbers and tighten up the seams. This would decrease the amount of water seeping through into the bilges, and help the boat's speed.

He checked the bilges, and was pleased there was not a lot to be pumped out; the hull caulking must still be fairly tight after the careening they had carried out earlier in the autumn.

At the top of a spring tide they had tied the boat to the hard, and at low water they had given the hull a good scrub and a coat of tar paint. Hopefully not much weed should have grown since then, and in a fair wind the boat should give a clean pair of heels to most other boats they were likely to encounter. At a pinch in calm weather, the boat was small enough to be rowed; the oars being below in the hold.

Since the mainsheet needed attention, John bent a light line onto the end of the existing sheet and pulled the line, followed by a new mainsheet, through the masthead block and back to deck level. Also he renewed one of the shrouds that showed wear. The sails were all stored below, and though he was not aware of any problems with them, he still had them out on deck to check them over and get rid of their musty smell, and ended up re-stitching some of the clew eyelets that were frayed.

Having satisfied himself that the boat was sound and in good condition, he set about filling small barrels with fresh water from a spring close to the hard, rowing them out to the boat and storing them below. This was time consuming, for the spring flowed slowly and it seemed to take an age to fill each barrel. But it was quiet and peaceful waiting, and he spent the time enjoying watching the patterns the breeze made on the water, listening to the rustling as it blew through the reeds near the water's edge, and the gentle sloshing of the little waves against the mud. He watched the many waders and ducks feeding along the water's edge, contentedly piping and whistling to each other. He too was contented, whistling softly to himself, unaware that there was a watcher spying on him, checking up on his activities.

The afternoon gradually became gloomy, the clouds were increasing and the wind was rising, whistling through the rigging and making the sheets tap and crack against the mast. As all the jobs were done he packed up and checked the mooring buoy, pulling on its rope to ensure that the anchor was well stuck in the mud. Satisfied, he returned to the shore, but as the tide was now low he had to wade across the mud to reach the hard, towing the tender behind him. It was filthy and smelly work. He put the tender back in the shed, and though he rinsed his boots and hands in a pool, he couldn't get rid of the horrible, muddy smell of rotten eggs on his hands and clothing.

The horse whinnied when she was caught up, knowing that she was now going to head back homewards. They returned home over the downs in the twilight with the almost full moon rising low in the east, to light their way, and the familiar stars of the various constellations above them.

* * * * * *

When John arrived home, to his surprise Frances was still downstairs, sitting in the dark gazing into the coals of the dying fire. He could tell she was upset. Though she was obviously bursting to tell him something, she welcomed him home with a kiss, and then went into the larder and fetched some cold meat, cheese, bread and butter, and a jar of the black currant jam she had made during the summer. She put them on the table, while he removed his boots and washed his hands free of the muddy smell. Then they both sat at the table and she started to tell him her woes.

'I went to visit Sarah Bulley again this morning,' she said dolefully. Then a torrent of words spilled out. 'It was fine when I arrived; just like old friends we started where we had left off. She played with the baby, and we had a cup of tea, and she seemed much happier than the first visit. But then she started to tell me of her husband's reaction to my visit. He had not been happy about it, and almost accused her of fraternising with 'the enemy', as he put it. He didn't want her to have anything more to do with me, and almost forbade her to open the door to me. She was upset to say the least, but over the following days had resolved to take no notice of him because he was being so irrational and petty about it. Apparently they had quite a row, but it hadn't affected her determination. She had thought that he might have raised his hand to her, he was so agitated. But, apparently, he is not that sort of man, and managed to curb his fury before it came to that.'

She paused to gain breath, looking at John to judge his reaction. He kept a straight face while he pensively chewed on a mouthful of bread and meat.

Then she continued. 'I was on the point of leaving, but just as Sarah had her hand on the knob, he opened the door. He hadn't been expected, and it was obvious what we had been talking about, as Sarah went quite white and stammered when welcoming him home. He in turn went red, and seemed to be making a considerable effort to keep his temper under control. He was very frosty and hardly even managed a curt bow to me, even though I curtseyed to him. He said nothing apart from, "Good day", and then pushed past us into the house. I left then, but Sarah apologised for his bad manners. I suspect they had another row after I'd left.' She fell silent, looking into the fire again, lost in concern about her friend's unhappy situation.

After some more chewing and a little contemplation, John replied. 'It seems to me that it's their problem. They have to resolve it between themselves. It's selfish for him to expect her not to talk to the local people, or to make her own friends. Perhaps it is the thought that your visiting her in his house put him under some sort of obligation. I suggest you leave it for a while, and see if she comes to visit you here, because you have made it plain to her that she can. That seems to me to be the next and the most appropriate move she can make, and it might not cause him so much of a problem if she were to do that.'

Frances thought it a sensible thing to do, and seemed relieved at this conclusion. She could see his eyes were drooping, and took his hand, saying, 'Come on, you look tired. It's time you were in bed. You've had a long day. You can tell me about it in the morning.' It was true, he was tired, and he had to be up early the following day to go fishing.

Chapter 5

John felt rather weary and thirsty as he returned from a day at Newport market. He had been to sell some lobsters they had caught the previous day, and was pleased because he had bartered a good price for them. In part, the trip was also an excuse to call at a number of possible wholesalers with the aim of selling some of the cargo they were imminently anticipating. In particular as he passed through Carisbrooke, he had visited Oyster Shell Cottages, a well known pop or grog shop, owned by the mother of some friends from Niton. He had been encouraged by the response he had from them; it seemed that demand was likely to exceed supply in the immediate future – good news for their plans.

He had walked a total of about eighteen miles in a stiff wind, and been soaked by several heavy showers. As a result he felt justified in calling in to the New Inn at Stroud Green for a thirst-quenching drink before going on home to his dinner. Brandy, who had accompanied him, was quite familiar with that inn, and knew he would get a bowl of water and even a biscuit or two. They both knew they were bound to get a good welcome from the landlord, Henry Ralph.

Being early in the evening, the bar was empty, except for a weather-beaten and grubby man seated by the fire having a quiet pint of ale in the warmth. He looked around when he heard the sound of the door latch, the shadow of his large, hooked nose moving sinisterly across the wall. John knew old Joe Bastiania well, having fished and traded with him several times over the recent years. Robert had thought of recruiting him to help with their run, but Joe had not been at his hut, and couldn't be found. When he did appear later, he said he was involved in activity elsewhere and agreed under the circumstances it would be too risky to help them.

Joe lived in a rough shanty of a hut he had built from shipwreck timber on the cliffs at Atherfield, but he moved around often, from one small hideout to another, a number of which he used as occasional accommodation. He was a colourful and interesting man with an unusual ancestry. His father was originally Italian, but had been rescued from a shipwreck as a lad. He was taken in by a local family, treated as one of the family, and had never returned home. He ended up settling down and marrying a local girl and having several children that, like him, were entirely independent spirits. His lineage accounted for Joe's nose and his thin face, black hair and dark skin. Old Joe must have been in his sixties, having grown up in a life of fishing, poaching, smuggling, and anything else that took him on the day. He had a wide range of contacts and friends so he always knew everything that was going on and was a mine of information, and he was good for an interesting story.

'Good evening, John,' he called. 'Come over here and warm

yourself. And hullo to you too, Brandy,' he added as the dog went over to him wagging his tail furiously, only to quickly settle down right in front of the fire with his muzzle on his paws. 'I've something to tell you that you might find interesting.'

'Hullo Joe,' John replied. 'Can I get you another drink?' Without expecting to get a refusal, he turned to the landlord who had just appeared through a doorway from the adjoining room. John greeted him, and asked for two pints of his best ale. Apparently he had newly tapped a recent brew that he welcomed them to try, and he went down to the barrel in the cellar to draw them.

John took a chair next to Joe by the fire, and held out his hands to the warmth. Peering at Joe, he said. 'I haven't seen you around for a while, Joe. Have you been busy?'

Before he could answer, Henry Ralph brought in two foaming mugs of ale, set them down in front of them, and went out to investigate the sound of hooves outside.

Taking a rather appreciative mouthful of the beer, Joe replied. 'Aye! I went to see an old friend in the West Wight for a few days, and that's where I learnt the tale I'm about to tell you.' John could read between the lines, and understood that in actual fact he had been involved in a run, but wasn't going to say so out loud, in case anyone could overhear. This must have been the other activity that he had been engaged in. John smiled and encouraged Joe to tell him, knowing that Joe would trust him not to tell others.

'I was at Totland Bay, and a run was being made one night only a week or so ago when conditions, to say the best, were marginal. The wind was from the south-west and blowing hard, but the cutter with the cargo had been waiting offshore for a couple of days, waiting for better weather and for a clear shore. They must have been having a hard time of it, standing offshore during the days and then coming close inshore at night, only to have to give up and retreat back to sea. Everyone was getting rather nervous, reckoning that the landing had to be done that night; they couldn't risk waiting any longer. The word was out that the Coastguard would be otherwise occupied, and the signal light was made to bring the cutter in. It was very dark with rain in the wind, and a fair sea running. Despite the fact that the Bay is largely sheltered from the south-west, waves were breaking heavily at the northernmost end of the beach. The cutter approached the beach at the southern end of the bay where it was more sheltered. You know, where the path comes down Widdick Chine through the trees from Middleton.'

John nodded for he knew the place. He had been in there before. 'Yes. I know where you mean.' There was a steep and normally muddy path beside a little stream running down through a grove of Holm oak trees. It ended at the shingle beach near where the rocks below Headon Warren started. The cliffs at the seaward edge of the Warren continually slipped, shedding limestone blocks into the sea; each slip providing a jumble of rocks and mud, jutting out into the water. Between the rocky promontories there were small and secluded sandy coves where it was easy to land a small rowing boat and temporarily hide kegs. John guessed that was probably their objective.

Joe went on. 'The landing party had assembled waiting for the rowing boat to come in with the line, so that the tubs could be hauled ashore. There were about twelve men waiting, listening, though the wind was strong enough to cover most noises. A Batman had been sent out along the cliff edge towards Warden Point, to give warning if any Revenue men approached. He was dressed in the normal black cape, hat and mask, and armed with a bat, or cudgel. All appeared to be peaceful as they waited for a light from the boat.

'Suddenly, from along the cliffs there were shouts and a number of gunshots. A lad who had also been posted at the top of the chine to warn of any approach from the other direction came running and sliding down the chine, saying that he thought a patrol was coming through the trees. He said that the carter, who had been waiting with the horses at the top of the chine to carry away the tubs, had gone off further up the hill towards the Warren to get out of the way.

'The noise had been made by the Batman who was doing his job well. He knew all the twists and turns of the track, all the trees and hiding places, and he could dodge in and out of the undergrowth, and shout and scream, frightening the Revenue men. Being all in black they could hardly see him against the surroundings. Wielding his bat he was hitting them whenever he could, and he was creating mayhem. The Coastguard were firing off their pistols at random, shooting at almost every noise. It is lucky the Batman wasn't hit, but I'm not sure they didn't hit each other. They were scared stiff and completely disorientated.

'We,' hastily corrected by Joe to, 'They, thought that the

Coastguard at Sconce Point, under Chief Officer Jenkin, had been bought off, or had been fed misinformation about when and where the run was likely to be. But there must have been another informer busy, because apparently the Coastguard, anticipating trouble, had even sent a message to Lieutenant Dornford at Freshwater Gate requesting help.

'There was much confusion amongst the beach party as to what should be done. Anyway, after a while the Batman appeared out of the dark on the beach, and said there were ten or a dozen Coastguards approaching, they were armed with cutlasses and pistols, and really meant business.

'The leader of the landing party immediately signalled to the boat that there was trouble, and they split up, with some men preparing to go over the rocks to hide and some up the chine into the trees. But they didn't go very far. It was very dark, and they assumed that the boat would pull away, but they couldn't hear any sound of oars over the noise of the wind. Presumably, the oarsmen were waiting, trying to work out what was happening, hoping it might have been a false alarm, and listening to see when it might be safe to land. It was surprising that they couldn't have heard the gunshots over the wind and the noise of the waves. Just then the Revenue appeared on the beach, and stood calling to the boat trying to entice it in, and waiting for it to ground.

'The leader of the shore gang realised that the whole run would be jeopardised if the boat was caught, so with a yell he and some others jumped out, and fell upon the Coastguards. The others then joined in. There was the devil of a fight, everyone vainly trying to keep their feet, slipping and sliding around on the stones, and falling into the water. Wet clothing then impeded their movement. There was grabbing and grasping, hitting and kicking, grappling and groaning. More pistols were discharged, until it was realised by the Coastguards that they were endangering each other more than their opponents. Luckily, no one seemed to be hit. But some of the Coastguards managed to unsheathe their cutlasses, and the fight became cutlasses against branches and bits of timber picked up off the beach. It was eerie because the fighting was done almost entirely without shouts or cries lest a voice be recognised.' Joe had been careful in his choice of words, but in his excitement it became more obvious that he had been directly involved.

John was both captivated and amused by the story, imagining the scene and the feelings of the men on both sides of the fight. He waited for Joe to continue after he had taken a deep draught of his beer. As he managed to empty it, John had to call for refills for both of them.

'All of the gang were strong and fit, not like the softer Revenue men who spend most of their time marching or sitting on their backsides,' Joe continued, 'and it was as black as pitch. The Chief Boatman caught hold of one of the men to arrest him, but in the mayhem he couldn't keep hold of him. At times it was even likely that gobbie was fighting gobbie, and smuggler fought smuggler. Everyone was trying to keep their feet on the stones, and they were falling over the boulders. Whenever you took a swing at a shadow in the dark, your feet would slide, and you'd lose balance and fall over. It wasn't long before everyone was gasping, and out of breath, and one by one the shore gang disappeared in the darkness either up the cliff or round the rocks. The fight must have lasted only about five minutes before the beach cleared, but it was a good night's entertainment.

'The poor Coastguards were left nursing their injuries without any trace of smugglers. Several of them ended sitting on the stones with their heads in their hands, with their senses knocked out of them. One was totally unconscious, and eventually had to be carried off the beach. There were several broken heads and black-eyes. Everyone had cuts and bruises, and one of the shore gang had a broken arm.'

In the dim light John hadn't realised that Joe had a bruise on his cheek, and one of his hands had skinned knuckles. But when Joe saw his glances, he ruefully touched his cheek and laughed. It sounded to John as if they had had a successful night, nevertheless. 'Was the cargo landed later then?' he asked, grinning.

'Oh, yes!' Joe replied, smiling. 'They ran into Alum Bay and landed beneath the coloured cliffs a bit later in the night, after the Coastguards had given up and gone back to their station to nurse their wounds. The cargo was carried to the cottage, hidden in the woods behind the manor, or at the inn.' John knew exactly where Joe meant without him having to say the precise locations. 'But, unfortunately, one of the boats was holed on Hatherwood Point, and wrecked. The Coastguard found it the following morning before it could be retrieved and repaired. They were so pleased about finding it that during their distraction the load was collected on a cart right under their noses and taken away to Newport. A good thing too, because after the fracas there was a lot of Coastguard activity all around the neighbourhood! They searched everywhere, but not a thing could they find. It seemed as if they were trying to recover their honour rather than the tubs.' He laughed again.

They both took a long draught of beer, and as it obviously was the end of the story, John said. 'Talking about Totland, I recently heard a verse that I would like to try out on you, Joe, you knowing the area so well.'

He paused while he ran through the verse in his mind to make sure he had it right. 'It's called Totland Tides, and it goes like this:

'When full or new you see the moon,
The tide's far out in the afternoon,
But when the moon's in either quarter
At tea the beach is underwater.
Six hours the water ebbs away.
An hour later every day.
Get down to the beach as soon as you can,
Time and tide wait for no man.'

'I like that,' said Joe. 'It really encompasses the feeling, the repetition of the tide, and the connection to the moon. But is it right? It doesn't hold everywhere along the coast, does it?'

'That's just what I thought too,' John said. 'If you go down to Cornwall, I think you'd find that the reverse occurs, with high tide in the afternoon at spring tides. I was wondering where else the verse might hold? Do you know?'

Before Joe could answer there was a rattle of the door, and a group of men and a couple of women entered the room, all fashionably dressed. The men were talking loudly, and called the landlord to serve them with glasses of brandy or wine. Brandy woke up and a low growl started in his throat. Joe grimaced at John and they both shrugged their shoulders, feeling that their peace and quiet, and privacy, had been invaded.

The visitors pulled a table across in front of the fire and without any word to the two local men, set their chairs in front of it, effectively blocking them from the warmth. One of the visitors poked his walking cane at Brandy who was forced to move away, his lip curled and his growls became warning snarls as he retreated under the table. Without anything more than a glance at the locals, and certainly no courtesy, the visitors continued their loud conversation about how frightful the conditions were that they had to bear, how bad the food was, and how the accommodation was not to be borne. This was a common discourtesy made to the Islanders by visitors; making out that they didn't exist, or could be ignored, and were in some way considered to be invisible. John was convinced their intention was to ensure they were thought to be superior, when in fact they felt out of place and distinctly uncomfortable and vulnerable. There was little that could be done about it except to charge them very high prices for the privileges they assumed.

The innkeeper came over to John and Joe, silently indicating that he would put a drink for them on the slate against the visitors' account. But John decided that it was high time he went home, as Frances would have the children in bed, and would be expecting him soon. He finished up his drink. As he rose he caught an appraising glance from one of the ladies in the group who seemed to appreciate his good looks. John was weather-beaten, tall and broad in the frame, with a neat beard, strong brown features, unruly hair and clear eyes, and dressed in worn but hard wearing, coarse dark blue serge. The contrast with the male visitors was marked. They were pale and thin, dressed in pastel coloured fine clothes, with powdered wigs and soft-looking slender hands. It looked as if the ladies were not over impressed by their companions. Still watching him, the lady whispered to her friend, and they both smiled coquettishly. John inclined his head slightly, so as to acknowledge their interest without appearing to upset the men. He smiled to himself, wondering what the response would be if he were to go across and start talking to the ladies and intrude upon their party. He was sure the men would be highly offended if he did.

Joe also stood up and they both moved to the door, leaving the floor clear for the visitors. Outside in the fitful moonlight, blustery wind and gusts of rain they stood for a minute and whispered a confirmation that the run was still on in a few days' time. As they went their separate ways into the dark night, John pondered on the implications that the recent skirmish at Totland might have for them. Had it alerted the Coastguard and put them on their guard for other possible runs, or would they now think that no one would dare do anything for many weeks?

John didn't get very far along the road to his house when he heard a horse coming up behind him at a fast walk. The most likely person to be on horseback, riding around in the dark, was Lieutenant Bulley, carrying out his rounds, checking to see what was about. John was in two minds whether to dodge out of the way and avoid being seen, or to carry on his legitimate and peaceful way. He was doing no ill, and had no reason to avoid the officer. John walked on, and was overtaken quite quickly.

The horse started when the Lieutenant realised that John was there and involuntarily pulled on the reins. He seemed to be unsure whether to ride on past without speaking, or to slow down and make acknowledgement. After a brief pause he said, 'Wheeler. I wanted to have a word with you.'

John stood to one side, feeling rather at a disadvantage, because the Lieutenant was looming above him on the horse in a very intimidating manner. Unsure whether it was consciously intended or not, John said nothing.

'I understand that your wife has been visiting mine, while I have not been there, and upsetting her.' He paused while the horse jiggled about, giving John the chance to reply.

'Quite the reverse, I have been told. I believe your wife has gained considerable consolation from the visits of my wife and children.'

But the Lieutenant carried on speaking without taking any noticeable heed of what John had said. 'I would be obliged if you would instruct your wife not to come again. It causes too much upset to my wife, who has many other more pressing concerns.'

John could feel his temper beginning to rise, even though he was normally a very even-tempered man. He felt that he needed to avoid a brusque retort, as that would immediately hand the advantage to the other man. So he resorted to extreme politeness in order not to let the situation get out of hand. 'I am not in the habit of instructing my wife to do, or to not do anything,' John countered. 'I might suggest, or ask, but in this case, as far as I am concerned she is a better judge of the desires and the needs of other females than I am. I would not dream of telling her not to do anything that she considers to be in the best interests of her lady acquaintances and friends. She has much experience of these matters, and I trust her judgement to be much better than my own in such affairs. If you don't want your wife to be approached by the women of the village, I suggest that you leave it to her to tell them not to.'

The Lieutenant obviously had a different attitude to his wife, and probably also to other ladies. John knew there was a common perception amongst upper class men that women, even of their own class, were inferior in some way, less educated, and less capable of being educated, with their minds entirely satisfied with trivia of gossip, clothes and needlework. But he did not agree with that thesis. It seemed that the Lieutenant may have been one of that persuasion, though John would not rate him as being upper class in any way. Perhaps the Lieutenant may have adopted this posture to try and impress or intimidate.

The Lieutenant blustered. 'Keep you wife away from mine. I do not want her to be contaminated by the philosophies of fishermen and common criminals.' With this comment, he dug his heels hard into the horse's flanks, and trotted off along the road.

John was furious at the obvious insult, and swore under his breath at the overbearing and intolerant nature of the man. He thought it would be a waste of time trying to reason with such an attitude. However, he thought he'd had the best of the confrontation, and would get his own back at some time.

He was still incensed when he reached his house and told Frances about the exchange. She too was very upset. 'I thought he would be happy that someone was taking notice of his wife, and trying to help her,' she said. 'I don't think that this will stop me visiting her, because she is desperately in need of comforting. Doesn't he realise that, if he carries on in the way that he is doing at the moment, not only may he not have the family that they want so dearly, but he may not even have a wife.'

Chapter 6

A week later, and four days before Christmas, if you were about the village early, you would have seen John leave Fulford Cottage before it was light, having reluctantly left Frances curled up, warm and gently snoring in bed. Luckily, the girls were still asleep too. Leaving Brandy behind, much to the dog's chagrin, he closed the door, saying a silent prayer that he would return triumphant, and would not be returning in chains.

As he went along the road first one man came out to join him, quietly shutting his garden gate behind him, and then another. They exchanged wordless greetings. Eventually there were five of them, tramping along the narrow, winding road towards Shorwell. They walked because it would attract less attention than if they were all on horseback or on a cart; groups of men tramping off to market, or to labour at some distant task were a fairly common sight. They were quite happy to walk the ten miles to Newtown to board the smack; walking that distance was not an unusual pastime, for they were all used to long distances. In fact they would normally expect to tramp to Newport market at least once a week, carrying heavy loads of fish or other produce as well. On this day they were carrying only enough food to last them for five days, together with a few important personal items. John carefully carried in a sack over his shoulder his essential and valuable brass compass, protected in a stout wooden box; without it they would get nowhere when out of sight of land, or on a dark, cloudy night. He also had the money wrapped up in a thick bag to prevent the coins clinking together.

Their boots made a steady tramping noise on the stones of the road, even though they tried to tread on the grass to make less noise. They made rapid progress. The intention was that the run would occur during 'the darks', the three days before and after new moon, which coincidently occurred on Christmas Eve. All being well they would be home just in time for Christmas.

The previous evening John had studied the clouds and the sky for signs of change, to try and forecast the weather for the coming few days, but in the sound knowledge that they would simply have to accept what came. He was particularly anxious because there had been a strong south-easterly wind for several days, and this was not a favourable direction; it would have meant beating across the Channel and an awkward entry into Barfleur, situated as it was on the eastern side of the Cherbourg peninsula. On the other hand, in those conditions the return would have been a broad reach across the wind, fast and lively, with a relatively sheltered beach to receive them at Blackgang. However, that evening John could see that change was due. There had been clear skies, but high, feathery clouds moving in from the west, foretold a change in the weather, and the possibility of westerly winds. When he had woken he was pleased to find that during the night the cloud had thickened, and it had rained steadily for several hours. The wind had veered round to the south-west, and settled to what he estimated was a steady Beaufort force five.

This was a much better direction for the wind. Once clear of the Island they would have a fair wind to sail to Barfleur with a minimum of beating. And, if the wind held, they would be able to sail almost the same course back, the only difference being the tides. A flooding tide would set them towards the east, and an ebbing tide would hold the boat against the wind. John made a mental reckoning that they had about 100 miles to go, due south as the crow flies. But, because of the tides their track would be somewhat longer. He reckoned the voyage would take about twelve hours, and, with luck, they would have about equal amounts of both ebb and flood currents. Of course, they would have to endure the conditions that fate gave them. Their arrival time at Barfleur was uncertain, though John was hoping they could reach the port soon in the early morning when observers would be few, and they might be taken for incoming fishermen.

As they trudged along John thought about the two options they had for leaving the Solent. He had discussed with Uncle James the alternatives and he saw no need to alter their decision. They had agreed to sail eastwards through the Solent and out through the Spithead; though this would be slightly further, it would avoid having to beat out through the narrow Needles channel against the wind. Also it would avoid them having to pass directly under the noses of the Coastguard at

Sconce Point. John surmised that, after the fight at Totland Bay that Joe Bastiania had told him about, they were likely to be alert and keen to keep a close check on vessels departing, and looking out for their return. It would be best to slip out of Newtown appearing to go on legitimate business at Portsmouth, or thereabouts, giving no cause for suspicion.

They had planned to arrive at Newtown at about low tide. This would mean they could use the major part of the flood tide to carry the *Sweet Frances* eastwards, to clear the Spithead well before midday when the tide was due to turn. With luck they would be in Barfleur the following morning, load the cargo and sail back to the Island that night. It had been arranged the landing party would watch out for them that night, which was the night before Christmas Eve, or if there was a delay, on Christmas Eve itself.

As anticipated, they arrived at the creek before low tide, and the five of them eventually loaded all their gear onto the smack. This took a succession of trips from the wharf to the boat, as the dinghy could only take two men at a time, one, of course, being the oarsman. The dinghy was then hauled aboard, and turned upside down on the foredeck. The gaff mainsail was hauled up the mast, flapping in the wind, and the jib sail was set. At the same time the anchor was raised. Grabbing the tiller, John managed to get steerage way on the boat before it ran onto the tidal flats, and with the last of the ebb current to help, they set off down the narrow creek and out through the narrow entrance into the Solent. There, because of a peculiarity of the tide, the flood current was already setting towards the east, and it would be a straight and fast run with the tide and the following wind. The topsail was broken out and they were soon bowling along at a combined speed over the ground of about eight knots, the water foaming at the boat's stem, and the wake spreading out behind. As they were travelling faster than the short, steep waves, the bowsprit occasionally dipped into the water, throwing spray over the boat, soaking the lower sails and the crew. The initial nervousness that John always felt at the start of a voyage disappeared under the familiar sounds and the easy movements of the boat. He was sure the others felt the same way.

The wind stretched the faded tan-coloured sails tight above their heads, and the spray darkened the foot of the mainsail. As they were running with the wind it was not particularly cold, especially when the fitful sun broke through the clouds, which was a good thing as there was little sail-hauling to be done. They quickly settled into the familiar routine of the boat's motion, the regular rise and fall, and the side to side swaying in the short seas the wind created in the confined waters.

Across the other side of the Solent several similar smacks were fishing in the shallows, dragging trawls and nets along the seabed, probably fishing for oysters and flatfish. Some they recognised as having come from Yarmouth and Lymington, determined to take advantage of the weather to supply the forthcoming Christmas market. But John kept the *Sweet Frances* to the deeper channel closer to the Island shore, where the current would be stronger. They shot past the *Lydia*, a smart, fast coastal trader from Yarmouth, tacking hard to make way westwards; she had been recently inherited by William Warder from his father. John and the others waved to them, wondering why they were pressing so hard, when they could have sheltered and waited for the tide to turn in their favour. They waved back probably wondering in turn what the *Sweet Frances* was doing going the other way.

A little further along they passed the entrance to the Beaulieu River on the north side of the Solent, where two ships were waiting to be towed up to Buckler's Hard, presumably for repair or disposal. Buckler's Hard had been a busy shipyard where many of the 'wooden walls' were built that formed the backbone of the Navy during the wars against Napoleon's France; Nelson's favourite ship, the *Agamemnon*, being one of them. The woods of the New Forest had been plundered for the best oak trees at that time. Since the end of the war, and the advent of iron for shipbuilding, it was losing its importance, and the slipways were now largely empty and decaying. James wondered whether smugglers still used the cellar beneath St. Mary's Chapel at the Hard as a hide, but none of the others knew.

As they drew abreast of Egypt Point John reckoned they were travelling at close to nine knots, with the coast rushing past. He thought they were making very good time.

A shout then came from James sitting comfortably near the bow with his back against the mast. He pointed to a vast pall of smoke arising from behind Calshot Spit, further ahead on the port side. 'That must be the steam packet from Southampton into Cowes,' he said. 'We don't want to get caught in that smoke – it almost suffocates you with noxious fumes, dust and grit.'

John replied, 'I think it'll be alright! We should be well clear of her before she comes across this far.'

They watched the packet boat appear from behind the spit, turn and plough her way down the channel directly towards them. The tall funnel emitted a heavy black cloud of smoke that the stiff breeze pushed towards the northern shore, completely obscuring it. The vessel breasted the waves, punching her way through bursts of heavy spray. John wondered how the passengers would be feeling in that uncomfortable motion; most being dreadfully sick, he thought.

Almost irrespective of the wind and weather the packet boats crossed the narrow stretch of water to a regular timetable, and the dependable traffic had made the Island very much more accessible. The wealthy and aristocratic could now spend their summers in the houses they had newly built on the Island. Also the boats had opened up the Island to more trade and commerce, rapidly destroying the Island's seclusion and relative independence. Cowes in particular had benefited, becoming a fashionable seaside resort and a focus for the new interest in sail racing. Many of the wealthy people owned yachts built at yards on the adjacent Medina River, and raced them from the elite Royal Yacht Club, recently renamed as the Royal Yacht Squadron, since the King, William IV, had been elected Admiral. The members were proud of having the distinction of being allowed to fly the white ensign of the Navy ships, but had the risk of their boats being commandeered for Navy service in times of war.

Appearing close on their starboard side was West Cowes Castle. This had been built in the time of Henry VIII to protect Cowes harbour and the approaches to Portsmouth against French attack. Built upon the northernmost headland of the

Island, where the River Medina joined the Solent, the battlements still housed cannons that could rake any invaders over the crucial waterway. But it was now the residence of Lord Anglesey, the Captain of the Castle, a fairly nominal position now that hostilities were at an end. Even so, the cannons looked very impressive.

John was still steering, and he had to avoid several anchored yachts as well as a number of smacks, sloops, cutters, pinnaces and rowing boats, all either going into or leaving the wharves and jetties in the crowded harbour; though quite small, Cowes was an important and busy place, even close to Christmas-tide.

He pointed to a three-masted fully rigged ship moored up the river. 'That's the *Falcon*,' he called out to the others. 'I've sailed in her as a crewman for several summers of racing. Her owner is Lord Yarborough.' Everyone knew of Lord Yarborough; he was a descendant of the Island family, the Worsleys, and was for a long time the Commodore of the Yacht Club. He was well known for lavish entertainment, and John was able to recount how, on one occasion, he had entertained 600 guests to a buffet lunch in a marquee under the cliffs in the grounds of his manor house at Appuldurcombe.

'The *Falcon* is really well fitted out, with the most splendid cabins and accommodation,' John described. 'Though it is only three hundred and fifty-one tons and is very tight for space, it was better than the Navy, even for a crew of fifty-four. We were captained by a Navy Lieutenant, and the discipline was as harsh as the Navy. Lord Yarborough wouldn't accept anything as second best. We had to sign articles in which we agreed to be flogged if there was any transgression of seamanship, or behaviour, but we were paid an extra shilling a week for it. Mind you, the threat was a very good incentive to make sure the need never actually did arise. We were a choice crew,' John added proudly. 'She was not unlike a twenty-gun ship of war, but the only guns were small brass ones for firing salutes – but there was a large arsenal of muskets and cutlasses, and on one occasion they were used in an argument with another ship about who had right of way. She was a well-found ship, and we won many races.'

As John knew the town better than any of the rest of the crew he thought he'd give them a tourist introduction as they swept past. 'Over there,' he pointed to the other side of the river, 'is Norris Castle, built for Lord Henry Seymour. And further over is East Cowes Castle that John Nash built for himself. He is the famous architect. You know the one that designed many important buildings in London, as well as the new town hall at Newport. He died earlier this year. Both he and Lord Henry were sailing men,' John added. 'I understand Princess Victoria, who will become Queen when our King William IV dies, loves it here, and has frequently been on the King's yacht. As a consequence, all the best houses in Cowes are being bought by the aristocracy and the fashionable.

'Don't get me wrong,' John said. 'Not all of the fashionable are yachtsmen. Most of them prefer to spend their time walking, talking and showing off. If they do take to a boat it is only for a short cruise in fine weather to view the coast and to be seen by others.' John's disdain for their indolent lifestyle was obvious, in marked contrast to his respect for those who loved the sea and relished the competition of sail racing.

But Cowes was not all stylish and good. It wasn't possible to see from where they were the poor hovels further along the waterside, and the squalid conditions in which many of the folks who served the wants of the wealthy had to live. Several families would be crammed into each house, each family having only one room. All the rubbish and sewage would be thrown into the sea; the stink of the water would be awful, even though the tides cleaned out the river reasonably well every day.

Though John spoke with familiarity about the famous people, he couldn't say he knew them. He hadn't met most of them, but he had seen them and had them pointed out to him; the others had not even had that close contact. Those John had met were in general straight speaking and fair-dealing people, and, as far as he knew, most of them were very lordly, gracious and civil people, provided those they considered inferior remained so.

However, some of the upper class were wastrels, and reputed to be 'wild bucks', not above enjoying fist fights with some of the hardy, local young men, butchers and draymen, and often besting them. Addicted to wagering, they would bet enormous amounts on horse and boat races. A thousand pounds seemed to be nothing to them, even though it was many times what a normal man would earn in a lifetime. Those men were generally oblivious to any damage they made, or injury they caused, believing it their right to be overbearing and inconsiderate to the less fortunate. Nevertheless, it was their money that ultimately paid the price for the trade that those in the *Sweet Frances* were engaged on that day; it was on their tables that the brandy would end up. But times were changing, and most people were aware that a new class of skilled craftsmen and moneyed industrialists was arising to challenge the superiority of the upper class. They appeared to have a stricter moral code and to be more philanthropic in attitude. John often wondered how different the world would be for his children, and their children, when they grew up, than it had been for him and his generation.

As the *Sweet Frances* swept round into the East Solent, the channel widened and the southern shore became lower and more wooded. Moored further along the channel towards the Spithead were several men-of-war, mostly second and third rate. John had served for a while on a second-rate ship. They had three continuous gun-decks stretching from stem to stern, mounting a total of about ninety-eight guns and being about 2,000 tons burthen, with a crew of 750. As they were only about 180 feet long, conditions were very cramped. A third-rate ship was smaller, having only two gun-decks, carrying sixty-four to eighty guns.

As they approached, the steep black and white striped hulls towered over the little smack, the tall masts appearing to reach up to the clouds. John remembered the sickness and dizziness he felt when he had first climbed to the truck at the top of a mast and looked down: it was not long before practice and necessity had made him cease to worry about it.

Between the ships a mass of rowing boats, pinnaces, lighters and gigs moved, carrying supplies, victuals, water, seamen and officers to and from the harbour. Some of the seamen had berry-brown faces and arms, and torn and faded clothing; a sure sign of recent tropical service. One of the ships flew a yellow flag, indicating it was newly arrived with fever on board.

John steered close in under the stern of one of the second-rate ships and he looked up at the ornate gilded counter decorated with dolphins and mermaids, capped by the naval white ensign stiffly flapping in the wind. The windows of the captain's cabin were open, and some of the gun-ports were also open with the guns run out. Men were cleaning the decks, the water pouring from the overflow ports, and some men were slung over the side on bosun's chairs freshening up the paintwork and hammering in the caulking. Others were up in the rigging renewing some of the ropes, sheets and stays, and clewing on fresh sails. It looked as if the ship was preparing to leave sometime fairly soon. A bell struck the hour, and a whistle shrilled for the watch to change. The immediate response was a sound of slapping of bare feet on the deck, and the rigging shook as the yardsmen rushed down the ratlines, or slid down the yards. The tricorn hat of the officer of the watch appeared at the gunwale as he watched the smack go past, perhaps wishing that he had a crew as experienced as John's was, as he would have to spend many hard watches drumming seamanship and discipline into a raw crew. At the bow the figurehead looked newly cleaned and a white painted finger pointed a leading way to the horizon. John shuddered as he remembered the hardship and the harsh discipline of mean and vindictive officers during his time in the service; officers who considered the seamen as disposable creatures on whom they could relieve their sadism, rather than men. He was glad to have escaped to become his own master, but, nevertheless, he had to admit he had come out of it harder, braver, and more self reliant; a real man.

Away on the port side, on the north shore, was the entrance to Portsmouth Harbour, the channel being well protected by twin forts that had defied many attacks by French ships. During Henry VIII's reign, his flagship, the *Mary Rose*, sank during a squall just off the harbour mouth in one such attack, with huge loss of life. Towering over the buildings of the town and the Navy yards were the many masts of ships crowded into the harbour. From the distance one could only imagine all the crowds, workers, artisans and seamen, and the victualling and chandler stores, the ropewalks, shot foundries, and noise, the smell and the dirt of the town itself. Portsmouth was the biggest and most important naval town in the Empire, always busy with ships leaving on foreign duty, and returning sometimes after years at sea in the tropics or the other side of the world. It took many thousands of men, women and children to make the ships ready for sea, to mend them when they returned, to feed the men, fleece them of their pay and satisfy their carnal needs.

John and the others had often entered the harbour to sell their fish and shellfish, and had to endure being pushed from pillar to post and harried by impatient people who could not wait, or even be civil to them. John, for one, was always glad to escape back to the clean air and the solitude of the water. He had long ago concluded that Portsmouth was probably best appreciated from a distance. Then the poverty, sickness and hunger were not visible, but the romantic concept of the British Empire remained. Nevertheless, the benefits always seemed to accrue to the very few rather than the many, and the mass of people suffered as a consequence.

Looking at the mass of masts in the harbour John wondered whether one set of them belonged to the *Waterwitch*. He recounted to the others the story of this fast brig that had been built for Lord Belfast. The noble lord had raced her many times and beaten all comers. One race was of 224 miles from the Nab, at the eastern end of the Solent, round the Eddystone Lighthouse and back, and it was reputed that Lord Belfast won the huge sum of fifty thousand pounds when *Waterwitch* won by almost half an hour. To poke fun at the Navy and to amuse himself, he used to have the vessel lie in wait outside the harbour for departing men-of-war, with the purpose of out-sailing them. He boasted that she was faster than any vessel of her size in the fleet. This strategy became such a success, and was so embarrassing to the Navy, that they had purchased *Waterwitch* the year before to test her against their own vessels, so that they could design modifications to improve them. It was amazing what lengths someone with money would go to in order to pander to their whims, and to score illusory points in the search for status and reputation.

The wind stayed constant in both force and direction, hastening the *Sweet Frances* further eastwards. The number of other vessels diminished, but there were still occasional isolated fishing vessels around some of the shoals and banks. Beating up in the other direction was a Revenue cutter tacking back into the channel. Through the spyglass James saw that it was the *Rose*, probably returning to their home station at Ryde. She, and the *Adder*, which was based at Yarmouth, were sister ships of fifty-three tons carrying crews of fourteen. They were the bane of the fishermen's lives, always trying to catch them when they were fishing, and insisting on boarding for a rummage for contraband, a search that was more intimidation than based on any real suspicion. John could see that a spyglass was being used to examine them, but they weren't stopped, not that they were doing anything wrong at that time. 'I only hope that they stay ashore for Christmas now,' John prayed.

The wind was rising as they were getting clear of the shelter of the Island, and it now played coldly around them, penetrating their necks and ankles. James passed around sets of oilskins that they donned for protection from the cold and the spray.

They could see in the distance the anchored hulk used as the Nab beacon, marking the end of the Spithead channel, the limits of the confines of the Island shores, and the start of the deeper water of the English Channel. The wind was stiffening, and veering slightly towards the north-west, and the waves were becoming longer and more regular in the deeper water. John reckoned it was now force six, and gusting seven. But this suited them well, as they now needed to point in a more southerly direction, they could remain running-free. The little smack started behaving with an awkward corkscrewing motion because the wind was now across the tidal current that had turned and was beginning to ebb. For a landlubber this movement would have made them seasick in no time, but the crew were enjoying the heave and surge of the boat, and the exhilaration of fast sailing in the late afternoon.

John pushed the helm further to port and the boat's heading became southerly. They rounded the end of Bembridge Ledge, passed over Princessa Shoal and kept clear of the tall white Culver Cliffs, around which innumerable seagulls and pigeons, the 'culvers', flew. The full horizon of the English Channel then lay before them, with the bare southern downs of the Island towering large on the starboard side. These hills would remain on the horizon for several hours yet, slowly sinking behind them in the twilight as they travelled across towards France. If it were lighter they could almost have seen the downs behind the village, with the Hermitage on top. Their day had been spent in going almost a full circle round the Island, and now they were committed to crossing the Channel and breaking the law.

It was gradually growing dark and the constellation of Orion began to shine brightly in the south-east sky. John looked upon this group of stars as friends, having seen them on many a winter's night, with three stars marking the man's head and shoulders, a further line for his belt and sword and others for his knees and ankles. To the left and a little lower was the single bright star of Sirius, a good leading mark on a clear night for the cross-channel voyager.

John asked his uncle to light the masthead lamp and hoist it; it would be essential to avoid them being run down in the dark by a fast clipper running up the Channel bound for London, laden with tea or grain. That is, if the ship had an adequate lookout, which couldn't be guaranteed after such a long ocean voyage. He also lit the small lamp in the binnacle illuminating the compass bowl; they would need it to keep a good heading so that they could make landfall on the other side. The glow was also comforting in the cold dampness of the night that was quickly penetrating, making them shiver.

With mutual accord they pulled out some of the food that their wives had so faithfully packed for them, and washed it down with some of the water that John had loaded a few days before, water already tasting of metal from the tank. They settled down as well as they could to several hours of cold wetness, for the spray was now coming aboard often over the starboard quarter. A lookout was posted before the mast for an unobstructed view ahead, and then John handed the tiller over to Uncle James; the two of them would be quite capable of handling the boat. John and the others went into the cuddy, or down into the forecastle, and wrapped themselves in blankets; braced against the motion, and securely wedged, the motion was nicely soothing. Quickly they were sound asleep, knowing that in too short a time they would have to be on watch and take their turn, and they stayed that way for the next four hours.

Chapter 7

Two days later, just as darkness was falling, they were in mid-Channel again. It was gloomy, a thin, misty drizzle was blowing across them in slowly falling drifts in the light southerly breeze; in fact breeze was too strong a word for the light breath that was moving the air. The sea was leaden green-grey with long, low, regular waves about two feet high slowly moving east. The visibility was only about fifty yards and getting worse. The mist was turning into a thick fog. There was not enough wind to keep the sails filled, and as the boat wallowed in the waves, the boom slatted from side to side. They were hardly moving. It was very quiet. Any noise they made seemed to be muffled and absorbed by the mist, and the direction of any sounds from elsewhere was difficult to locate.

They were not absolutely sure where they were, because they had seen nothing since they had left Barfleur at the break of dawn; eight hours on a compass course, being swept sideways by the tidal currents. They carried on steering northwards. The foggy drizzle settled on the sails, ran down in rivulets and dropped onto the deck or onto the men. Everything was clammy and covered with a film of moisture, even down below decks. Cold and wet to the touch, droplets reformed quickly after they were wiped off. Woollen sweaters were covered with tiny beads of moisture, and even beards and eyebrows were covered in dewy diamonds. The tubs were all roped together and lined up on deck and in the hold, ready to be weighted and thrown overboard should the Revenue appear; they were covered loosely with a tarpaulin to hide them from view. Little pools of water collected in the folds, cascading from one to the other as the boat moved.

James, leaning against the mainmast was the lookout, scanning ahead, straining his eyes through the fog. Occasionally he ducked his head to peer round the jib. All on board were alert, ears and eyes concentrating on locating the slightest noise or disruption to the even greyness of the miserable twilight. After several hours straining their eyes they felt that they were becoming hypnotised, seeing all sorts of imaginary fantasies.

They were considerably later than they had anticipated, not that it mattered as delays had been allowed for in the plans. During the first night of the crossing to France, they had made good progress in the steady wind. The lights of only two other boats had been seen within their limited horizon, both of them running eastwards. One must have been a large, fully rigged ship, as it was showing several lights on deck as well as at masthead. The other smaller boat was beating back northwards across the Channel showing only a single masthead light; they speculated whether it also might have been on a smuggling errand.

Early in the morning of that first day they had reached the

French coast without any trouble and had found the entrance channel to Barfleur Harbour through a swarm of small, departing fishing boats. In the harbour it took quite a while to find a gap at the wharf where they could moor, but once they had tied up, John Parker appeared to welcome them. John was particularly relieved to see him, because he had not relished the thought of bartering with the French merchants, not knowing a word of their language. The factor had been there several days and had successfully finished his business, arranging the sale of some English wool with the local merchants. But he had bad news for them. He had been informed there had been a delay in the supply of the cargo, and only part of the load was ready; there had been a cutter in from Sussex that had bought a larger than anticipated cargo, loaded it and departed the previous night. However, the merchant was expecting further supplies to be delivered later that day which would complete the load for the *Sweet Frances*.

The choice was either to depart immediately with a part load, or wait. It would take several hours to load and stow away the tubs that were ready, and to depart then would involve arriving on the English shore in daylight; probably to have to wait in the Channel for darkness and risk meeting the Revenue. So they waited.

Fortunately the full load appeared as promised, and they finished stowing the tubs in the late afternoon, under the watchful eye of a group of sullen and dirty French youngsters. John took the opportunity of a visit to the shops, where he bought a Christmas present for Frances, and toys for the children; these would have to be carefully hidden in case they were boarded by the Revenue for a rummage. In addition he bought some fresh crabs and lobsters, so that if they were stopped on the English side they could show proof they had been legitimately fishing. As they were still alive they were placed in the holding tank which was refilled with new salty water; this would keep them alive and fresh for several days, at least until they could be cooked. Then, satisfied with their day's work they went to a bistro on the quay for a meal, followed by a good sleep, before setting off on the return trip at the crack of dawn. They were about a quarter of the way across when the mist came down, and they had spent the rest of daylight slowly feeling their way northwards in very light and variable winds.

A few minutes before, John Rayner had heard the regular sound of a ship's bell being rung as a fog signal. But it was faint, and it was difficult to know where the sound was coming from, as it echoed in the fog, appearing to come from one side and then another. It seemed to have been on the port bow when he first heard it, but after that he was unsure where it came from. They were worried because there was little time to avoid collision with a large ship, and if it were a Revenue cutter they really didn't want to have a close encounter, considering their load of contraband.

Just then the bell rang out clearly directly in front of them. A low call came from James, more of a grunt than a call. He pointed ahead to a slight intensification of the darkness, and a swirling of the fog that might be indicating disturbance by a large, moving object. A slight clearing gave a short glimpse of a ship's hull moving eastwards. The dark shape looked like a large clipper heading directly across their bows, on a course up the Channel. John leaned against the tiller to pull the boat's head to port to pass astern of the ship, and face into any wake it may have created. There were no shouts, no calls of 'Who are you?' or 'Where are we?' It was obvious that they hadn't seen the *Sweet Frances*, which said something about the quality of their lookouts. The shape passed quickly out of sight, leaving only whirls and eddies in the fog, and a few low waves in its wake that set the smack bobbing. The bell rang again, to starboard this time, and the sound diminished quickly thereafter. Close, but not too close. They had been lucky. John relaxed slightly and flexed his shoulders and neck, tight with the tension. With that ship out of the way their immediate worries were relieved by the thought that the chances of meeting another soon were slim.

It was approaching midnight and it had been fully dark for many hours, when they were beginning to anticipate making a landfall. But neither John nor James could be sure how far off the coast they were. They could see no lights, nor any stars, the fog was still thick and cloud was too low. But the drizzle was easing, and there was the hope that visibility might improve as they approached land. They might then be able to see the loom of the land against the stars. The problem then would be whether the Coastguard were out. Should they stand off and wait for an improvement in visibility, or continue?

John had been steering by the compass and by instinct. At the same time he had kept a close eye on the water surface, watching the flow and colour of the water, the swirling of eddies, and the movement of weed and flotsam. He sniffed the air, as often one could smell the proximity of the land, and each coast had its own distinctive smell. He had a peculiar feeling that convinced him they were close off Rocken End. According to his pocket-watch the tide should be on the ebb, and should carry them westwards towards their destination.

James, who was still forward and had acute hearing, whispered, 'I think I can hear the sound of waves breaking.' They all listened intently, with mouths open to help their hearing, and turning their heads from one side to the other. There was no sound of wind in the rigging or on the sails, just the creaking of the rigging and the faint slapping of the boat passing through the water; they were probably doing about a knot through the water. Eventually they could all hear it, a low susurration, a gentle murmur of waves breaking, a sound rather like the sea was breathing. Now the question was, which bit of coast was it? Was it rocks, or a sandy beach?

The mist was definitely thinning, but it was too dark to see the shore. Suddenly, the sound of a dog barking came from ahead; not continuous, just the occasional single bark. John recognised the distinctive sound, and smiled. 'Good dog! That's Brandy barking. I'd recognise his bark anywhere. Robert would have him out to give warning if the Coastguard were about. But that's not his normal warning yap, he's barking for us. Calling us in.' He steered towards the sound. 'They will now know that we are coming, and should be waiting for us at the foot of Blackgang Chine. Now, is that luck, or just good judgement,' he added with a laugh, relief clearly in his voice.

John turned to Charles. 'You had better get ready, lad. When we get in close enough, and the shore party indicates the coast is clear, it is up to you to take the rope in to the beach. You're not to swim it today. It's too cold. Get ready to lower the dinghy.'

Charles was a strong swimmer and could take a rope to the men on the beach, who could then pull the tubs in. This technique was often used when the sea conditions were calm, and the water warm. But today the water would be far too cold; a swimmer's muscles would quickly seize up and he'd risk drowning. Instead, Charles would take the rope's end ashore in the dinghy, and pass it over or float it across to those on shore.

Charles and John Rayner quietly lifted the up-ended dinghy off the deck and manoeuvred it to the side where, without too much of a splash, they slid it into the water attached on a long painter. The smack slowly crept closer to the sound of the breaking waves. John was confident there was plenty of water under the boat providing they didn't get too close to the breakers.

James was in the bow staring into the gloom. He had to constantly blink to keep his eyes clear. He turned and whispered just loud enough for the others to hear, 'Breakers ahead, about forty yards.' John immediately put the helm up to bring the boat parallel to the shore and heading into the ebb current.

A blink of light, just a narrow pencil beam, shone out towards them. As they had previously arranged, the landing party were using a snout, a lantern with a long tube to point the beam of light only in one direction. The shore gang had either seen or heard them, warned by Brandy's barking, and were giving the boat the signal for coast clear. James acknowledged it with a small, shaded lantern he had hidden in the cuddy.

Charles clambered down into the dinghy while John Rayner held the painter. When he was safely balanced Charles was handed the rope for the tubs and fastened it round one of the thwarts. He cast off, and started rowing towards the beach, the rope uncoiling off the deck as he went. He quickly disappeared into the gloom and the two Johns started lowering the tubs off the deck into the water. When those were all in the water, they brought the others up from the hold so that those too could be lowered in, when necessary. No matter how hard they tried to be quiet there was quite a lot of splashing, the knock of tub against tub, and stifled grunts and curses. Once in the sea the tubs floated quite happily, bobbing about and gently banging into each other until they were drawn out by Charles' efforts at paddling to try to stem the current.

It must only have been a couple of minutes, and, to those on the boat, the oarsman and the dinghy were outlined against the pale strip of the breaking waves. On the beach the landing party would be walking along the shingle keeping up with the movement of the dinghy as the tide swept it along. Charles had to work hard to pull the rope and the first tubs through the water, but eventually the dinghy was in the surf and one of the men waded out to take the rope's end. He quickly transferred it to those waiting on the beach and they started to haul the load in. The long train of kegs began to slowly move towards the shore. After a brief word with the men Charles turned the dinghy and rowed back to the smack.

Luckily he could see the lighter patch of the smack's sails, so that there was no risk of missing it in the darkness.

The cloud above must have been lifting slightly and the fog thinning, because a vague change of colour, a faint lightening of the darkness, was becoming apparent beyond the line of surf. John could now vaguely see the beach, and on it the moving darker patches that must be the shore party hauling on the rope and heaving the tubs up the shingle out of reach of the waves.

Charles clambered back on board, and tied the painter to a stern cleat. 'All seems to be quiet on shore,' he said. 'Apparently there's been no sign of the gobbies. Robert says we should get the hell away, and leave it to them.'

'Righty-ho!' John said, with relief flooding through him that one of the most difficult stages of the operation was successfully completed. He put the helm over and headed the *Sweet Frances* back out to sea, while the dinghy was lifted and stowed back on board.

James turned to John and suggested, 'As the weather is so good we could lift a few pots on the way to the Needles. We can then add a few English shellfish to the French ones we bought. Then our consciences will be clear, and if we are seen from the shore, we are busy fishing,' he added with a grin.

John thought it was a very sensible suggestion. It would only delay them two or three hours, and would be a moral justification for being at sea, should the Revenue appear; not that they could have much to say now the cargo had gone, unless a rummage were to reveal their hidden presents. So he set a course due west for the outer edge of Atherfield Ledge where some of their pots were, and where they could wait for dawn. Looking at his watch he saw it was well past midnight, and realised it was now Christmas Eve. He shouted that fact to the others, and they all smiled with joy, knowing that they would be home again for the festival. If they were not in church on Christmas Day their absence might raise a few eyebrows, particularly amongst those who were adamant that no work should be done on the Lord's birthday.

As the stress of the last few days dispersed, John felt tiredness creeping over him. He was sure the others felt exactly the same. For obvious reasons they hadn't kept any of the liquor on board, and John for one could have done with a stiff drink to warm him and keep him going. Though they couldn't splice the main-brace, they could sing a shanty or two in celebration.

* * * * * *

This was the second night Robert and the landing party had come to the beach. The first night was only in half expectation that the *Sweet Frances* would be back. But they had to be there and be sure, otherwise the boat would have to spend the dangerous period of daylight waiting about under the noses of the Coastguard, inviting investigation.

During the afternoon when the mist had rolled in from the sea, Robert was certain that fortune was smiling on them, and he was convinced that the cargo would arrive that night under the protection of the poor visibility. He had total faith in John's ability to find his way home. The Atherfield Coastguard had been surreptitiously sent on a wild-goose chase towards Brook by some veiled hints made in John Bulley's hearing, and there was little chance that the landing would be seen.

Since dark the men had been waiting at the foot of Blackgang Chine, spread out along the beach so that they had the best chance of hearing or seeing the boat. Towards midnight, when dampness was penetrating their clothes, and they were getting cold and depressed, thinking that the boat would not come after all, they heard the faint creak of boom and rigging close inshore. Robert was relieved when Brandy barked and wagged his tail, knowing instinctively that his beloved master was close at hand. Once they knew precisely where the boat was, the all-clear signal could be made with the snout lantern.

When the rope was ashore, Robert and the other men struggled with the tubs, slipping and sliding in the loose shingle as they tried to keep their footing. They untied the ropes that strung the barrels together, but left the ropes that tied the tubs together in pairs. Now the hard work started. Each man picked up a pair of tubs and slung them across his shoulders, with one tub hanging down in front and the other behind. The mere raising of the weight to their shoulders caused their feet to slide, with the avalanche of shingle making unwelcome noise, and making them lose balance. Carrying a hundredweight on firm ground was hard, but on the moving stones, where there wasn't a firm foothold, was a huge strain on muscles, ankles and knees. Despite having a thick pad of sacking beneath the rope, it cut into the shoulders and quickly made the back ache. Though there were a dozen men to carry the fifty or so barrels, each had to carry their share several times over.

To start with they carried all the tubs to the back of the beach where the ground was flat, and somewhat firmer, and then took them along the base of the cliff to the foot of the chine. This was done in silence, apart from the inevitable grunts and groans, and muffled curses. They had already planned where they were going to temporarily hide the kegs, until they could get them away to their final destinations. Each man knew where he was to go.

Once they had all of the barrels assembled at the foot of the chine, Robert indicated to Brandy that he should go up the chine to wait at the top. He understood his task was to keep watch there with the carter, and bark warnings if necessary. He raced off with his tail wagging, happy to have something specific to do.

From the beach there was a flight of steps that climbed about seventy feet onto a terrace formed by a thick outcrop of harder ferruginous sandstone. The stream responsible for cutting the chine fell over the resistant rock in a thin waterfall, splashing onto the stones below. During westerly winds even in full spate it could hardly reach the beach, all the water blowing away as a feathery mist. Behind the waterfall the continuous wetting and seepage had cut a semicircular cavern in the dark marl; at one time it was reputed that the notorious 'Blackgang' of smugglers used to hide their contraband there, but it wasn't to be used today. It was too obvious to be a real hiding place.

Each of the shore party picked up a pair of tubs, took a

hard look at the succession of steps they had to climb, took a deep breath, and in procession climbed the steep flight. After a brief pause at the top to gain breath and let the strength flow back into their legs, they went to the west along a narrow path on the terrace.

After a hundred yards or so there were several fishermen's huts, containing nets, pots, ropes and collected flotsam. Even further along, near the path up to Chale, some of the huts, including that of John Richards, were lived in. Within one of the nearer huts a large pit had been dug; most of the soil having been carefully distributed in the marshy patches. About half of the first load of kegs were put in the hole and covered over with wooden beams and a tarpaulin, followed by a layer of soil, and then a pile of nets. The rest of that load of tubs were put in a nearby thicket of stubby willow and thorn bushes, and covered with branches. When it became daylight the footprints they had made would be smeared over or obliterated, and their tracks covered. The kegs would lie there safely for several days, with the passing fishermen keeping an eye on them.

Having disposed of about half of the cargo in this way, the men returned to the foot of the chine and started to carry the rest of the kegs up the steep footpath to the terrace. From there they had to go over 300 feet all the way up the chine to the road. The path wended its way up the bottom of the chine beside the brook, which tumbled and splashed down the rocky bed. Flights of steps, a dozen or so at a time, were interspersed with almost level sections, revealing where the alternating bands of sandstone and clay occurred in the underlying rock. The steps were slippery from recent rain, and the path had shallow puddles of soft mud. In the dark it was difficult to see where to step, but, if they could, they wanted to avoid leaving tell-tale footmarks in the mud.

Each time a laden man reached the top of a flight of steps, his legs would be weak and wobbly, he would be gasping for breath, his throat would feel as if it had been rasped with a file, and his lungs would be bursting. He would have to take a short rest for a couple of breaths, and then would plod up the level section, before facing the test of the next set of steps. The night was still dark and the steps were uneven, the footing was not firm, and puddles and muddy patches made the going treacherous; the sticky mud built up on the soles of their boots so that with each step they had to lift much more than the normal weight of a boot. But they were hardy men, used to extreme physical labour. However, it was demanding when silence was imperative and the tubs were so heavy. There was one slight consolation, the fog was lifting, and the wind was being funnelled up the valley behind them, helping push them along. The incentive to keep going was the thought of the cart waiting for them at the top, and the necessity of getting everything clear away before dawn, providing that the Coastguard were still elsewhere and not waiting to catch them red-handed. But the spies they had watching the gobbies had given no indication that they were anywhere in the neighbourhood, and Brandy was still quiet.

One after another they arrived wheezing and coughing at the top of the chine and set their loads down to lean exhausted on them. As soon as they appeared, Brandy leapt up at Robert, his tail wagging furiously. At that point the lane was wide enough for parking visitors' carriages, so that the ladies could admire the ruggedness and beauty of the view from within the comfort of their carriages. Also, there was a hut where the visitors had to pay to enter the chine, if they were adventurous enough to want to climb down.

The carter had been resting in the shelter of the hut, watching with Brandy for the gang to appear up the chine, but once he heard them coming he had gone to fetch the cart from behind a barn further along the lane. It came creaking down the hill pulled by an ancient chestnut carthorse with a comforting nosebag over her muzzle, and with shoes muffled by sacking. At a flick of the reins the horse stopped obediently in front of them. The cart was high-sided and about half full of rotten and stinking potatoes.

Several of the men clambered onto the cart and moved some of the potatoes aside. The tubs were then passed up and covered over with potatoes. When no sign of the tubs could be seen, the carter pulled out a tarpaulin to cover over the lot. To a cursory inspection it looked completely innocent. The men and the cart then set out down the lane, where possible avoiding the gravel of the track, picking their way down the grassy verges, with Brandy trotting contentedly beside Robert. There was only the quiet plodding and an occasional squeak from the wheels of the cart as they bumped over the stones. If any of the neighbours heard anything they would simply turn over and go back to sleep, conveniently forgetting they had been disturbed. Comments later in the morning by the two solitary visitors at the Blackgang Hotel were dismissed by the landlady as being pure imagination; she had heard nothing, and she knew of no one who would be about at that time of night. The procession went towards Blythe Shute, the steep, narrow and winding hill down to the village of Chale, leaving the sickly sweet smell of rotten potatoes blowing on the wind behind them.

Their first stop was at the church, where an often used and convenient hiding place had been prepared in one of the table tombs in the churchyard. The sexton, Alfred Shepard, was as usual one of the gang, and he took charge of opening the tomb.

Normally the curate would be in charge of the upkeep of the church and churchyard, but the keen, new curate, the Reverend John Saunders, was an unknown quantity. He was inclined to be eager and fussy, and it wasn't clear whether he would be sympathetic to the free traders' cause. If he wasn't it could become a major problem in future. Until he had been tested, Andrew Gothen had sent him away to his family for Christmas, determined to keep him out of the way for the time being.

The tomb was one of a group of three, just inside the churchyard wall, only a dozen feet from the road junction, but set fairly well away from the path into the church, so it could be seen, but not under regular, detailed scrutiny. Each tomb was about six feet long and three feet high, with a flat table-like top; children always thought they were ideal for sitting on and imagining they were at sea, or just for looking over the wall to watch the world go by.

The cart was driven close to the wall so that the tubs could be handed directly over into the churchyard, the ground level in the yard being much the same height as the floor of the cart. The end slab of the tomb furthest from the road, the easternmost one, was loose and could be easily pulled out; the table top being fully supported by the other three sides. The end slab was taken off and carefully placed on one side so as not to scrape off the lichen which encrusted it. Even though the gap revealed was only about two and a half feet square, it was possible for a small man to wriggle in and stand on the stone coffins within. Thomas Dove, the smallest in the party, crossed himself, hoping that the occupant, Robert Weekes, would not resent the intrusion. He then clambered in, carrying a candle lamp to light the inside, and the tubs were passed down to him using the rope harnesses. Eight of the kegs were lowered in and he stacked them as a pile so that he could clamber back out easily.

The first light of morning was beginning to lighten the sky in the east and the wind was stronger, buffeting around the church tower. They needed to hurry because soon people would be stirring about their daily toil. The slab was carefully replaced and they removed the sacks that had been put over the grass to protect it from their muddy boots. They congregated round the cart where the carter had been holding the horse's head to prevent her whinnying. During the activity in the churchyard, the potatoes had been redistributed and the load recovered. There were only sixteen kegs left, two of them standing beside the cart.

Robert signalled that half of the men could go back to their homes, as the major part of the work had been done. George Walsh and Thomas Dove between them took the two tubs, and set off for Abbey Farm. One of the tubs was for the farmer,

William Jacobs, for whom they worked and the other tub would be shared between them, the cost being taken from their share of the profit. The six men who were left could cope with the rest.

Their next move was to carry on along the road towards Chale Street and Stroud Green, but before they had gone more than a couple of hundred yards, a youth came running towards them. Breathless he blurted out that he had seen the Coastguard on their way from Atherfield. They were armed with cutlasses and pistols, but it wasn't clear whether they were carrying out a routine patrol or whether they suspected something was afoot.

Robert had to make a quick decision about what to do. 'David,' he called up to the carter. 'You had better carry on by yourself. We'll keep out of sight. If they stop you we'll come up and divert them. But, wait a moment! We'd better take the sacking off the horse.' Not that there was much left on the horse's hooves; it had mostly worn away, but the tatters round the fetlocks would be bound to raise suspicions.

No sooner was that done than voices could be heard in the distance, blown on the wind. Robert signed for the shore party and the lad to leap over a gate into the nearest field. After a click of Robert's fingers, Brandy burrowed through the hedge. They crouched down out of sight to await developments. David Cheverton shrugged a thick sack over his head and around his shoulders and put his head down, letting the horse plod on at its own pace. Before he had reached the next corner three gobbies appeared at a fast march.

'Ho there, carter,' the Chief Boatman called. 'What have you got in the cart there, and where are you going at this time of the morning?' David jerked upright, as if he was half asleep and surprised to see them.

'Why, Zur,' he replied. 'I've got a load of teddies and I'm takin' them up to Billingham Manor. They'm got too ripe, and they'm only good for cattle feed.' The men hidden behind the hedge held their breath, wondering whether this would satisfy the nosy, officious officer.

'Let's see,' came the reply, and the Coastguard clambered onto the hub of the wheel to look over the side of the cart. He lifted the tarpaulin and peered beneath. The stink of part-rotten potatoes wafted out, making him jerk his head back, appalled at the smell. He jumped down, thinking better of burrowing into the load. 'You'd better go on,' he said in a broad Irish accent. 'But have you seen anyone else along the way?'

'No, Zur. Not a soul,' the carter said. 'Were you expecting owt?'

'No! Not at all! Just wondering!' He gestured to his patrol, and they marched on along the road, past the gate beyond which the shore gang were hiding. David drove the cart on.

Once they had gone out of sight, the gang let out a collective sigh of relief, and climbed back over the gate. 'That was a close one,' Robert said, as they quickly caught up with the cart. 'Well done, David. That was a good bit of quick thinking.'

'Well, I didn't tell 'em any unthruths now, did I, Robert?' David replied with a laugh, not revealing the quaking of his knees and the sickness that he had felt inside.

'At the next turning we can drop off a couple of tubs for Gotten Manor.' Robert reminded them of the next stop. Then he turned to the lad, saying, 'Well done, youngster. Here is something for your efforts,' ruffling his hair, and giving him a sixpence. 'You can go off home now.' The lad joyfully departed across the fields with more wealth in his hand than he had ever seen before.

After a couple of hundred yards the cart stopped again and they unearthed two barrels from under the potatoes. One of the men hefted the tubs onto his shoulders and with a wave of the hand staggered up the lane to the right, having a steep walk of half a mile to the Manor. The others pressed on through Stroud Green towards Billingham Manor.

It was now almost plain daylight with heavy grey clouds, a strong wind and the beginnings of rain in the air. There were a number of people busy about the houses and shops at the Green, and the smell of freshly baked bread wafted from the bakery, making them feel hungry. Little notice was taken of the cart and the two men and the dog walking behind it, except to wave and call a greeting to the familiar faces.

A well known Island parson, Reverend James Worsley, a relation of Lord Yarborough, lived at Billingham Manor. He was the vicar of Thorley, a parish near Yarmouth, so he had a well worn pony trap that he used to travel back and forth to the services and other parochial duties that the curate could not perform. He was now in his sixties, but his second wife Elizabeth was much younger, in her thirties. He saw nothing wrong in enjoying a glass or two of brandy with his dinner and had, at Andrew Gothen's behest, even put some finance into the present cargo. Ironically, his son, Jonathon, was studying to become an attorney, and may have had a different view. But he was away most of the time and must have known nothing of his father's involvement in receiving smuggled goods. In contrast, the younger son, William, knew what was happening, and was excited by the occasional periods of local activity. When he could he spied on the shadowy figures carrying heavy loads across the Manor lawns in the depth of night, and he dearly wished he was old enough to take part in some way. But he had been sworn to keep his own counsel, and enjoyed hugging the secret to himself. On the other hand, his Aunt Jane, who lived with them, was disapproving but daren't go against her brother's wishes, him being the head of the house, and she dependent upon his goodwill.

There was a very extensive hidden cellar room at the Manor that must have been built at the same time as the house. It probably had been used as a priest's hole where travelling Catholic priests could be hidden during the time when the religion was banned, and the priests were searched out and executed. The way in from the outside started at a turf covered trapdoor behind some shrubs in the garden close to the pond. It was well hidden, and difficult to find, unless one knew where it was. Behind the trap a passage extended about seventy yards under the gardens to the house, where it entered the cellars through a small doorway, heavily bolted and barred on the inside. From the cellars was a further flight of stone steps to the ground floor, where entry could be gained to the drawing room by a sliding section of the panelling. The steps went on up to the first floor, where there was a private way into one of the bedrooms, possibly more recently used for surreptitious night-time visits by the amorous.

CHAPTER SEVEN

The cart stopped on the driveway out of sight of the house, and the tubs were lifted down and carried across the dew-covered lawn to the pond. David went off in the cart to tip the potatoes into the farmyard where the cattle would eventually be allowed to eat them, and Brandy went off for a sniff about. The grass covering the trapdoor was curled back and the trapdoor lifted, revealing half a dozen steps down into the passage way. A gust of musty, damp air billowed out, but, surprisingly, the walls and floor of the passage were comparatively dry. Once the tubs had been carried down the steps they were rolled up the passage into the cellar, the door of which was not fastened. The noise they made was quite deafening, the sound being amplified within the walls, but Robert had been assured that little could be heard within the house itself or outside. It had been said that the occasional nocturnal noises had led to rumours of ghostly visitations; a very useful way of deterring unwanted intruders.

Robert and the others were stacking the kegs in the cellar when they were startled by a figure descending the steps from the drawing room above, carrying a candle. It was the vicar, rather portly, and black clothed with a red face and bald head. He would be setting off soon to spend the day in his parish. 'Good morning, lads,' he said. 'I trust that you have had a satisfactory journey with the cargo.'

'Yes, Sir,' Robert replied. 'All has gone very smoothly. I don't think that there'll be any trouble caused by this load. We'll come and move these kegs on within the next few weeks; just as soon as we can. I believe that you are to have two of them, though. Is that so?'

'I am contracted to take two, as you say. But I would like you to carry them up the steps, so that I can have access to them from the dining room.' He paused. 'What is the horrible smell?' he asked. Once it was explained how the kegs had been covered by the delivery of potatoes, he laughed loudly. 'Well, then. You had better leave all the kegs there, where the smell won't be offensive to the ladies. But I am sure that you could do with some sustenance after your labours. When you have finished come round to the kitchen door and I will ensure that cook gives you something for breakfast,' he offered graciously.

He held the candle high while Robert and the others went down the passage, and then he locked and bolted the door behind them. Once out of the passage they were greeted by Brandy who had been guarding the entrance, and they carefully replaced the turf and removed any trace of their having been there. After a quick drink and a bite of bread and cheese at the kitchen door they walked home for some further breakfast before starting their proper day's work, pleased that they had accomplished their task without being caught. They could now look forward to enjoying their Christmas the following day.

* * * * * *

Meanwhile George Walsh had lagged behind Thomas Dove while walking towards Abbey Farm; a large blister had formed on his heel, and it was giving him a great deal of trouble. On the way he had spied a sack in the hedge. Having pulled it out, he put the tub in it, thinking that it would be less conspicuous even though more difficult to handle. As he limped along, he became aware of someone hurrying along behind, rapidly catching up with him. He looked around, but couldn't see anyone in the half-light. Nevertheless, he thought he'd better be careful, so, as he came up to a gate into a field he jumped over it, dropped the sack into a ditch and started running off. It was a good thing he did, because the man was a Coastguard.

Fortunately for George the field was full of sheep, being tended by the shepherd, Jacob Blow, who recognised his fellow labourer. Realising what was happening he pointed out the Coastguard to his dog and said a few unintelligible words. The sheepdog ran straight at the Coastguard, who was just about to climb over the gate, and jumped snapping round his ankles, growling, snarling with its lips curled, barking and thoroughly frightening him. This was all despite shouts from the shepherd, who was making out the dog was not under his control.

By the time the Coastguard had managed to get over the gate, George Walsh had disappeared, and because the Coastguard hadn't seen him throw the sack in the ditch, he rubbed his ankles and waited for the shepherd to come over to him. The gobbie was annoyed, and told him in no uncertain terms to keep his dog under control and not to obstruct him carrying out his official duties. The shepherd, in reply, said that he had been calling the dog, who probably didn't like the colour of the Coastguard's uniform, or his long beard. The Coastguard had no choice but to return to his station to report failure, while the shepherd took the sack and its contents on to the farm, where it was destined. When George and Jacob got together later they had many laughs about it, especially when they shared the joke and a compensatory glass with William Jacobs the farmer.

* * * * * *

The Coastguard must have been alerted by something or someone, because there were several of them snooping around in the vicinity of Gotten Manor Farm later that morning. Though why they should suspect the farmer, David Brener, was hard to contemplate. He rented the farm from the very wealthy merchant, Michael Hoy, who owned extensive property in the area. He had been at one time Lord Major of London, and had made his money from trading with Russia; it was he who had erected the monument on the down above to commemorate the visit of the Tsar of Russia. He had so much influence that his tenants would be considered above suspicion of infringing the law.

Luckily the farmer had seen the Coastguard coming up the lane. But the tubs had not been well hidden; they had just been put down out of the way, as he was busy. On the spur of the moment he had to find somewhere to put them, and the only safe place he could think of was in the cow cribs in the yard. He immediately got his men to put the tubs into the cribs, cover them with hay and let the cows in to feed. So that, while the Coastguard were searching the buildings, the cows were standing in the thick muck of the yard, stamping their hooves, bellowing and belching as they ate the feed from around the tubs. The Coastguard eventually left empty handed, not knowing how close they had been to a major discovery, had they dared to go in among the cattle.

* * * * * *

After dropping off the cargo, the *Sweet Frances* headed on a compass course back out to sea. It was still dark, but the fog was lifting fairly quickly as the breeze stiffened. Even so they were soon out of sight of the cliffs. But John was used to sailing or rowing over these seas, and knew instinctively to within a few yards where they were. But, as they now had time in hand, they circled around until dawn had lightened the sky enough for them to see their fishing ground.

They stopped near to the rocky ledge off Atherfield where cork floats marked the location of the pots; it was only occasionally that they were swept away and when they were, the pots could still be retrieved by grappling. Every fisherman could recognise his own and other's marker flags, and there was seldom any trouble with thieving. Because the wind was gradually increasing it took several attempts for Charles to snag the float with a boathook, and with the mooring rope beneath they raised the pots, while John endeavoured to stem the tide by playing the tiller against the sails. In the pots were several crabs and a couple of good sized lobsters, which were added to the shellfish already in the holding tank. The pots were re-baited, and set again, and the crew departed with relief for the Needles.

While they were beating westwards to the Needles against the rising wind they could see the rocks at the foot of the cliffs beneath High Down being intermittently covered by breaking waves and spray. They were forced to take a long starboard tack out to sea, to avoid being trapped against the lee shore. Eventually John was able to go about onto the other tack, ease off and they could run down into the Needles Channel with the flooding current behind them. On their starboard side was the huge jagged stack of the Grosse, the outermost of the Needles, while on the port side there were now ferocious waves breaking over the Shingles Bank, sending spray high into the air, and making the shingle roar. With dark grey clouds low overhead, it was rather like entering the gates of hell, with catastrophe on either hand, and only a narrow channel to safety ahead; not something for the faint hearted.

It would have been impossible without the tide behind them. The *Sweet Frances* was catching the waves under her stern and lifting, accelerating hard down the front of the wave, with the bowsprit under water, and John fighting the tiller to keep her straight. The wave would then overrun the boat, which would slow down suddenly, the bow would abruptly rise, and her bowsprit point to the sky. They would then wallow in the trough, and the steersman had to be careful to make sure the boat took the next wave square on the stern, to shoot forward again. It was exhilarating travelling like this, but demanding on the boat and also on their tired nerves. In this fashion they swept up towards Hurst Castle and, with the increasing shelter of the land, the wind eased and the waves became more manageable. There were few other boats about, and those were all hurrying for shelter too.

They sped up the channel past Sconce Point and Yarmouth, and were thankful to see the Revenue cutter, *Adder*, at her moorings in the Roads; the Captain, Thomas Morgan, and the crew were obviously on land, about to enjoy Christmas with their families, and they were unlikely to want to detain the *Sweet Frances*. The familiar outline of Yarmouth, with the tower of St. James Church peeping over the roofs of the houses, and the castle, sternly guarding the harbour, felt almost as good as home to John and the others. They could see the harbour was crowded with ships, their bare masts pointing at the grey sky, but they had to press on further yet.

Off Hampstead Point they turned to starboard and in the lighter wind in the lee of the high land, they took the mainsail off the boat, and under jib and topsail sailed over the bar and into Newtown Creek. A few minutes later they had moored in the creek having sailed a round trip of at least 200 nautical miles.

They were squaring up the boat, taking the remaining sails off her, sloshing water over the salty decks, and pumping out the bilges, when James remarked on a Coastguard gig approaching. 'I think we may be having some visitors. Be careful now, lads,' he said in a low voice, so as not to be heard across the water.

When they came closer the Coastguard Chief Boatman, whom they recognised, shouted. 'We are coming aboard.' Then, when they were closer alongside he added, 'Where have you been, and how long have you been out?'

'We have been lifting our pots off Atherfield,' James replied, for John was below decks checking that all was shipshape. 'We have been out for several days. Because of the mist and poor weather we had to hold off the land overnight, otherwise we would have been in yesterday. We have been having trouble with our compass too, and that gave us concern over night-time sailing.' He was as honest as possible.

'Are you the Captain?' the Boatman asked.

'No! My nephew here is,' he answered as John's head appeared out of the cuddy, and he clambered back on deck.

'In that case, Captain, we will have a look around.'

The Coastguards clambered aboard and searched the whole boat, but found nothing but the crabs and lobsters, and some broken crab pots put aside for mending. They had missed the presents John had bought, which he had wrapped in oilcloth and poked into the bilges beneath the holding tank. They also didn't find some cigars that one of the others had hidden in the folds of the mainsail. The disappointment showed on their faces as they rowed away. They were probably hoping that they might have earned a Christmas bounty in terms of prize money or perhaps a bribe of some contraband liquor instead.

After the gobbies had left, they quickly congratulated each other on another successful run. But each of them was hoping that the cargo had been safely stowed away. If so, all that would remain was to carry the tubs to the paying customers elsewhere on the Island.

Chapter 8

It was rather late on Christmas Eve by the time John managed to reach home after the weary tramp from Newtown. Besides being tired, each of the crew was additionally laden with bags of crabs and lobsters, which disguised their other illicit burdens. These bags were left with John Richards, who, as usual, would cook them up in the large pot over a driftwood fire just along from his hut. As a last minute thought John took out two of the best looking crabs, which would make a nice Christmas treat for his mother, who loved crab. It always surprised him that she hadn't grown tired of them, being married to a fisherman for so many years.

As soon as John put his hand on the latch of the door, Brandy yelped, and Frances came rushing to meet him, her eyes shining. He hardly had time to put his load down before she threw her arms around him. Her warm and supple body moulded itself against him, but he could feel little of her femininity through his thick coat. She held him tightly for what seemed ages before looking up at him with tears in her eyes.

'I have been so worried,' she revealed. 'For the last two nights I had a horrible, recurring dream that the boat had been run down in a fog, and that you had drowned. When the fog came in last night I thought that it may have been a portent, and the dream was bound to come true. I knew I was being silly, but I couldn't help it. But you are home, safe. I thank the Lord.' She closed the door behind John and led him into the kitchen. 'Thank goodness the girls have kept me busy getting ready for Christmas, and your mother came round to help. When I told her about the dreams, she said she knew the feeling well from the times your father was away. But the feeling kept on returning whenever I wasn't occupied.'

As far as John was aware, Frances wasn't normally prone to worrying, as she was a very practical and matter-of-fact woman, so he was surprised to hear her concerns so readily expressed. 'Don't worry now, my love,' he said as he stroked her hair to calm her. 'We did have a dense fog on the return journey, but we avoided other ships without any problems.' He carefully said nothing about the near miss with the clipper. 'Running a cargo is actually less hazardous than fishing. Then we are busy handling nets or pots over the side, get tired more quickly, readily losing concentration, and are at the mercy of the weather. This time our main concern was the Revenue cutters catching us, but we saw nothing of them, apart from when we were inside the Solent. So we were relatively safe.' Changing the subject, he asked if the children had been any bother, and was pleased to hear they were well and safely tucked up in bed.

He whispered a few endearments in her ear as he squeezed her, and she responded by rubbing his salty whiskery beard. After holding her for a minute or so and giving her several kisses, he broke away when his stomach rumbled. 'I'm famished. Is there anything to eat? By the way, there are some crabs here that need cooking up tonight. I will give them to mother. It has been some hours since they were in the water.'

She looked at him knowingly, turned and went to the stove. Opening the door let out a waft of delicious smells. 'I knew you'd be hungry, as usual, and I've made one of your favourites, a rabbit stew, with potatoes, swedes and carrots. You'd better wash your hands while I serve it out. I had mine with the children earlier. While you eat you can tell me all about the trip, and I'll put a pot of water on the stove to boil for the shellfish.'

Frances sat opposite him while he ate, looking a little guilty with her eyes down. 'John,' she said. 'Before you say anything, I have a confession to make.' She paused, obviously trying to formulate her thoughts. Then she looked up, directly into his eyes. 'While your mother was here looking after the children one morning, I thought I'd pay another visit to Sarah Bulley, despite what the Lieutenant had said to you the other day. I knew he would be out on duty, and she was pleased to see me, but worried that if he found out he might be upset, as he was the previous time.

'Anyway, we sat down with a cup of tea, and I noticed that she kept her face partly to one side, not looking directly at me, but out of the corner of her eye, as it were. Eventually I realised that she had a bruise on her cheek that she was trying to keep me from seeing. She had tried covering it up with powder, but it was still quite dark blue underneath. I wondered how she had come by it.

'She saw me looking at it, and said that she had walked into the edge of a door in the dark and bruised her cheek, and tried to make light of it. But I still wonder if he had hit her in the heat of an argument. I didn't say that, however.

'We were talking about the children when there was a noise outside, and the door handle rattled. Sarah seemed to dissolve into a trembling fit, shaking and clenching her hands. "Oh dear," she said. "It must be him coming home. I wasn't expecting him until this afternoon."

'The door opened and the Lieutenant walked in. As soon as he saw me he stopped abruptly, and a frown came over his face. He was obviously not pleased to see me there, but he made a little bow, and said, "Good morning, Mrs. Wheeler. I trust that you are well, and your children?" Then he walked in and throwing his hat on a chair he blurted out, "After the discussion I had with your husband the other evening, I am surprised to see you here today. I know that your visiting is with honourable intentions, but it does not agree with my wife's equanimity. It upsets her."

'Sarah tried to say that she enjoyed my visits and hearing news about the village and the children, but he waved a dismissive hand and shut her up with a scowl and a gesture with his hand. I thought it better to take my leave, than try and argue the point with him. He didn't appear at that moment to be open to other opinions. So I moved towards the door, and Sarah followed to show me out. The Lieutenant didn't move, or say anything more, even though I almost had to brush past him; he didn't even say "Good day".

'As Sarah came with me to close the door behind me, she

whispered to me not to worry, it would be alright eventually, and that she would see me again. Perhaps she would visit me. But as I walked down the lane I thought I could hear their raised voices.'

John could see from Frances' troubled countenance that she was upset by the memory of the occasion; she had obviously been brooding about it. 'What do you think I should do now? Or do you think that I should let her take the initiative next time?'

John had a feeling the situation was beginning to brew up into something that could cause trouble. It could make the Lieutenant even more determined to take out his ire on anyone he thought might be involved in smuggling. At that moment he could think of no clear way in which the Bulleys' problems could be defused. 'I think we had better let time be the judge, and see how things develop. You never know, it may be that Sarah will become pregnant, in which case the problem may disappear completely. Leave it to her to make the next move.'

Still pondering, they washed the dishes, and John took the crabs out of the pot, as they were now red and well cooked. Then sitting down in his favourite chair with Brandy at his feet, he told Frances about the main events in their trip to France, and she told him that Robert had called in earlier to return Brandy, and he'd said all was safe.

With a feeling of relief and great satisfaction he was just about to get his pipe out for a last smoke, when Frances came over and sat on his lap. She put her arms round his neck, looked slyly into his eyes and smiled bewitchingly. She rubbed her hand against the stubble of his beard, and wrinkled her nose disparagingly. But she didn't protest when he kissed her, softly at first, then with increasing ardour. He reached up to her neck and softly started undoing the buttons on her blouse. She wriggled in anticipation as his hand searched beneath the cotton material, sliding down and tickling her soft skin.

* * * * * *

The following morning was Christmas morning. John was very tired, and he slept much longer than normal. Frances had been awakened by Lottie excitedly coming into their bedroom looking for Christmas presents. Frances had managed with great difficulty to get her out before she woke John up, and took both the girls downstairs to have breakfast together in front of the range. Lottie could not understand why she would have to wait until after church to have a present, but it was normally their tradition to give thanks to the Lord before they celebrated themselves. Today John would break it though.

When he did awaken it was with a start. He had been dreaming a complicated and unlikely mixture of events involving French merchants, Revenue men, and smugglers, which led to opening the cargo of kegs, only to find them full of salt water and crabs. John got out of bed cursing his imagination and hoping that the tubs were still actually full of brandy. Downstairs in the kitchen he ate a quick breakfast while bouncing Emily on his knee. To keep the girls quiet, and as a special treat, he gave each of them a present from France.

While Frances cleared up, John amused the children by stropping his cut-throat razor and shaving off the stubble around his beard and trimming it up. In the mirror he could see Frances applying some powder to her red chin, but he thought it better not to comment.

After breakfast they dressed in their best clothes and walked along the road to join the throng heading for the morning church service. It was a wild and cold day, with the north-westerly wind gusting around the buildings and trees, ensuring everyone hurried. Frances proudly wore the silk scarf that John had bought her in Barfleur; the pleasure and relief that he was back safely shone in her eyes whenever she smiled up at him. John too was proud of her beauty, and full of the wonder that such a lovely woman should love him above all the other men that she could have had, men of much higher standing than a common fisherman. Lottie happily trotted along holding her hand, carrying her new doll, while John carried the bundle of clothes within which Emily snuggled, comfortably half asleep. Brandy sniffed along several paces behind.

There was a stream of villagers heading for the church, and many of them looked at John with curiosity, knowing that he had been away for several days, and expecting that a cargo had been landed. He was sure that they would also be thankful for the extra money that it would bring into the village. It was a cold morning, but the bells cheerfully ringing gave a real atmosphere of Christmas celebration for everyone.

At the church gate they encountered Robert and Charlotte. Under the pretext of wishing him a Happy Christmas, John drew him to one side with a raised questioning eyebrow, enquiring whether all had gone well with the shore gang, and that the cargo had been safely stored away. Robert gave a little affirmative nod, at which John smiled, blew out his cheeks with relief. Robert similarly wanted to know whether the voyage back to Newtown had been uneventful. Once their worries were satisfied, they wished each other a Happy Christmas, shook hands, and embraced the women and each other's children.

The chorus of bell ringing abruptly stopped, and the minute bell started tolling the seconds to the start of the service. John told Brandy to wait, and he obediently lay down and put his head disconsolately on his paws. They quickly passed into the church, acknowledging friends and acquaintances on either side, and found seats in their accustomed pew where their mother was already waiting. She was seated primly with a stony face, which lightened once they appeared safely. The church was well decorated, with candles on every window sill lightening the gloom. The brightly lit altar was half hidden by greenery, as if in a grotto, and boughs of holly filled the windowsills, and long trails of ivy wound round the pillars. It was very festive.

They were kneeling to say a brief prayer when there was a commotion by the doorway as Lieutenant Bulley and his wife came in. He was smart in his uniform, and she was demure in a long brown coat. John happened to glance round as he rose from his knees and resumed his seat, and caught the Lieutenant looking at him as they crossed the Manor Chapel. The officer scowled and looked quickly away; it was as if he wasn't expecting John to be home, or was hoping he wouldn't see him there. Sarah, on the other hand smiled at Frances, and gave her a little wave of the hand.

The bell ringers had by then assembled in the gallery, and were tuning up their instruments. The church resounded with squeaks and scratches from the violins, and blasts from the trumpets and flutes, much to everyone's amusement. They were used to it happening every Sunday, and today it was probably worse because the players were likely to be still suffering from the drinks they would have been offered and accepted at each house during carol singing the night before.

Nevertheless, Reverend Andrew Gothen conducted a lovely service, with appropriate carols, such as 'We saw three ships', and an admirably short sermon, which made a strong point of brotherhood, tolerance and charity. Afterwards, on the way out, Andrew, smiling broadly, with Anne beside him, greeted his sister with a kiss on the cheek, and shook John and his mother's hand. Lottie immediately ran outside. After the rest of the mutual greetings, Andrew extended an invitation to them all, including Robert and Charlotte, and Hannah Wheeler, to join them for tea and Christmas cake in the late afternoon; he obviously was hoping for a blow-by-blow account of their recent exploits.

As they went out through the porch door John looked for Lottie and was surprised to see her crouching on the ground beside one of the table tombs up by the churchyard wall, with her fingers tracing out the letters carved into the side of it. Brandy was sitting by her side, trying to lick her face. Robert reached her before John could, and lifted her up, but then stood waiting. John went over to him to take charge of the boisterous child, and find out whether anything was amiss. Without replying Robert surreptitiously pointed to a bright mark on the end that he was trying to conceal by standing in front of it. The lichen and moss had been scuffed off in a long score mark, and fresh stone had been revealed beneath. Quite obviously the end slab had been damaged during its removal and lowering of the tubs into the tomb beneath. It was very noticeable, and looked plainly suspicious; it cannot have been visible the previous morning in the twilight. John immediately realised what had happened, as he knew the tomb was one of the hiding places. Robert was obviously waiting for the other people, and in particular the Lieutenant, to leave the churchyard before doing something about it.

Seeing the Lieutenant coming down the path, John took Lottie and sat her onto the tomb, and made as if her shoelace needed doing up. Robert and he stood in front of her, effectively covering the mark, and this meant that John conveniently had his back to the Lieutenant, avoiding any chance of contact. The two ladies were behind them, with Frances holding Emily. Though they were wondering what was going on, they were talking to each other and thankfully diverting attention from the activity at the tomb.

John was aware that the Lieutenant glanced over towards them as he walked past. Sarah Bulley looked at Frances, hesitated and smiled, appearing to want to stop and talk. However, her husband seemed disinclined to let her stop, and looked resolutely ahead. As her hand was firmly tucked in his arm, he pulled her on down the path. John wondered whether he had suspicions of the previous night's activities, or whether he just resented Frances' contact with his wife. Nevertheless, they all breathed a sigh of relief when the Coastguard had moved on.

It was only a couple of nights later that the tubs were moved out of the tomb, and up to Billingham Manor where they would be safer.

* * * * * *

Over the next few weeks they had to move the majority of the cargo from the temporary hiding places and get the tubs to safer places or sell them on to the consumers. As happened often, there were many incidents that made the process difficult and worrying, as well as memorable. So much so that they were always good for recounting round the fire of a winter evening, especially when there was the consumption of the spirit involved.

The first priority was to move the tubs that had been put beneath the floor of the hut down by the beach. Being close to the beach there was a high risk of the Coastguard snooping into the hut. Their suspicions would be aroused if they were to thrust a sword into the soft soil, only to encounter the sound of solid wood. The landing team were assembled again one dark night, when it was known that the Coastguard were likely to be well occupied elsewhere. They had to carry the tubs up to the top of Blackgang Chine, in the same wearying way that they had done on first landing. It was not a popular task, but it had to be done, and the many footprints they made had to be obliterated and tracks covered.

Again, the carter, David Cheverton, was waiting at the top with a load of potatoes, good ones this time, and some stored apples, both destined for market in Newport. He would take the tubs with the potatoes and apples, and return with a load of coal that he had on order. It was arranged that Charles would accompany him, and on the way they would stop at a pop or grog shop, and drop off the kegs. The shop would either act as wholesaler to sell the liquor on to retailers on the mainland, or sell it directly to their thirsty customers. The tubs were put in the cart and the potatoes used to cover them up, with baskets of apples packed around the sides, and the whole lot sheeted over to protect it from rain. This was done smartly, and the carter and his assistant had set off for the market before daylight, as they would have done normally. Charles had a job to do at the market for his father but could provide a strong arm to help with the loading and unloading and earn himself an extra crown as well.

They had made good time and were progressing along the road towards Bleakdown and Rookley, about half way to their destination. Though not the shortest route it was probably the flattest, and was less tiring for the horse. At the fast walk the horse was managing to keep up it would take about a further two hours and a half to reach Newport. In the twilight of the morning, a horseman appeared, coming down the road towards them. With a shock they realised it was Lieutenant Bulley, presumably out on his rounds; he was supposed to have been with his men on the cliffs out to the west of Atherfield, entirely the other direction. Their hearts sunk into their boots. Why was he there? Did he suspect them? Had he been tipped-off? They had no choice but to plod on, as they couldn't avoid him. 'You let me do the talking, lad,' David whispered.

Instead of stopping and waiting for them to come up to him, the Lieutenant continued to walk towards them, then pulled over to one side as if to let them pass. But, when he came abreast of them he stopped, looking curiously at the cart and the contents. 'Wait a moment, carter,' he said with a dark scowl. 'Where are you off to today?'

'We'm goin' to markit in Nippert,' David replied, reining in the horse, who gratefully halted for the brief rest and started nibbling the hedge.

The Lieutenant moved his horse closer to the cart and lifted the corner of the tarpaulin. Seeing the produce beneath, he pulled out his tuck-stick for a prod. The tuck-stick was essentially a walking stick with a curved handle that opened up to become a sword. As well as an aid to walking, it could be used for prodding to investigate for suspected contraband, or for defence, if necessary. He unsheathed it and was preparing to plunge it into the load.

'Don't ye spoil th'apples,' David shouted. 'They'm valuable. The farmer will be after you if they'm damaged.'

The Lieutenant raised an eyebrow, and drew back a moment, but then leaned over and plunged the blade several times into the potatoes. He looked quizzically at the blade, and the depth it had penetrated, wrinkled his nose and appeared to be deciding whether to try again. Luckily it had missed the kegs, which had on purpose been mainly put around the edges beneath the apples, but that luck could not last long if he went on prodding.

However, while he was looking at the load, and pondering whether to risk further probing and the ire of the farmer, he was distracted by a clatter of hooves in the distance. A pony trap appeared round the corner behind them going at a fair pace. Driven by Andrew Gothen, with Anne as passenger, they were also on their way to the market, the vicar to buy some altar wine and collect a new book he had ordered, and Anne to search for some pretty material for a new dress.

'Good morning, Lieutenant!' Andrew called brightly. 'It is unusual seeing you out and about this time in the morning, and so far from the shore.' It was in fact more unusual to see the vicar out and about so early, and it was only about two miles as the crow flies to the beach; the Chief Officer's work involved roaming far and wide at all hours, looking for contraband inland as well as at the coast.

'Good morning, Vicar and Mrs. Gothen,' the Lieutenant replied with a bow of his head, doffing his hat. 'I have been up across St. Catherine's Down watching for anyone signalling to vessels at sea that might be smuggling. Not that I have seen anyone this day. But it has been a very nice, clear night, and the stars have been so bright. It reminded me of my time in the Tropics, when I was in the West Indies as a midshipman, though it was much warmer then,' he reminisced.

He had obviously lost interest in the cart and seemed prepared for a long chat with the vicar to help relieve the tedium and loneliness of the day's work, and make a social contact. The carter, with a slight smile, gave a gentle shake of the reins. The horse pricked up its ears, lifted its head and started plodding up the road. The Lieutenant looked around as the cart moved off, but did nothing to detain it any longer. David looked at Charles, grinned and shrugged his shoulders. Charles in turn breathed a quiet sigh of relief.

Five minutes later the pony trap caught up with the cart, and swept past, with the vicar waving a salutary hand. They could see Mrs. Gothen holding her bonnet with one hand, as well as tucking the rug over her knees with the other. She had a satisfied smile on her face. Whether they knew that they had helped to run the cargo, or not, was never clear. As a consequence of the timely interruption the cart's valuable cargo was despatched, and Newport market was reached safely and the business satisfactorily concluded.

* * * * * *

At the village of Carisbrooke, near to Newport, there was the afore-mentioned grog shop called Oyster Shell Cottages. It was always well patronised, particularly on market days, with a succession of clients having a ready demand for spirits. The landlady had agreed to take several of the tubs, and Robert had arranged to deliver the kegs to them; not all at once, but over the period of a few days. One of the gang had agreed to do it, provided he was recompensed for the effort and the risk involved. As the task would have to be done at night, the agreed fee included one of the landlady's renowned square meals and a bed following successful delivery.

The first time the porter set out it was a very dark and windy night, and he decided he would only carry a single keg; certainly enough of a load for such a distance. He had been warned he would have to be careful if he was passing through Rookley, as a Revenue Officer lived there and it was well known he was prone to riding out after dark on his black horse. This made him difficult to see, and he was liable to pop up anywhere without warning.

However, all went well. The porter crept through the village of Rookley and up the hill past Pitsford Manor, without any trouble. But as he was staggering down Blackwater Hollow on the other side with the wind on his back, he heard the sound of horse's hooves soft in the sandy lane behind him. He wasn't sure whether or not he had been seen, so he slunk into the hedge and got ready to drop the keg and jump over a gate. He kept absolutely still, and tried to stop his knees knocking together. But neither the officer nor the horse can have been aware he was there, for they rode past without making any indication they had seen him. After a while, when he felt certain the officer was out of the way, the porter carried on and delivered the tub to the grog shop. Relieved, he claimed the meal that had been promised him, and eventually returned home the richer by a shiny crown in his pocket.

A few days later the porter had to try again, and after the success of the first trip, decided to take two tubs, a very heavy load for the best of men. Again, it was a pitch black night with heavy cloud and no moon. The porter had reached much the same place on the road, when he heard footsteps behind him. As they were not hoof beats he thought it couldn't be the officer, but he hid the tubs by the roadside hedge and hid some way from them, just to be sure. When the person came abreast of him, the porter, thinking that he must have been seen, shouted out 'Good night' at the top of his voice. The poor fellow, startled, cried out, nearly jumped out of his skin, and ran off down the lane whimpering with fear.

After he had gone, the porter laughed heartily, picked up the kegs and proceeded, only to be stopped near his destination by a drunken man, who wanted to help him carry the tubs. By that time it was getting light, and the drunk insisted he should be taking them to Newport, and a quarrel ensued. They argued for several minutes, and the drunk became increasingly aggressive. It was plain that the porter would either have to fight for them, or lose possession of the kegs completely. The porter grabbed a pole from out of the hedge and was preparing to fight, when a woman and two other men came up. They quickly realised what was happening, and intervened. The woman asked the drunk what he was up to, and a row then erupted between the drunk and the woman. While they were occupied in the new argument, the porter hastily took the kegs on to his destination, which was nearby, and pushed them through the door before they could be seen. Luckily, the drunk can't have seen where they went, and he must have forgotten all about the incident when he sobered up, for nothing more was heard about the incident.

Because of the problems he had had near Rookley, the next time the porter had to take more tubs to Oyster Shell Cottages he decided to take a more roundabout route; thereby hoping to avoid further trouble. Unfortunately he wasn't certain about the direction, and lost his way in the pitch dark, ending up in a boggy area near Merston. Staggering about in the marsh under his heavy load, which was beginning to tire him exceedingly, he fell over what he thought was a large mound, only to find it immediately rose behind him, bellowing, and preparing to chase him. He had inadvertently fallen over a bull, which leapt up, and came thundering after him, snorting and roaring, with wide horns lowered menacingly. He had no choice but to flee, lightening his load by throwing the kegs into a pond as he went. Luckily the bull didn't seem to be too fond of water, and once the porter had himself fallen in a ditch, he found himself standing safely but wet on one side of the ditch, while the bull stood snorting and pawing the ground on the other. Eventually the bull got bored and wandered off, at which point the porter rescued the kegs and set off to complete his journey, thoroughly soaked, and muddy, cold, tired and hungry.

Luckily, that was the final chapter of the saga. All of the tubs had been distributed, and there was no further call on the porter to carry more on that occasion. Had there been more, he would have refused to take them – he had had enough, and thought his luck would run out if he did it again. Anyway, the stories of his escapades were told and retold many times over, probably suitably embellished, through the following weeks and months. They earned the hero many warming stiff drinks in the process of retelling.

Chapter 9

January was a terrible month. The wind seemed to hold at gale force for days on end, and there was lashing rain. There were only a few days when John managed to go fishing, and the damage to their gear was enormous, and it took a long time to mend the nets and pots. Robert, Uncle James and John spent hours weaving new pots with willow wands. It was very hard on the fingers; a job that couldn't be done for long at a time without them aching, or developing calluses or blisters. What with this and cold sea water it is not surprising that fishermen were prone to develop arthritis when they were old.

It was towards the end of the month during one of the occasional meetings between John and Andrew, that Andrew showed him a summons he had received via Edward Webster, a letter carrier from Yarmouth. He handed it to John to read for himself. It was an Official Notice to Witnesses, informing Reverend Andrew Gothen that he would be required to attend a formal Court of Inquiry to be held at Yarmouth. The inquiry was to investigate various charges against Lieutenant Josiah Dornford. He was accused on a number of counts relating to collusion with smugglers, accepting bribes, and dereliction of duty. Andrew was required to appear in the Lieutenant's defence to present evidence of good character and probity. Andrew was surprised that he was being involved because although he had known the Lieutenant for many years, he didn't consider that he knew him that well. As far as he was aware, John probably knew him better because of their mutual experience of naval service, but that probably didn't carry much weight.

It was stated that the prosecuting officer was Commander Charles Deare, the Lieutenant's immediate superior as Inspecting Commander at Yarmouth. Though the inquiry was to start on 22nd February, Andrew was not required until 2nd March, presumably when the defence witnesses were to be heard. Since in the normal circumstances he would not be allowed to hear the prosecution witnesses, he suggested that John might go, and let him know what transpired, and he offered to pay any expenses John might accrue to do it.

John had heard many tales of the personal antipathy between the two senior Coastguards, though he hadn't realised it had reached such a state of animosity. After some consideration, he agreed to Andrew's proposal, thinking that he might give his old naval acquaintance some support by being there. Though it might turn out to be a tedious chore, it wouldn't really interfere with the fishing and might give John useful information, and help him make up his mind about whether he should give up smuggling. February was often colder and there was less productive fishing than in January, and he thought an interesting diversion might be welcome, providing it didn't cost too much.

It will not be sensible to bore you with all of the evidence and other goings on at the inquiry. But it is an important illustration of the state of the relationships between the Navy officers, the developing Coastguard Service and the general populace. The inquiry turned out to be a notable occasion for the Island and it seems also to have had important repercussions in the Coastguard Service, and the way it was organised.

The inquiry lasted ten days, and became very involved, with many local personalities called to take part. Though John attended at the beginning for a few days, he had to leave and return to his work and family, having passed on to Andrew a narrative of the events. Andrew himself attended for a few days during the defence, so that between them they managed to attend a majority of the important proceedings. They gleaned much of the rest from the reports in the local newspapers, as well as from other attendees and witnesses. Because it was the main talking point on the Island for many months after, most of the proceedings were replayed many times as a continual source of enjoyment and speculation, though they probably became considerably exaggerated or distorted in the process.

It was apparent from these various sources that a number of old grievances were aired, and scores were settled, as well as some favours being delivered. Accusations were made about people who did not appear in the court, and, of course, the court was not able to examine them to prove or disprove the accusations. Consequently, it is only possible to present the highlights and the general gist of the proceedings so that the reader can get the essential facts and the flavour of the arguments. You must then judge for yourselves the merits of the case, and whether or not Lieutenant Dornford was guilty.

The inquiry was to be held in the main room of the George Inn in Yarmouth. Fronting onto Quay Street, it was one of the most imposing houses in Yarmouth. The inn, which could be more sensibly called a hotel, was conveniently situated for the ferries across to the mainland and was popular as a centre for visitors wishing to spend a few days viewing the beautiful scenery of the West Wight. Being wintertime there were few visitors, and the landlord was grateful to have so much extra trade.

The inn catered for the best tastes, attempting to achieve the standards of luxury to be otherwise found in London or Bath, with elegant bedrooms, and stylish public rooms. The frontal elevation had been recently remodelled with well-proportioned windows and tall chimneys, and a pleasing aspect in the up-to-date classical style. The rooms had high ceilings and fashionable and ornate mouldings and architraves, with well-made carved marble fireplaces and elegant wooden panelling, creating a warm, comfortable and pleasing ambiance. To the east side of the inn, adjacent to Pier Street, was a picturesque cobbled courtyard with coach houses and stables for horses on three sides, and access to a popular tavern bar in the inn on the other. John knew that the proceedings would provide a quite memorable occasion.

John set out early on one of Andrew's horses through the bitter frost of a morning that offered to be calm and sunny later. It was barely light when he reached Yarmouth. But he went straight to the Wheatsheaf Inn, where he stabled the horse and ate a leisurely breakfast in front of the fire, and talked about the coming inquiry to an old acquaintance, Susanna Plumbly, the landlady; he had dealt with her on several occasions involving the availability of illicit liquor. She told him that she too had a summons to appear for the defence as a witness, presumably because she knew Lieutenant Dornford and most of his men. Probably the court assumed that she was likely to know a great deal about smuggling too, as she might have heard idle chatter in the bar or been asked to handle some of the liquor.

When it came near the time for the inquiry to start John walked through the alleyway that ended in Quay Street opposite the George. The street was busy with people of many classes. There were many in seaman's garb laden with gear, heading for the quay, or the bars behind the Inn, and others more elegantly dressed, some in naval uniform, heading for the inn's main entrance.

John, who had donned his best suit for the day, so as to not appear or to feel too out of place, climbed the three steps and went through the doors into the hallway, where he stood for a moment to take in the atmosphere. Though he had been inside the inn before, he was impressed anew by the smart tessellated floor which was formed of large white marble slabs, diagonally placed, with contrasting smaller black marble squares across the intersections, and a surrounding black edging; altogether a very pleasing and harmonious effect. The walls were panelled right up to the moulded ceiling and the doors were also panelled and the surrounds deeply moulded.

All was painted in modern pale blue and cream colours, following the Wedgewood fashion.

The hall was thronged with people of all classes of distinction, though the better class men and ladies were gathered round the foot of the broad oak staircase that led up from the side opposite the front door. There were many smartly attired naval officers standing in a group round a door at the back on the left, with their hands hovering where their sword hilts would normally be, watching the ingress of people. A scattering of local aristocracy talked quietly, and covertly watched to see who they could recognise and comment upon. Other local people found their way quickly through to the tap room and bar at the back on the right, the refreshment needs of the gentry and officers being catered for in upstairs rooms. A number of men stood nervously in the doorway of a room on the right-hand side indicated as reserved for the witnesses.

Another notice indicated that the inquiry was to be held in a room on the left. John wound his way through the throng, acknowledging a number of acquaintances on the way, and entered the designated room. The room was very large, normally functioning as a ballroom; very popular monthly balls were held there, drawing the gentry from a wide area. Otherwise it served as a large, special dining room, as well as a meeting room, the normal dining room being upstairs. Again it was tastefully panelled and decorated in pale green and cream, with swags of expensive looking curtaining hanging around the windows. Though it had several windows on two sides, it was illuminated against the February gloom by two large candelabra, as well as catoptric wall candle lamps, that reflected light across the room. Especially long candles had been put in; long enough to last all day. A log fire burned brightly in the large fireplace on the long inside wall adding further light, and it was notable how many of the chairs near to the fire had been reserved with cloaks flung over them. The continual flickering of the fire and the candles lent a rather surreal glow to the growing crowd and their tense faces and excited eyes.

At one end a heavy table stood in the middle of the room, with chairs behind for the three Court members, and the two prosecuting officers. In front of the table was an empty chair in which the witnesses would be required to sit when they were being questioned.

To one side was a small table for the recorder, a scribe whose task it was to take down a transcript of the proceedings. A pile of paper was beside him, and various pens and pencils in front. Two uniformed Coastguards stood to one side. Obviously they were to act as stewards, and to call witnesses.

The room was already filling rapidly with people, and John knew that it wouldn't be acceptable for him to try to find a seat near the windows or the fire, where the gentry would expect to sit, but few seats were unoccupied or reserved. He looked around and eventually found a seat at the back, just behind one of the doors, which happened to be next to an old friend from Yarmouth who had been involved with him in crewing for the sailing races at Cowes. He was pleased to see John as they hadn't met for several months, and they quietly exchanged a few reminiscences. Around the room there was a continual buzz of conversation and expectant laughter.

CHAPTER NINE

The main defendant, Lieutenant Josiah Dornford, already sat alone in a chair to one side, smart in his best undress uniform, with white hose, shiny buckled shoes, and his jacket buttoned to the neck, though it was strained by the middle-aged spread beneath. Today he looked older than his fifty years, the stress showing on his face as he stared pensively at the floor, his beard tucked into his chest. As he had temporarily been removed from his post while the charges were being heard, he must have been worrying about his reputation and his family's future, and had many sleepless nights. He was not acknowledging any of his friends or acquaintances, maintaining a withdrawn stony immobility. Seated beside him was a smartly but soberly dressed middle-aged man. He had a prematurely balding head, and he constantly peered over the top of glasses perched on the end of his nose, giving him a studious appearance that he obviously was keen on cultivating. John learned later that he was the Lieutenant's legal advisor, an attorney at law, Mr. William Hearn of Carisbrooke. Seated on a bench behind them were the other accused members of the Freshwater Gate Station – the Lieutenant's Boatmen.

The rest of the room soon became packed. As expected, the best chairs were occupied by various gentry, notables and local aristocracy, as well as naval officers, who talked quietly amongst themselves. They had come along expecting some noteworthy entertainment, to provide moral support for the defendant, or for the prosecution. Some benches were aligned along the walls and they were crowded with various local people. Others, who were too late to gain a seat, stood, leant against the walls, and packed the doorways.

There was a rustle of movement at one of the doorways, and the crowd suddenly fell silent. Two Naval Officers, also in undress uniform, entered and took the two seats at the end of the table. They were introduced as the Prosecuting Officers, Captain Samuel Sparshott R.N., who was the Deputy Comptroller General of the Coastguard, and Commander Charles Deare R.N., who was the Inspecting Commander for the West Wight area, and Dornford's immediate superior.

Captain Sparshott was in his mid-fifties, tall and gaunt, looking rather drawn, hollow-eyed and pale; probably looking forward to the peace and quiet of his retirement on a good naval pension. Though he was to take a minor role in the proceedings, his eyes were always bright and alert, sharp and watchful. As he was very high up in the service, he perhaps thought it inappropriate to take a major role, preferring to sit back and listen and assess the performance of his subordinates.

In contrast, Commander Deare was younger, in his mid-thirties, bouncy, energetic, and bumptious, radiating enthusiasm and aggression. He obviously considered that he was still climbing the ladder of command, and he was out to impress and climb further. It was generally known, from inspection of the Navy lists, that he was born in 1801, had been made Lieutenant in August 1824, and Commander in 1829. He had therefore achieved promotion unusually quickly; whether by influence or ability was unclear. He had been made Inspecting Commander in March 1834, so he was still comparatively new in the post, having been in charge for barely two years. His appearance caused whispering amongst the local people who knew that he and the defendant did not get on, having had public disagreements and private arguments in the past. It was common gossip that it was personal animosity that caused the laying of the charges by Commander Deare against Lieutenant Dornford.

A few seconds later, following a sharp rap on the table, everyone was required to stand for the President of the Court, Captain S. Meredith R.N. He entered, soberly pacing, as if in slow marching time, with his hat beneath his left arm and his hand tucked into his jacket. John's neighbour whispered that he had been in Yarmouth for several days, having been collected the previous week from Swanage by the cruiser *Adder*. In the meantime he had hired a horse and been seen riding around the district, presumably to familiarise himself with the area.

He was followed by two younger Navy Lieutenants, Lieutenant William Weekes R.N., and Lieutenant Henry John Carr R.N., who were the other members of the tribunal. They carried their papers under their arms, and looked rather embarrassed and uncomfortable as every eye focused upon them. One of them stumbled over a floorboard and almost fell down, bringing forth titters of amusement from the public. But he recovered and, red-faced, took his chair beside the Captain.

Captain Meredith sat in the middle chair behind the table. He was resplendent in his full undress uniform, one that must have been newly tailored for him, with his insignia bright on his shoulder. A powdered grey wig sat squarely on his head, but with some of his own dark hair escaping wantonly beneath. He was a short and portly man with small, beady eyes, a rather florid complexion, a large red nose, and a double chin. But he had a benign and cheerful look about him. His eyes constantly flickered here and there, as if he were seeking amusement from the proceedings or the location; but, as he was the Inspecting Commander of the Coastguard in the Swanage District, he would have been used to imposing the formality of the court through official proceedings.

Everyone sat. Captain Meredith picked up his gavel and hammered unnecessarily on the table for silence. He cleared his throat and looked down at the papers spread before him. 'This Court of Inquiry has been convened by order of the Commissioners of His Majesty's Customs to hear charges against the Chief Officer and the Boatmen of the Freshwater Gate Coastguard Station. The charges are in respect of erasures in the journals, bribery by and collusion with smugglers, and general misconduct.' There was a murmur of concern around the room, as people were astonished at the enormity of the alleged crimes, the breadth of which had not been apparent before.

When the hubbub had died down, he said, 'The Comptroller General will administer the oath to the court.'

Captain Sparshott rose, with the volume of General Instructions for the Coast-Guard in his hand, and turned to Appendix No 55 from which he read the oath. The members of the court repeated it phrase by phrase. 'I do swear that I will duly administer justice, according to the several Regulations and Instructions issued by the Lords Commissioners of His Majesty's Treasury and the Commissioners of Customs, for the government of the Revenue Coast Guard, and at this time in force, without partiality, favour, or affection; and if any case shall arise which is not particularly mentioned in the Regulations and Instruction, I will duly administer justice according to my conscience, the best of my understanding, and the custom of the service in like cases. So help me God.' He sat amidst a chorus of coughs and clearing of throats, and scraping of chairs on the wooden floor as the crowd made themselves comfortable.

Captain Meredith resumed. 'Lieutenant Dornford, you are the Chief Officer of the Freshwater Gate Station, and have been in post for ten years. I understand that you have been authorised by your men to speak on their behalf. Is that true?'

The Lieutenant stood up, held his head high, and looking the Captain said clearly, 'Yes, Sir. That is correct.'

'And how do you plead to the charges?'

'Not guilty, Sir.'

'Right, Lieutenant. You may sit down.' Then leaning forward and turning to the prosecutors, he said, 'I understand that the prosecution will be presented by Commander Deare. Is that correct?'

'Yes, Sir.'

'Very well! You may proceed,' then added as Commander Deare started rising to his feet, 'You may remain seated.'

Commander Deare smiled thankfully, put on a pair of spectacles, looked down at his papers and glanced round the room. He paused to add emphasis to his words. 'Thank you, Sir,' he said. 'Before I go further in summary of the prosecution, with your leave, Sir, I think it appropriate to present a brief account of the state of smuggling in the Isle of Wight as a context in which the charges need to be considered.' Captain Meredith waved him to continue. 'The Isle of Wight is a difficult coast to guard. The force is allowed a complement of only sixty-eight men, and the coastline totals seventy-six miles. Of these men, eighteen are employed to look out during the daytime, leaving only fifty who can be sent out at night. In my view this is totally inadequate to prevent smugglers running their goods almost whenever and wherever they please, and there is no relief for the men who have to be alert for sixteen out of twenty-four hours. There is nothing or next to nothing that can be done to prevent the smugglers running their goods.' He paused again for effect, and to let the whispered comments die away. Whether or not he intended to, he had given the impression that the Coastguard were carrying out an impossible task.

'Nevertheless, since 5th April 1834 the inadequate force under my orders has seized eighty-one smugglers, ten sloops, in excess of three thousand tubs, as well as tobacco and tea, and yet this does not appear to have decreased the amount of smuggling. There are at least thirty vessels concerned in the activity, most of which are notorious, as well as many more suspected of being engaged. Catching them and proving their involvement is another matter.' He glanced round the room, and could see he had everyone's attention.

He continued. 'Now I would like to explain the extent to which I believe the Revenue is being defrauded. I have been told, and hold it on good authority, that eight out of every ten people in the Island are consumers of contraband spirits, tobacco and tea, and that they see no wrong in this. It seems that they have no regard for the law in this matter. The total population of the Isle of Wight, including the crews of the yachting club and visitors is estimated to be about forty thousand. This means that if only one in four, that is ten thousand people, drank a gill of spirits each day, it would require a supply of thirty-three thousand tubs a year. 'But,' he paused again dramatically. 'But, that is exclusive of the amount that leaves the Island by the steam packet boats to Southampton, Lymington and Portsmouth. Again, I am reliably informed that it is likely to be three times the amount consumed on the Island.

'We have little control over this re-export since we cannot search every person on every ship. Nevertheless, we have ventured to arrest eighteen individuals in the act of conveying spirits from the Island. I am within the truth when I say that there are fifty individuals who are constantly going backwards and forwards to the mainland. If they do it five or six times a week and one person can conceal the equivalent of a tub about them each time, and that they can clear twelve shillings for each tub, they will be quite rich. Conservatively then, ten thousand tubs leave the Island in this manner.

'Additionally, there are likely to be even larger quantities sent in boxes, parcels, bags, etc to various places on the mainland. For instance, some months ago a large seizure of casks in Hampshire was traced to a respectable hotel in Ryde. Two days ago an informer told me that there are ten wholesale dealers in Cowes alone, and they sold the equivalent of five or six tubs a day. Consequently, we have to consider a 'trade' that is likely to be worth at least forty thousand pounds a year in which the Island is involved. This is the context in which we have to consider this disciplinary action against some of our men. The temptations to benefit from part of this trade are strong, and the rewards are probably large.

'I would like to add that the particular shore that we will be considering in this inquiry is unique and has special problems for adequate surveillance, especially in view of the intense shipping and fishing activity prevalent. In my view, two Coastguard stations are insufficient, and they should be augmented by two further stations, specifically at Alum Bay and at Totland Bay.'

At this point the Commander stood, with some of the papers in his hand. 'In the case we will be considering here, the accused are Lieutenant Josiah Dornford, and his Boatmen at Freshwater Gate Coastguard Station, namely: Charles Yeates, Maurice Blackford, John Taylor, William Herbert, Hugh Rainey, Isaac Young and James Thomas.' Each Boatman looked uncomfortable as their names were read out, and eyes focused on them.

'It is alleged, and I will call witnesses to prove it, that on a recent winter evening there was a fierce fight between smugglers and the Coastguard at Totland Bay. Signals had been sent to Lieutenant Dornford that the Coastguard needed assistance, but none was forthcoming. During the fight a number of the Coastguard were severely injured. I will bring forward evidence of those injuries. I am certain that had the cry for help been answered, those injuries would not have occurred. That evening a cargo of spirits was landed. It has been alleged that Lieutenant Dornford did not render assistance because of an agreement with the smugglers. It has been stated by witnesses that I will call, that money had changed hands to ensure that support for the Coastguard would not materialise. It is also alleged that the official reports of the encounter were falsified so as not to give an accurate account of the battle, and its consequences.

'This is not the only instance of falsification of reports. Several witnesses have deposed that there have been other occasions when the entries in the reports do not represent the actual events as they occurred, and this has allowed smuggling activities to be discounted or covered up, to the detriment of the lawful collection of taxes, or eventual prosecution of malfeasants.

'I have also been told that there have been other instances when landing of cargos has been made easier by the Coastguard being told to be absent, or being conveniently directed to focus their activities elsewhere, in order to allow the smugglers to complete their illegal activities without being apprehended. I have been reliably informed that bribery has been involved, specifically of James Thomas, one of the crew, and that a person will come forward who can evidence having seen a ten-pound note paid to him. This bribery is a dereliction of duty, an offence against sworn allegiance to His Majesty, and collusion in avoidance of due taxes.

'Specifically, it has been stated that on Christmas Day past Lieutenant Dornford had given liquor to his men and told them not to come on duty at four-thirty p.m. as they were due to, but to sit by the fire in their watch hut until seven-thirty p.m. It is alleged that during this time a cargo of spirits was landed and secreted away by the smugglers, effectively right under their noses, and in the process one of the smuggler's boats was wrecked, it being found the following morning.' That's strange, thought John. Joe had told him that a wrecked boat was found by the Coastguard several weeks before Christmas; unless a second boat had been found then.

Commander Deare continued. 'This practice of landing contraband has become so widespread that it has been estimated that many thousands of pounds' worth of taxes are being avoided, and the stretch of coastline that should be guarded by the Freshwater Gate Coastguard has, by the inefficiency of the station, become a major route by which illegal contraband enters the country. We must stamp on all infringements of the laws under which our country has succeeded in benefiting our people and defeating our enemies to become the guiding light to principles of good governance.' On this emotive note he ended his opening speech, and sat down, taking off his spectacles with apparent satisfaction.

There was an immediate buzz of conversation from the audience, coughs, and shuffling of feet. John was aware that the story that Joe Bastiania had told him of the fight at Totland was probably the one the Prosecutor was referring to. But, if, as he had implied, another run had been made into the West Wight only a day following their own, it had been truly lucky for both of them to avoid capture.

Captain Meredith cleared his throat, looked at Lieutenant Dornford, and asked. 'Is there any response that you wish to make to the accusations at this stage?'

The Lieutenant, who had his head inclined, listening to something his legal advisor was saying, sat up and looked round at his Boatmen. Then glancing at the piece of paper on which he had been scribbling throughout Commander Deare's statement of the accusations, replied in a confident voice, 'Yes, Sir, if I may. Firstly, I trust that you understand the relative dispositions of the stations and the coastline. If you allow me, I will explain. The West Wight is almost an island by itself, being separated by the River Yar from the rest of the Island. It is only physically connected by the beach at Freshwater Gate to the main island. It can only be reached from Yarmouth by ferry or by a very roundabout route via the causeway at Freshwater, a distance of at least five miles, or by a further three miles to the beach. As a consequence of its isolation there are two Coastguard stations. The first at Freshwater Gate has a watch hut overlooking the bay, which is a prime site for smuggling, as there are many caves in which contraband may be hidden. The cliffs to both east and west of the bay can be scaled by the locals who have created footpaths for the collection of seagull eggs. The cliffs stretch for a total of about six miles. The Freshwater Gate Station abuts that of the Brook Station which is about four miles to the east.' He paused to clear his throat.

'The second station is at Sconce Point, overlooking the narrow Needles Channel between Hurst Castle on the mainland, and their main responsibility is for the north coast. The north coast is lower, and has three wide open bays with many landing places, again totalling about four miles of shore. There is also about two miles of creeks and hiding places on the western shore of the River Yar.

'There are at present no purpose built cottages for the

Coastguard, and in order to cover the entire coastline as well as can be done with so few men, I have assumed the policy of distributing my men in twos or threes in rented property at various places, as favourably located as can possibly be managed. However, their disposition does depend upon where accommodation can be found. I schedule the patrols of the Boatmen so that they cover as much as possible of the shore, and can meet up with the patrols from the other stations at different times. Of course there are occasions when all my men have to meet up together at the lookout to obtain orders, and to take account of the weather or relay information. My men also frequently encounter those of the Sconce Station by chance on their patrols. It is not normally possible to organise any joint action, unless important and reliable information is received, and even then it is difficult because of the distances involved. I generally use my horse and ride around in order to control the patrols, gain information and help in anticipating and dealing with any unforeseen events. This policy is accepted by Lieutenant Jenkin of the Sconce Station, and has been agreed by the Commander.' He glanced at Commander Deare, the person involved. 'In this way I believe that the whole of the coastline is covered as well as it can be with the resources available, and the activities of the local people are adequately observed.'

'I see,' said Captain Meredith. 'And where were your men accommodated at the time of the incident which involved the fighting at Totland?'

'Two Boatmen were housed at Totland, two at Colwell, two at Norton Green, and two men and myself in Freshwater, Sir.

There are two men from the Sconce Station also quartered at Colwell, and the rest at Norton itself.'

'I understand.' Captain Meredith nodded. 'It seems an eminently sensible arrangement until the new, special Coastguard cottages are completed. Please continue.'

'Well, Sir. During the fight at Totland Bay it was a combined group of Boatmen from my station, as well as some from Sconce Station, that were in conflict with the purported smugglers. This had not been organised in agreement with the Chief Officer at Sconce Station, Lieutenant Jenkin, but was an entirely accidental meeting of Boatmen who lived in the same vicinity and were acting on their own initiative. I knew nothing about it until after the event, and therefore I was unable to provide any assistance. The rest of my men were watching and guarding the rest of the coast. In many cases such fights are often started as attempts to divert interest away from the point at which a landing might have been made. To ensure that was not the case, I wouldn't have been able to commit all of my men to the fight anyway. By the time it became apparent that injuries were resulting, it was too late to contact my men to assist, and have them reach the location. The situation was so confused that it was not clear who was involved in the fighting, and I believe that the reports written separately by myself and by Lieutenant Jenkin, based on the men's versions, may contain discrepancies on that account.

'There is no evidence that any landing of contraband at Totland was made during the fighting, and the assumed band of smugglers dispersed and could not be caught, partly because of the darkness, and partly because of the injuries sustained by the men.

'Regarding Christmas Day, I recollect that it was a very cold, wild day with a heavy sea running. I considered it was unlikely that any attempt would be made to land a cargo under those conditions. As it was Christmas Day, I gave them well watered grog and allowed them to stay in their hut for a few hours of a beastly night. It is true that the wreckage of a dinghy was found under the cliffs the following morning, a boat marked with the name William Lane. He is a well known local fisherman, and has been imprisoned for smuggling in the past, but he now insists that he has reformed. However, there was nothing to show that any landing had been made, and when questioned about it, Lane stated that the boat had been missing, and had been wrecked several days previously.' He looked towards his attorney, who nodded. 'The charges can therefore be explained by a conjunction of the unusual circumstances and misrepresentation of the facts because of confusion of events. I think that is all I wish to say at the moment, thank you, Sir.'

'Thank you, Lieutenant Dornford,' said Captain Meredith. 'I think we have heard enough for today, and I adjourn the inquiry until ten o'clock tomorrow morning when we will proceed with the prosecution witnesses.' He rose and the other Court members gathered up their papers and the whole assembly rose to their feet while the officers followed him to the door.

The crowd poured out of the room chattering loudly, heading to the bar or the dining room for refreshment. After talking to a number of acquaintances John went back to the Wheatsheaf, where he spent a convivial evening with old friends speculating on the things they had heard that day.

* * * * * *

The following morning, when all had gathered again in the room set aside for the inquiry, the press of people was even greater than the first day; word had obviously got about that fireworks might occur. Though John was prompt in getting there, it was only because a seat had been saved for him that he managed to get in.

After the customary preamble, Captain Meredith started the proceedings. 'We will now hear the prosecution witnesses. Commander Deare, call your first witness.'

'Sir, I call on William George Sullivan.' A man came into the room and stood before the chair in front of the table. He was of medium height, but stooping. Dressed in ordinary clothes, shabby but clean, there was nothing one would remember about him, apart from his nose, which was long and hooked. He appeared to be an insignificant person, one who suffered the difficulties of life with resignation if not fortitude. When he responded to the request to swear to tell the truth, he spoke with a very distinct Irish accent, with his eyes flicking round the room.

'Sullivan, you are twenty-five, and born in Ireland,' stated Commander Deare.

'Yes, Sorr.'

'How long were you a Boatman at Freshwater?'

'Four years, Sorr, and then I was transferred to Alverstoke.' Alverstoke was adjacent to Portsmouth.

'Was this at your request, or that of your superior?'

'It was at my request, Sorr. I just couldn't stand the way in which the station was being commanded, and the way in which we were being treated.' Captain Meredith looked surprised at this, and glanced at Lieutenant Dornford to see his reaction. The Lieutenant was entirely nonplussed, but made a note on his paper.

'Explain what you mean by that,' Commander Deare demanded.

'We had to be on duty sixteen hours a day, with only the occasional Sunday free, and even then we were on call. On our pay it is difficult to support a wife and growing family, though I don't have that encumbrance at the moment. As for prize money, when did we get any?' he added bitterly. 'Some of the Boatmen resorted to accepting bribes to make up for it. The Chief Officer was aware of this, but to my knowledge he did little to prevent it. My colleagues considered that he was being bribed as well.'

Sullivan continued, looking at the ceiling. 'The Chief Officer was never on duty at night. He gave us instructions and then disappeared. If we wanted him to help us or give us further instructions, he couldn't be found. At one time I know that he was at home in bed. As a consequence of the lack of supervision many of the Boatmen used to spend their time drinking with friends, asleep in the watch house, or at home with their wives. The recorded entries in the journals did not accurately show what we had been told to do, or what had been done.'

Commander Deare looked down at his notes, then peered

intently at the witness. 'Do you have any personal knowledge of the Chief Officer being bribed?'

'No, Sorr.'

'But you have deposed that you were a witness to ten pounds changing hands as a bribe with Boatman Thomas. Tell the Court about this incident.'

'Well, Sorr. I was told by my wife that Thomas's wife had told her that Marshall had received a bribe.'

Startled, Commander Deare immediately asked. 'And when was this incident?'

'It was about two years before I came onto the station, four years ago.'

Commander Deare looked horrified, hearing his major witness cut away the whole foundation of the major charge. That was not what he expected to hear, but he recovered asking, 'Were there any more specific incidents that you can tell us about?'

After some thought, Sullivan said, 'About nine months ago I overheard a man, William Lane, offering the Coastguard a sum of ten pounds for every one hundred barrels safely landed. Later I saw Thomas talking to the Chief Officer, who said something like he was sure that it could be arranged, though I was not sure to what he was referring.'

'Was it Thomas whom you heard being offered that sum by Lane?'

'I cannot remember, Sorr.'

'Are you sure you do not know what it was that Thomas asked for?'

'I think it may have been for the patrol to be directed to a particular place two days hence. And when the time came we were told to go to Freshwater Gate watch house, and stay there all night. During that night we understood that a cargo was landed beneath High Down, and we never were told to look around there, or search for it in any of the hiding places we knew of.'

'Do you mean to say that a bribe was accepted to allow a cargo to be landed without hindrance?'

'I think so, Sorr,' Sullivan replied.

'Did you see money change hands?'

'No, Sorr.'

On being questioned about dates and locations of the arranging of the bribe and of the landing he was vague, and couldn't remember details. Sullivan then went on to describe other occasions when he thought that bribes had been taken to avoid particular places at specific times to allow the smugglers free rein, but he insisted he had never received a penny himself. One thing he was sure of, though, was that Lieutenant Dornford was seldom on night duty at the times in question.

Lieutenant Dornford declined to question Sullivan on the grounds that the evidence had been so vague that the Court could gain little by him doing so.

The next witness was called, a former Coastguard named as Isaac Young. This man stated that he was forty years of age, and that he too was aware that bribes had changed hands. He thought that the smugglers had certain members of the station 'in their pockets'. But his whole demeanour did not inspire confidence, he was small, shifty eyed and snuffled incessantly, wiping his nose on his already filthy sleeve.

Commander Deare asked Young, 'Was the Chief Officer negligent in his duty? Did he, for instance, regularly not appear on night duty?'

'No, he was thorough. He caught me sleeping on duty twice, when I'd had a little to drink.'

'Were you very drunk?' Captain Meredith interposed.

'No, Sir, not drunk, only stupid in the head.'

'In that case, how would you define being properly drunk?'

'When I could neither speak nor stand, Sir.'

The whole room burst into laughter, and Captain Meredith, with a twinkle in his eye, said, 'I don't think anyone here would disagree with that.'

When the humour had died away Lieutenant Dornford asked Young, 'Have you ever been in jail?'

'Only twice, Sir. Once in Winchester Gaol, and once in Newport Bridewell.'

'And I suppose that was for being drunk?'

'Yes, Sir.'

'Was that the reason for your being dismissed from the Coastguard Service?'

'Yes, Sir.'

'And what do you do now for a living?'

'I am now an agricultural labourer at Newbridge, near Shalfleet, Sir.'

When asked by Dornford whether he had any particular friends amongst the other Boatmen at the station, he replied that one of his friends was Sullivan, and another was called Rochford. He was dismissed from the Court, but left the distinct feeling behind him that he had never been a credit to the service, and in leaving he was likely to have changed sides, and become a smuggler to support his drinking habits.

The next witness called was the aforesaid John Rochford. He also had been dismissed from the service for being in trouble with the authorities for insubordination. He was aged sixty and retired, living at Newchurch, near Ryde. He too stated that Dornford had seldom been on duty at night. When asked what information he could present about smuggling, he gave several instances where it was believed that smuggling had taken place. He also stated that he had heard that Farmer Rogers of Compton gave every help to smugglers, and that on a Sunday of the previous November, a band of sixty to seventy men were seen, each carrying two tubs of brandy and marching from Freshwater to Compton. However, it was pointed out that the farmer was a yeoman of highest respectability, who rented his farm from Lady Holmes for four hundred pounds a year. Captain Meredith thought it would be absurd to connect such an eminent person with smuggling. Anyway, he was informed that Farmer Rogers had recently died.

The next to be called was James Fudge. After being sworn in he declared that he was thirty-five years old, and had been a Boatman at the Sconce Station. He said that he had been badly injured in the fracas at Totland Bay and was now very hard of hearing. In proof of which he waved an ear trumpet, and held it to his ear when he was not talking himself. Since receiving the injury he had been transferred to Weymouth and had become a tide waiter, standing guard and rummaging for dutiable goods on ships waiting to berth. He stated that he still had intermittent pain from his injury, but could do his new job satisfactorily.

Upon being asked to relate the happenings at Totland, Fudge gave a brief account, but said that he did not have a clear recollection of all of it because he was knocked unconscious fairly early on in the fight. When he regained consciousness he had such ringing in his ears that he couldn't hear anything, and was dizzy and disorientated. However, he did remember hearing before the fight started, that a message had been sent to Lieutenant Dornford asking him to send help at once. He did not know by what means the message was sent, or why help did not arrive. He had no direct knowledge of any bribes having been offered or accepted by the defendants, nor could he name any of the smugglers involved that night.

A very similar version of events was given by John Kendall, who was also a Boatman at Sconce. He had been badly beaten in the fight, and had spent six weeks in bed as a consequence, before he could resume duties. His evidence did not add much to the strength of the accusations, but helped to illustrate the fury of the fight between the smugglers and the Coastguard, and the strong incentives for the latter to avoid getting in the way of the smugglers should they be at all faint hearted. He admitted that the temptation to accept bribes was high but didn't know of any being offered or accepted.

John was interested to hear the account of the fight by Kendall and Fudge, because there were significant differences between them and the version he had heard from Joe Bastiania, of which you have already been given an account. Admittedly, there are always discrepancies between witnesses of an event, especially one occurring during a wild and dark night. But there seemed to be no agreement on where precisely the fight took place, or what happened afterwards.

Lieutenant Jenkin was the next to appear for the prosecution. He was the Chief Officer at the Sconce Station, and though he did not take part in the fight, because he had been ill at the time, he was able to recount the events that had been related to him by his men. He stated that as far as he was aware a message had been sent for assistance. However, he said that he had never experienced any problems of communications or understanding with Lieutenant Dornford, and he had the highest regard for him as an officer, and of his previous work. He concurred in giving Lieutenant Dornford the highest character, and believed that he was incapable of accepting a bribe or being implicated in anything dishonourable. When questioned by Dornford, Jenkins admitted that Rochford had been removed from other Preventive stations too, for misconduct and suspicion of bribery.

A further witness against the accused was the supervisor of excise, a Mr. William Harland from Newport. He was in his thirties, and was an austere man, pale and thin, looking as if he never saw any sunlight, or exercise. He gave the court many statistics about the amount of revenue collected on the Island from taxes on spirits, the amount he estimated should have been due, the amount of drink he calculated would be consumed, and the volumes supplied legitimately. It sounded as if he was the source of many of Commander Deare's introductory remarks about the state of smuggling in the area. He further stated that, in his opinion, the volumes of liquor being intercepted and confiscated by the Freshwater Station was significantly less than many of the other stations under his purview. He admitted the implication was that the station was either not well commanded, or that a blind eye was being turned to the criminal activity. However, when questioned by Lieutenant Dornford he admitted that it was possible the smuggling could have been restricted because the station was alert and efficient, thereby causing the smugglers to avoid the area. When he eventually left the stand, the crowd seethed with angry whispers and scowls. As ever, tax collectors were reviled, and he was a typical specimen.

Several other witnesses were called, but without presenting any significant new evidence. The prosecution then declined to call any more of their witnesses, ending their presentation with a summary.

Commander Deare drew breath and summarised the prosecution. 'You have heard evidence, though unfortunately somewhat circumstantial, that the Freshwater Gate Coastguard Station has not been well directed. There have been lapses in command, so that smugglers have been able to land their cargos without undue hindrance. There has also been evidence presented that bribery has probably been countenanced. There may not have been proof presented of money changing hands, but there has certainly been the probability of collusion between the Coastguard and the smugglers. A measure of the severity of the problems has been that certain Boatmen have left the service, others have been discharged. Even though the morale of the station seems to be much improved since I have been in charge, it should never have been allowed to get so bad, and this must be a serious criticism of the conduct and abilities of the Officer in Charge. Acceptance of collusion with smugglers appears to have been part of the spirit of the station. If no fundamental changes are made the situation may still revert to its previous state. Lieutenant Dornford, despite his experience, undoubted abilities, and standing within the community, must take the blame for the poor performance. Since he was in command, it is his responsibility, and it is he who should be reprimanded. I recommend that he is found guilty as charged.'

With a frown Commander Deare looked accusingly over his spectacles at Lieutenant Dornford, swept his gaze around the crowd, and sat down. There was an immediate buzz of comment within the crowd, with many people shaking their heads, and mumbling negatively at the blatant attempt of Commander Deare to save face by not accepting the fact that some of the responsibility for the situation should be his, or his predecessor's.

At the end of the prosecution on Saturday, 27th February, Captain Meredith closed the proceedings. The inquiry was set to resume on Wednesday, 2nd March. John could not afford to spend more time at the inquiry, and had to leave the rest to Andrew. The necessity of earning some money was pressing, and he felt he could not accept any more support from Andrew. Also, being away from Frances and the girls had laid heavily on his mind, despite his enjoyment of the inquiry so far. He felt he had imposed too much already on Frances' good nature to demand more time apart.

Chapter 10

After church on the Sunday, John relayed to Andrew the essence of the proceedings so far. Andrew was upset that he hadn't attended the beginning, as it sounded as if it would have been interesting, entertaining and informative. So he firmly intended to attend when the court resumed on the following Wednesday. John gave his opinion that, on the evidence presented so far, there seemed little likelihood of the charges being successful; the prime witnesses had been pretty thoroughly discredited, and most of the evidence that had been presented was circumstantial. However, John did express his concern about Lieutenant Dornford's future, because he was being made out to be ineffective and had, in the least, appeared to close his eyes to collusion of his Boatmen with the smugglers. But it was difficult to judge how the Court, in the light of their wider experience of the Coastguard Service, would see the implications, and judge them. John felt that the result was still in the balance, but they would be able to predict better after presentation of the defence.

But before the Wednesday came Andrew had a letter from the Court saying that he would not be required to attend, as there were many others due to appear to be dealt with in the restricted time available. Nevertheless, following John's comments he decided to carry on with his plans as he would now be able to attend the whole of the proceedings, rather than be barred from hearing the rest of the defence, as witnesses normally would be.

Following a warning from John of how busy he expected the court proceedings to be, Andrew arrived in plenty of time. Even so he had difficulty in finding a place to sit. The court was arranged just as he thought it would be, based on John's description.

After repeating the preliminaries, Captain Meredith opened the proceedings. 'And now to hear from the defence,' he said. 'Would you first present a resumé of your defence, Lieutenant Dornford? And then I would like to hear what the accused Boatmen have to say.'

'Thank you, Sir. I would request that a statement of my defence is read for me by Mr. Hearn.'

'Very well! Please proceed if you would, Mr. Hearn.'

Mr. Hearn rose to speak, convinced in his bumptious manner that he needed to stand, wave his arms and move about to emphasise his words and endow them with conviction and passion on his client's behalf.

'It is with great sorrow that I feel obliged to speak to you about myself; having served as an officer in all parts of the globe; having borne the fatigues and joined in the exertions of maintaining the superiority of the flag that has flown triumphant; having been the companion of gallant and distinguished officers, receiving from them their approbation and esteem as a gentleman and friend; one who, when the peace made employment afloat difficult to obtain, was deemed worthy of a situation of trust on shore, and who has for sixteen years executed that trust with zeal, with discretion and with success; one who has been the guest, friend and associate of the highest and best in society in the neighbourhood; one who had long passed the meridian of life with un-impeached honour, and has now supposed for paltry lucre to have degraded himself as an officer, a man, a husband and father. If the allegations were deemed to be true, then my aged mother, my wife and six children would sink with shame, and I would be forced to accept the unfair statement on my life, my principles, my upbringing, and my future, to my everlasting dishonour and aggravation.

'My father was at one time Deputy Commissary General in the West Indies, and my uncle at the same period was the Commissary General. I joined the Navy as a volunteer midshipman in 1795 at the age of only ten years, and served in many ships. I was promoted to Lieutenant in 1802. I was captured by the French while in charge of a prize, but released after the peace of Amiens. From 1807 until 1814 I was in charge of the gun-brig *Thresher*, being present at the siege of Flushing in 1809. Following the final defeat of Napoleon Bonaparte in 1815, my future in the Navy became less certain. In 1920 I was appointed to the Coastguard, serving at Southwold before transferring to Freshwater. My background and experience all go to illustrate my honourable discharge of trust and responsibility.

'You have heard the evidence exposed at length within this

Court. Evidence that has been presented before God as faithful and correct, but I will prove it to be totally unworthy of credit. Man is ever unfaithful and scheming for his own ends. Much can be said about hearsay and rumour that can turn desire and supposition into fact and truth. Such evidence is totally unworthy of credit and being hearsay would never have been received in a court of law or in a court-martial. In support of that opinion I can quote the opinions of several judges, as well as McArthur's Treatise on Courts-Martial, Volume II, page 108. The Coastguard have to work in situations of conflict between the law and the needs and aspirations of individuals. There are some that have the opportunity to twist the law, or to operate outside the law to gain benefit, power or money that they do not deserve. We must guard against them in order to maintain our honourable and Christian society.

'Within the station at Freshwater Gate, I have had a very good and faithful group of men, who have worked hard to do their duty at all times, and under the most dangerous and difficult circumstances. Nevertheless, there are always bad apples within the barrel, bad apples that can undermine discipline and good order. I have had to propose dismissal of two of the men, those who have appeared in this court as witnesses of the prosecution.

'These men have been weak and have been influenced by the prime witness, William Sullivan, who has been shown by local people to be devious, greedy and manipulative. He was the only member of the crew who was ever seen associating or drinking with reputed smugglers, and he had actively sought out a smuggler and offered to connive at the running of contraband goods. I will bring forward further witnesses to support this. It is my opinion that if anyone has sought bribes from smugglers, it is him; he has been shown to have asked for them. He is the bad apple who has created trouble, conflict and strife. The evidence is in the different stories of the witnesses and in the injuries that have resulted. Against such duplicity it is difficult to ensure good discipline and honourable practice. It is not myself and my men who should be on trial here today, but him.

'The witness, Young, has admitted that I had found him drunk and asleep on his watch, and that he had been in gaol for drunkenness. Because of this I had written to Commander Deare requesting that he should not again be sent to Freshwater Station as an extra man, and was unsuitable for employment in the service.

'Rochford is another one in the same mould. He admitted that when he was on duty, he was visited as regularly by myself, as any other officer he had served under. Yet he is also saying that I was seldom on duty at night. These two statements are blatantly contradictory. His evidence should be considered questionable as Lieutenant Johnston, the Chief Officer at Bembridge Station, has stated that Rochford has twice been removed from stations because of misconduct and suspicion of bribery.

'Further to the charge of negligence, Fudge, another witness for the prosecution, has sworn that during the time he was under my command, which he had been before transferring to Sconce, the duty I performed in visiting the guard was stricter than any other officer he was ever under.

'As to the charges of erasures in the journals, I will prove to the court that they were merely corrections of clerical errors, similar to others to be found in the journals of other stations and in the journal of the inspecting commander himself.

'In support of the defence of my good character I offer a number of testimonials, certificates and recommendations.' After this presentation Mr. Heard sat down, looking rather relieved.

Captain Meredith then read out the vast number of letters, testimonials and recommendations that the Court had received from various people. First of all there were a number from highly placed Navy officers under whom Dornford had served at various times. They all praised his bravery and skill, particularly using as an example his actions when he was only twenty-three years old, and in charge of the gun-brig *Thresher* at the siege of Flushing in April 1809. He had then joined in an attack on a strong division of the Boulogne flotilla, a great part of which was captured, destroyed, or greatly damaged.

Other letters were read which had been received by Dornford after his heroic effort in saving passengers and crew from the wreck of the *Carn Brae Castle*. That ship, an East Indiaman, had driven ashore at Brook on 5th July 1829 while bound for Bengal with a cargo of manufactures and stores for the East India Company. The crew had to cut down the main and mizzen masts to avoid her becoming a total wreck. The swell was too big for the local fishing boats to be launched, but Lieutenant Dornford had managed to reach the vessel in the Coastguard cutter and rescued all, apart from the Captain who decided to stay on board to try and salvage the vessel.

The ship had eventually become a total wreck before the gale abated. There was a letter of thanks from the commander, Captain Barber, and also an address from the eleven passengers, whose lives Dornford had saved, and from whom a plate of considerable value had been received. Additionally there was a letter from the secretary to the Admiralty to Captain Bowles, the Comptroller General of the Coastguard, conveying the thanks of the Lords of the Admiralty for the Lieutenant's conduct, 'which they will not fail to remember.'

There were letters from many eminent people: Admiral Sir Edward Owen, Captain Peake, and Lord George Stewart. Also a letter was received from Lieutenant Francis Dornford, the defendant's younger brother, who, it was stated by Captain Meredith, had shown exemplary service in the Americas. He had taken part in the storming of Washington, in an attack on Baltimore, and had assisted in the capture of a flotilla of five American gun-vessels on Lake Borgne, near New Orleans, after an intense battle. Additionally, a warm commendation was read from Captain Edward Sparshott, brother of the chief prosecutor, Samuel Sparshott, who was in the court acting as a prosecutor. He had been the Inspecting Commander of the Southwold Station when Lieutenant Dornford was stationed there, before transferring to Freshwater Gate.

Andrew thought the list was very impressive. It revealed aspects of the Lieutenant's character and past activities that he had never suspected before. It was particularly striking that so many of the testimonials were totally unsolicited. He thought it would be difficult for the court to convict someone with such a glorious past and such powerful friends and acquaintances

Captain Meredith brought everyone back to the present by saying. 'I would now like to hear what the other defendants have to say for themselves.'

One by one the Boatmen stood, swore their oath, and stated their amazement and horror at the charges that had been levelled against them. They insisted they had not accepted bribes, they had not been mutinous against their officers, and had worked in appalling conditions to do their duty to the best of their abilities. They were aware that Sullivan had been disruptive and each agreed that he had continually fostered trouble and tried to spread discontent, which, though largely ineffective, had a bad effect on discipline and on the relationship between the Coastguard and the local populace. Each man defended their records as being exemplary, and one of them, Hugh Rainey, in a strong Scottish accent, stated that he had served twenty-six years, since he entered at the age of fourteen, without a stain on his character, and without ever even having been fined a day's pay. He was not going to risk that record for a measly bribe.

A total of twenty-one witnesses were called for the defence, but it was apparent that the Court had lost interest in hearing a defence against the charges, having decided already on their verdict. Much of the questioning degenerated into a general investigation into the smuggling activities of the common people, as well as defamation of the characters of the main prosecution witnesses. As was to be expected, there was a great deal of duplication in their support for the Lieutenant, and bore testament to his character, as a strictly honourable, conscientious, indefatigable, zealous and brave officer. During the examination mention was made by Lieutenant Dornford of an event in July 1832 when seizures of spirits and boats, and the conviction of three smugglers was effected. Commander Deare was unaware of this fact, but the veracity of the statement was confirmed by written request by him to the Acting Collector at Cowes.

The first man to be called was George Conway, a well known local personage. After he was sworn in, questioning continued by Lieutenant Dornford. Conway stated that he was a carrier by trade and aged forty. He was then asked, 'How well do you know the accuser, Sullivan?'

'Only as an occasional drinking companion, Sir. But not of late.'

'And why would that be?'

'Well, Sir, I had been instructed by Commander Deare to dispose of a number of tubs of brandy that had been found on the High Down. He wished to avoid them being taken away by the smugglers who had brought them in. I did as I was told and threw them over the cliff.'

'You were paid for doing your duty then?' Conway nodded an affirmative. 'But how does Sullivan come into this?

'When I met him later, and he learned of what I had had to do, he said that if he had been present he would have shot the Commander, and thrown him over the cliff instead. Then he could have taken the tubs.'

'And what was your response to this blood-thirsty comment?'

'I answered "Oh, Fie!", and walked away. I have not spoken with him nor drunk in his company since.' Conway had to answer no further questions; he had done sufficient damage to the accuser's veracity in those few brief words.

The next to be called was Hannah Lane, wife of the alleged smuggler, the waterman William Lane, whose wrecked boat had been found. She was not asked her age, but willingly volunteered that she was thirty-five years old, and five years younger than her husband. She recollected Sullivan calling at her house one evening. He asked her husband for a mug of brandy, and after a great deal of discussion and some aggravation Sullivan was given one. Sullivan then said that if her husband cared to land tubs of liquor on their section of coast he, Sullivan, would make sure it was alright.

'What was your husband's response to that offer of a bribe?' Lieutenant Dornford asked.

'Oh, Sir! Bill would have nothing to do with such a proposition. Bill was adamant that whatever he did, he would only act fairly and squarely. He would not then be afraid of any consequences. Many of Bill's friends have been unjustly accused of being smugglers, and have had to endure the Coastguard snooping around and watching everything they did. Bill did not want himself, or me, to have to suffer such privation. Admitted, one or two of his friends have been found guilty of free trading and fined, or even jailed, but that lesson has made them careful not to do it again. Still, why don't you ask him yourself, Sir? He is in Yarmouth today.'

Captain Meredith indicated that he did not wish to have William Lane called at that time, despite the fact known to many in the crowd that he was propping up the bar in the adjacent room. Andrew could only suppose that the

Prosecution decided that he would be unlikely to be truthful, even under oath.

Instead of calling him, the Captain called Lane's mother, also called Hannah, a seventy-year-old farmer's wife to give evidence about her son.

'Your son, William Lane, is a waterman. Tell us what he does,' said Lieutenant Dornford.

'He's always around boats, does some fishing, and ferries people from Yarmouth across the Yar to the West Wight at Norton, or to Lymington. He does help out sometimes around the farm, especially at harvest,' she said. 'But he sometimes goes off to sea for several days at a time, around the coast to various ports, I suppose.'

'You don't know where he goes or what vessel he goes in?'

'No, Zur. He don't tell me things like that, and I'm not that interested anyways. I'm only too glad to see him come safely back home again.'

'Can you tell us whether you know if your son has had a hand in landing illegal cargos of liquor?'

'I cannot swear whether he has landed any spirits on the Island, or not, Zur. Would he be likely to tell me such things?'

'Has he ever given you any smuggled brandy?' Captain Meredith broke in, with a smile.

'Now how would I know whether 'twas smuggled, or not?' she replied with a grin. 'Of course he has given me brandy! He often does, for my health, and to help me with my rheumatics. But I'm not to know where he gets it from. I don't ask.' With a laugh the Captain dismissed her.

The next person to be called was Maria Bright. She was

fifty years old, and aunt of the innkeeper of the George Inn, Phillip Bright. As she kept the bar at the inn, she was known to everyone in the room. Lieutenant Dornford took up the questioning again.

'Presumably, Madam, you sell spirits such as brandy in your bar. Where do you purchase it from? Do you buy smuggled liquor?'

'Sir, I have little trouble in purchasing brandy. There are many sources, including the wholesalers in Newport and Cowes. I also buy some from local people. Some of it may be smuggled, I wouldn't know. But as you are aware, Sir, it might be illegal to smuggle brandy, but it is not illegal to sell it,' she said slyly.

'So you may purchase direct from the smugglers?'

'It is possible that I do. I would only buy from respectable people, those who are unlikely to be involved in an illegal activity. However, it is my nephew who has the final say on when we replenish our stocks of liquor, and where we get it from.'

'In the conversations you overhear in your bar, Madam, there must be mention of smuggling, of runs, of cargos, and landings. You must be aware of smuggling being planned, and carried out and where successful landings have taken place. Can you give us any instances?'

Mrs. Bright went on to give many instances of conversations about smuggling that she had heard, and of details of landings that she believed had been successful, mainly because of celebrations that had taken place in her bar. However, she made the point that the smugglers would not come and pay to drink in her bar when they had ready supplies elsewhere.

Also they would not want everyone listening to them discussing their plans, because of the possibility of informers overhearing.

When asked whether she knew of any times when the Coastguard at Freshwater had prevented runs, she answered that spirits had been seized on many occasions, and local men had been arrested, and fined or put in prison. She was sure that there were records somewhere of these instances, but she thought that if the Coastguard were not present, there would probably be a run every week. As it was, when pressed, she considered there was probably only one every three months or so.

Susanna Plumbly, the landlady of the Wheatsheaf Inn gave a very similar response to much the same questions.

Amongst further defence witnesses was Joseph Callaway, who stated that to his knowledge a crop of tubs had been landed at Red Lake, a side creek off the Yar River, though he called it the Ere River, its old name. Joshua Stark, the tenant of Freshwater Farm, the farm owning the land surrounding Red Lake, stated that he had no knowledge of that incident, and nothing had crossed his land. Nevertheless, it was possible that any contraband had been taken away elsewhere further down the river. He had, at various times, been asked if he would hide tubs in his barns, or in his ditches or hayricks, but he had refused. Nevertheless, it was always possible that it had been done briefly without his knowledge.

The Reverend Andrew thought that the proceedings had degenerated into a general investigation into the extent to which people were willing to be honest about their involvement in smuggling, despite being under oath. This feeling was obviously echoed in the Court, for Captain Meredith refused to contemplate any further witnesses, despite the fact that there was a throng of people waiting outside who wanted to testify to Lieutenant Dornford's honesty and good character. Many of the prominent people from the Island were present and gave written or verbal support to the Lieutenant. Amongst them were many Naval men, and men of the cloth: Captain George Hayes; Commander Thomas Robert Brigstocke, a previous Inspecting Commander for the area, and senior officer to Dornford, then the Magistrate for Ryde; Commander McCoy; Captain H. Love, a resident of Yarmouth; Reverend Samuel Wilberforce, vicar of Brighstone, well known locally as 'Soapy Sam' because of his habit of rubbing his hands together, and son of the opponent of slavery, William; the Reverend George Burrard, from Yarmouth, and the late High Sheriff of Hants; Henry Powell Esq; as well as business men and seafarers; altogether a massive approbation.

Instead Captain Meredith shuffled his papers, looked over the top of his glasses at the other two Board members, and said, 'If you have all done, I will call this Court of Inquiry closed. The court will now be cleared, the Board will confer on the facts we have had presented to us, and our recommendation will be sent to the Comptroller General for the final decision, of which you will eventually be informed. You will now forthwith return to your places of employment.' The Court members then rose and walked out while the public stood in silence. Captain Meredith engaged in deep conversation with Captain Sparshott, but Commander Deare looked like thunder, obviously upset by the light-hearted way in which the proceedings had ended, and the defeat he must have felt was coming.

As soon as the door closed behind them there was a burst of chatter, and many people, including Andrew, made their way over to Lieutenant Dornford to congratulate him on his delivery, and to reassure him that they thought the verdict would go in his favour. Andrew shook the Lieutenant by the hand and wished him luck, but received the reply that he hoped luck was not needed, it was only justice that was. Dornford looked drawn after the tension and worry of the last ten days, and said that he hoped his wife and children would not have suffered in the way that he had. He made a quiet comment to Andrew that he thought the inquiry had illustrated some of the many inadequacies in the service that needed putting right. Andrew could only agree.

Many of the others present in the room went through the hallway into the tap to refresh themselves with beer or spirits, and anticipate a welcome dinner. They then had hours of discussion of the many days of fact, fiction and speculation they had heard. The considered opinion was that it had been an entertainment better than many a good London play.

Chapter 11

It was several weeks later when the news came through of the verdict of the inquiry. To the joy of almost everyone the Court said that all of the defendants were found not guilty on all charges, and had a full and honourable discharge; there would not be a stain on their records.

The only person who was possibly a little aggrieved was the prosecuting officer, Commander Deare. He must have been annoyed at losing the case, which he thought would make his mark on a post that he had been in for less than two years, and set him up for further quick promotion. He had put a lot of time and energy into it, only to be made to look a little foolish when his star witnesses couldn't support his accusations, and appeared to be culpable themselves. But he was still convinced that he was right, and that there was guilt amongst the Coastguard, and there were some who agreed with him.

However, at the same time as the decision was made, it was announced that the Commissioners of Customs had decided to do away with the Sconce Station and create two new stations at Alum Bay and at Totland Bay in its place. They obviously considered there was too much smuggling in the area for the present establishment to cope with, and the station was too difficult to man, and was ineffective. The very fast tidal currents close to the shore, which raced through the Needles Channel on both flood and ebb tides, made launching a boat hazardous and a danger to the men. Both of the other bays were relatively sheltered from the currents, and though exposed to waves they would be less difficult to launch from. Besides that, they were the sites most favoured by smugglers. Also road communication would be easier between the stations and with the senior station at Yarmouth. This decision certainly mollified Deare's position, and helped him to save face.

A few days after they heard the welcome news about Dornford, Andrew had an unexpected visitor. It was a Sunday, and it was a lovely early spring day. The air was balmy, and the breeze light. Daffodils nodded in the greening hedgerows and primroses peeped through the grass. There was a hint of summer to come. At the morning church service who should appear but Lieutenant Dornford himself. He walked in through the doorway just as the service was due to start, accompanied by his colleague Lieutenant John Bulley. Their appearance in the church caused quite a stir, with murmurs spreading along the pews as the two men looked for spare places to sit. Many craned their necks to look round at him when they realised who it was. At last a number moved up to make room for them.

After the service the vicar stood at the church door to greet and talk to his parishioners, as was customary. The two Lieutenants came out together, and Andrew welcomed them both. However, Lieutenant Bulley quickly excused himself and rushed off, saying that his wife was not well, leaving the vicar shaking Lieutenant Dornford's hand warmly. He insisted that the visitor returned to the parsonage for refreshment; an invitation that was readily accepted. The Lieutenant went to collect his horse from the side gate, where it was tethered.

Frances and John, the children and his mother were not far behind in the queue to leave the church and were also prevailed upon to join them. While they waited for Andrew to finish his duties they talked with Dornford, the ladies enquiring about his wife, Elizabeth, and their children. But the conversation was continually interrupted by villagers wishing to congratulate the Lieutenant on the successful conclusion of the inquiry. For all his being one of the despised Revenue, they respected him for his bravery in saving the crew and passengers of the *Carn Brae Castle,* and for other notable actions. They considered him to be a truly honourable adversary. After they managed to break away, they walked along the road to the parsonage together, the Lieutenant leading his horse, with an excited Lottie sitting in the saddle.

Once comfortably seated in the library before the fire, Andrew poured out liberal measures of sherry or brandy in their glasses, and said, 'It is good to welcome you again to our house, Josiah. We are only sorry that Elizabeth and your children are not with you. It has been too long, and I hope it won't be the last time.'

The Lieutenant replied that it may well be the last time, because he and his family were leaving the Island. Even though he had been cleared of the charges, he made it plain that there was obviously still a cloud hanging over his continued presence in charge at Freshwater; to remain under Commander Deare would be an impossible situation for both of them. Consequently he had requested, or it had been suggested that he request, a transfer to another station. As a result he was being transferred within the month to Worth, near Sandwich in Kent, still as Chief Officer. He and his family were due to leave in a fortnight, and he was travelling round his old friends and acquaintances to say farewell. He had been on the Island for twelve years, and all his children had been born there, and considered themselves Islanders. It was obviously going to be quite a wrench leaving after such a time, and with a cloud over him. But he seemed to be quite resigned to it as being probably the final act in his career.

Andrew, John and Hannah were devastated to hear it, and were warm in their condolences. John was dismayed as it was always better, when smuggling, to be opposed by someone whose habits and reactions could be predicted, someone who could be respected. Smugglers bore no ill-will to a Coastguard who did his duty in a way they understood, but if one did not play the game, they could be very harsh. This was part of the problem they were having with Lieutenant Bulley; they could not yet predict his reactions or movements. It would be better if they could get him to develop a regular pattern of habits; if he were to have a family it could be a good distraction, preventing him becoming so apparently obsessive.

The women left the library to help Mrs. Shepard to prepare an extended luncheon for them all, and took the children with them. They also had the intention of allowing the Lieutenant, Andrew and John to be alone for a while to drink in peace, and talk about topics of mutual interest. It was then that the Lieutenant took a folder of newspaper cuttings from the breast pocket of his tunic, and laid them out on the table, smoothing the creases out lightly with his strong fingers.

'I am glad I have you both together, because I've something I would like to show you, and have your opinion on. These articles appeared over the space of several weeks under the pseudonym of Numa in The Naval and Military Gazette. I am sure you know of the paper, but I doubt that either of you are likely to read it regularly, or even see the occasional copy. I am sure that you'll not have seen these items, or even heard of them. They are an expression of many of my feelings, but they could be considered subversive in many circles.' He immediately had the attention of both the other men.

'You can read them, and you will see why they have been published anonymously. To be honest I've been very concerned for a long time about a number of weaknesses and deficiencies in the Coastguard Service, and I decided that something needed to be done about it. I had been searching for a way of expressing them without causing undue repercussions, but these letters are obviously an attempt to bring the worries to a wider audience, and start a debate that might lead to remedial action being taken.' He took a sip at his brandy, and cleared his throat, obviously prepared to elaborate further.

'The service has been operating for at least fourteen years, and I have been in it from before the beginning. It needs to change soon to improve its effectiveness, and the morale of the men. I have had the inquiry hanging over me for many months, and after the traumas I have been through I felt that I would have nothing to lose in expressing these concerns in some way. The question was how to make my feelings known to the wider service without incurring the wrath of the Comptroller General, Captain Bowles, or the Board, and putting my whole career on the line. But these letters have done the job for me; they echo my thoughts perfectly. They raise the problems for general consideration and comment, and perhaps may even lead to remedial action. The question I have for you both is your independent opinion on the content, as you would see it, and whether you think the arguments are sustainable, and the conclusions adequately supported.' He took a strong pull at his glass. 'If not, then more must be done.

'Anyway, I must put the problems to you in a nutshell. There are a number of main points that are raised. The first is that the Coastguard Service appears to be under the control of a number of clerks and paper-pushers, all petty bureaucrats, who are more interested in receiving formal records and passing out decisions than getting the main task of the service done. They make it plain that they doubt the word of the officers in charge, even though they are officers of the Navy and men of integrity. These officers are used to being trusted and honoured by their superiors, and left to organise their men's activities in a responsible way, as needs be. Instead, they are showered with forms requiring details of time and resources spent, with estimates and plans for the future, which are weighed against apprehensions and seizures in a purely numerical exercise. Even the Comptroller-General finds he is unable to carry out his own recommendations without interference by the subordinates attached to the Board of Customs. There seems to be a separation between the Customs, who are civil servants and intensely political, and the Coastguard, who are Naval and act on military terms and procedures.

'There are between three and four hundred commissioned officers of the Navy who are placed under the direct control of a civil department which can know nothing of the discipline, regulations and procedures under which they are trained to customarily work. Their reports of what they need to do the job asked of them have to be referred to, and vetted and agreed by a civil collector of taxes, who has to separately report on the truth and correctness of what has been said. It is disgraceful that the word of men of rank, education, conduct and character cannot be relied upon without corroborating evidence from a civil administrator.

'I recently had a good example of the dichotomy between the Customs and the Coastguard that is salutary. One of my men requested from the Collector of Customs at Cowes a service certificate, a certificate of years served, when and where, and in what capacity. The reply came back saying that they couldn't issue one as 'we do not consider Coastguard officers immediately under our survey or inspection.' I consider that to be a gross insult to a faithful officer, even though he may have been a simple Boatman.' Dornford was becoming rather impassioned, red in the face and agitated, his blue eyes glinting and his beard bristling as he glared in turn at them. He sat back in his chair and pensively twirled his empty glass in one hand while smoothing his beard with the other.

John looked at Andrew with wide eyes. This was fervent stuff. He could see why Dornford wanted to share it with an audience familiar with his own predicament. Andrew sought to calm the atmosphere by pouring some more brandy in the Lieutenant's glass, saying, 'It is difficult to credit how someone can be so inconsiderate of others' needs.'

'The next point,' the Lieutenant continued, gathering momentum again, 'is that Lieutenants as Chief Officers of the Stations are expected to give military honours to those who have no military standing. As an example, I have been expected to salute various Collectors of Customs when they have visited the station, and they have wished to inspect my men and comment on their dress and appearance, as if they were their commanding officers. This is entirely unwarranted, and gives the men a false impression of the scale of command, and to whom they are responsible. It creates many problems with morale and motivation. In many cases it results in the men bypassing the Chief Officer when they have a grievance and going instead to the Collector, rather than the Commanding Inspector, as they should.

'It has been known that men have been disciplined and even dismissed from a station often to reappear at another one, having been re-employed without any notice having been taken of their previous record. This is done by civil administrators without recourse to enquiring of their behaviour or character from the Chief Officers. Often in this way we have to cope with the imposition of an extra man of a very poor sort, and though they may only be temporary expedients, they often turn out to be more of a liability than an asset. You have only to consider the instance of Rochford, who appeared at the inquiry. He had been dismissed several times for insubordination, and certainly once within the Isle of Wight, and yet still was being employed, until I finally had him dismissed.'

John remembered well that he was not impressed by the man, and was surprised that he had been considered good enough to be a Coastguard.

'Now we get to a very annoying and most galling problem, that of pay,' Dornford resumed. 'When you consider the long hours we are required to work and the conditions we have to put up with, it is iniquitous that the pay of the Lieutenants in the Coastguard Service is less than their naval counterparts. It is only right that our emoluments should be fully compatible with our naval rank. In transferring into the Coastguard Service we are in effect acting as a reserve Navy. In case of a further outbreak of war we would have to serve again, and would be expected to be precisely equivalent in all ways to those in regular service. My younger brother, who is the same rank as I, has been retired on half pay for years, but is paid almost the same as I am, and yet, because of my duties, I have extra costs to carry, such as supporting a horse, and all that goes with it; feed, grooming, farriering, etc. We receive no extra allowance for those costs.

'As far as pay is concerned, one of the regulations is that pay is stopped when the men are unwell, ill, or on leave of absence. It is totally unhelpful. It drives the officers' income downwards, reduces them to poverty, and makes them more prone to accepting bribes. I believe that this is the only branch of government service where this is applied.

'There is another extraordinary regulation that doesn't appear to hold anywhere else, and that is that officers are required to pay considerable sums for their commissions. Promotion is not just a matter of being good at the job and worthy of promotion. It can be achieved by being sufficiently wealthy, resulting in the possibility of an incompetent being above their justified level.'

Perhaps this barbed comment could be considered to refer to Commander Deare. He had undeniably obtained rapid promotion to his present post, faster than many more able Lieutenant Chief Officers. It must have created considerable disappointment, annoyance and grief to many of his older colleagues who could have been effectively bypassed, and see no reward for their hard work. But Lieutenant Dornford ploughed on regardless; perhaps on purpose not emphasising the relationship of the comments he was making to any of his own circumstances.

'A similar inequity occurs in the distribution of the rewards of seizures of contraband. There is a system of 'flank-sharing' whereby the prize money earned from seizures is shared by all grades. This means the Inspecting Commanders get a share which is often greater than the men who have actually risked all in the face of violence and injury. This is unfair and blatantly iniquitous.

'Also, there is a scheme of inducements that are offered to informers. This is open to frequent misuse. Often an informer, who more than likely is a smuggler himself, may say that a run is being done at such and such a time at a certain point, knowing full well that a much bigger run is being done elsewhere. It is a common diversionary tactic among smugglers who stand to gain very much more than what is seized as a result of the information they give. Thus the informer is rewarded for his part in the seizure of some of the contraband, as well as having a share in the successful landing of the main load.' He laughed somewhat bitterly, John thought, as if he was aware that he had been duped in this way himself.

John was beginning to wonder whether the Lieutenant had in fact written the letters; too much of what he said was close to home. If he had, the anonymity could just be a clever cover to avoid recognition and accusations of seditious intent or insubordination. He thought it all sounded a little too well thought out and unhesitatingly put, and so very close to the facts that Andrew had heard in the inquiry, and their implications. John looked quizzically across at Andrew, but couldn't catch his eye. He was intent on every word the Lieutenant said.

But the Lieutenant wasn't finished yet. He went on commenting further on the role of the Inspecting Commanders, the level of seniority above him. 'The duties of the Inspecting Commanders need to be better defined. In particular there is a system of secret reports that they have to make at regular intervals on their subordinate officers. This can lead to accusations of defects in behaviour or in character that, if they were to come into the open, could be unsubstantiated or proved fallacious. But they are held in confidential files and always count against the individual, who, unless he knows about them has no opportunity to seek redress or to change them. The opportunity is therefore there for personal differences and animosities to be used to the detriment of the junior officers.'

This was even more telling, as it appeared to apply exactly to the position Dornford had found himself in. Though he had been able to test the accusations against him in the Court of Inquiry, and been found not guilty, the mere fact that the accusations had been made would remain on his record, they would not be expunged, and the suspicion would always be there under the premise that 'there was no smoke without fire'. He was becoming quite heated with his exposition, his face was flushed, sweat was appearing as little beads on his forehead, and he was waving his hands so energetically that his brandy was in danger of spilling.

'There is a very common feeling that the whole system is inefficient, and the public have a right to expect much better returns from the outlay of their taxes. It must cost in excess of half a million pounds a year to run the service, and it doesn't achieve a great deal; it is unlikely that the cost of the service is recouped by the seizures. Though there are many seizures of contraband, it can only be a small fraction of that successfully smuggled. As a case in point, the Revenue cruisers are hardly a check on smuggling at the moment. The numbers of vessels they capture and confiscate are few compared with the number thought to be involved. This is because they are badly manned, with seamen who are not up to the standard of training or efficiency that held when the vessels were under the Navy. In other words, inferior appointments are made. Additionally, the supply of stores is open to abuse by embezzlement. Top quality materials and provisions can be ordered and paid for, but only sub-standard ones supplied. The value of the difference is then pocketed by the merchant and by the officer. There is also widespread pilfering that is not prevented, or may go unrecorded because of poor checking. The result is that the cruisers cannot keep station for any length of time, or in bad weather, and cannot stay at sea long enough to act as a real deterrent to the wily smugglers.

'It is the opinion of the writer of the letters that the only way to correct these deficiencies is to remove the Coastguard Service from the Board of Customs and place responsibility for it entirely with the Admiralty. They would then have total control for the conduct, operation and success of the service. This is a conclusion that I would heartily endorse.' He sat back in his chair with a satisfied smile on his face and his hands folded on his stomach. He waited expectantly for the reaction while he finished his glass of brandy, probably realising that it was probably smuggled.

There was a pause as Andrew and John looked at each other. Who would speak first? Andrew cleared his throat and asked the pertinent question that was on both of their lips. 'From what you said and the way you said it, Josiah, I get the impression that you might have written the letters.' He leant forward purposefully, with a glint in his eye. 'Did you?'

Dornford smiled, somewhat embarrassed, and dissimulated, screwing up his mouth and clearing his throat. 'I agree with all the sentiments expressed in the letters, as I am sure most other Chief Officers would, though there are some parts that have been perhaps poorly stated and not well exemplified. It is possible that some significant parts have been edited out,' he said carefully.

It was obvious that they were not going to get a positive

response. But Andrew, hoping to find out more of the authorship then asked, 'Have you discussed these letters with any of your colleagues in the Coastguard? You could get a measure of their support for the sentiments, and further factual information.'

After a brief pause, when the Lieutenant was considering how much to say, he replied, 'I have talked about it with a number of other Chief Officers, including John Bulley, my wife's cousin, but not with anyone senior to that. I obviously couldn't broach the topic with Commander Deare.' This was said with a touch of irony. 'All of them were of the same opinion, but with the emphasis varying on different topics depending on their own experiences.'

John was astonished to learn of the relationship between the two Lieutenants: he didn't know before that Josiah Dornford was Bulley's great uncle. It certainly gave him a whole new insight into Bulley's behaviour. He wondered whether those discussions might have been the cause of some of the problems that Frances had heard about from Sarah Bulley, about the Lieutenant's distraction and poor temper. If he had those concerns in his own mind, talking about them with colleagues might not ease them, but could keep them in the forefront of a man's thoughts to worry at like a dog with a bone. In so doing it would be easy for them to grow out of all proportion.

John had sympathy with the criticisms that Josiah had expressed. He had seen at first hand how the Coastguard behaved, and they were usually well respected for their part in the saving of lives of shipwrecked mariners. But, in general, they were relatively easily outwitted by the locals involved in smuggling. Looking at it from their point of view, John thought it must be very galling and discouraging for them to know they could do a better job with different management structure, conditions of service, better pay and less internal strife. In contrast, he, both as a smuggler and a fisherman, worked together in a team with individuals who had a good mutual understanding and respect, and a unity of purpose. That would always prevail over a system where flexibility was missing and initiative frowned upon. Admittedly, smugglers would have less success if the Coastguard were better organised and better motivated, but they were always likely to come out on top because desperation and necessity drove them. However, breaking the law always led to the prospect of escalating violence, and that never would be tolerated, no matter what the cost.

John broke into the ensuing silence. 'If the government want to save the expense of paying for a costly and inefficient Coastguard Service, perhaps the best way to reduce the incidence of smuggling may be not only for the Admiralty to take over running the entire system, but to look at the causes for smuggling in the first place. For instance, if the duty on imported corn were relaxed, the poorer people would be able to afford bread to eat, without having to resort to smuggling and breaking the law to earn extra money. Then much of the incentive for smuggling would disappear. Additionally, their health would improve and there would be less people needing to be put in the poor house, which would remove a burden from all of us. Without the smuggling the Coastguard could be less numerous and the expense reduced. Just look at the number of special Coastguard cottages that are being built at the moment. There are at least twelve terraces of six or so cottages being constructed on the Island. That does give some work for a few local men for a while, but it wouldn't do as much good as putting more food in everyone's mouths for longer.' He was becoming rather heated and despite Andrew nodding in agreement, he thought he had better not let his feelings run away with him, and he ought to shut up.

Luckily at that point Anne came in and announced that luncheon was ready, if they would come into the dining room. Andrew rubbed his hands and gestured that they should precede him to join the womenfolk and the children, who could be heard laughing merrily in the other room.

In front of the ladies the topic of the letters was not mentioned again, the conversation being all about the Dornfords' pending move, and about his ten-year-old twins, Emma and Alexrina whose misbehaviour was causing his wife a great deal of worry. However, John continued to turn over in his mind how it might be possible to use the information he'd just heard to improve the relationships of the Coastguard with the villagers, as well as via Frances improve the situation and happiness of Sarah Bulley.

Chapter 12

Frances was worried when she heard, at the church the Sunday of Dornford's visit, of Sarah Bulley's illness. She realised she hadn't seen Sarah for some while. The next day she left the children for an hour or two with John's mother at Walpen and walked the half a mile further to the Bulleys' cottage, carrying in a little basket some cakes she had made. She was hoping that the Lieutenant would be on duty, as she didn't want to have a confrontation with him. The cottage was quiet, with some of the curtains unopened. It had a brooding atmosphere, as if the cottage was waiting for something to happen. She realised that, unusually, there were no birds singing, even though, being the end of March, spring was just around the corner. The hedges round the garden were showing green, except where exposed to the wind, and in secluded spots primroses were carpeting some of the banks with yellow. With trepidation she knocked on the door, the sound echoing away into the silence.

She waited half a minute and, thinking no one was in, she turned, partly with relief, and was just preparing to leave, when the door was opened by the Lieutenant. He looked rather drawn and dishevelled. His hair was uncombed, as if he hadn't slept much the previous night, he was unshaven, and his shirt was partly undone exposing a woollen vest beneath. He fumbled unsuccessfully with the buttons. His hands were shaking, and there was a persistent tic around his left eye giving him a shifty appearance.

'Oh! It's you,' he said with a worried frown and a downward twist to his mouth. He brushed a hand roughly through his hair, as if to comb it into some sort of order. Disappointment was clear in his red-rimmed eyes; he had been expecting someone else. 'What do you want?'

She was taken aback by the lack of gentlemanliness; to be welcomed with such an offensive reception made her regret coming. But she gave a slight curtsey and put on a smile to disarm him. 'I know you would prefer me not to visit, but I heard that Sarah was not well, and wondered if there is anything that I can do for her.'

He visibly gave a start, pulled himself more upright, and gave a slightly more gracious bow of his head, and replied. 'She has a bad fever, and is very weak, but I think that the worst may be over now.' He hesitated. 'At any minute I am expecting the doctor from Newport to visit her. I have looked after her the best way that I can. I suppose you had better come in. Some female company may cheer her up, but you will have to forgive the conditions, as I have had no time to attend to the house.' He stepped back a pace and made for her to enter.

As she passed him, Frances could smell the reek of alcohol on his breath and on his clothes; he had been drinking. She began to wonder whether she was safe alone with him in this state. He waved his hands vaguely in the direction of the stairs. 'She is in bed upstairs at the moment, but I don't think she is asleep, I have just been with her. You can go up if you will, but please excuse the state of the house.' He again waved a hand vaguely, blinking his eyes several times and frowning. He then appeared to overbalance backwards to lean heavily against the wall. Frances was now sure that he was fairly far gone with drink. She looked around with eyes freshly open to the reality of Sarah's situation.

The living room, that had been so neat and clean when she last visited, was now very untidy. An unwashed plate and cup stood on the table, beside an empty beer bottle and glass. The Lieutenant stood watching her as she walked around the table and avoided an armchair which was covered with papers. She wondered whether he might try and intercept her as she went towards the stairs in the far corner of the room, but he didn't, he stayed where he was. The staircase was so steep that she had to support herself with a hand on the wall, while with the other she lifted the hem of her skirt out of the way of her feet. Definitely not a sensible task for a sick person to have to continually climb and descend these stairs, she thought.

At the top she turned into the larger of the two bedrooms. There she saw Sarah lying on the top of the bed, dressed in a white shift, with a thin coverlet over her legs and the bottom half of her body. The bed almost occupied the whole room, leaving little room for a dressing table, a small wardrobe, and a single upright chair. The window looked out westwards with the prospect of enjoying afternoon sun. Quite a pleasant room,

Frances thought, casting a quick glance around the floral wall covering and noticing the attractive watercolour landscape on the wall above the bed.

Sarah looked pale, and thinner than usual. Her hair had lost the shiny gloss that it normally showed, and there were dark hollows round her eyes, red from recent tears; but a welcoming glint came into her eyes when she realised it was Frances entering. The invalid's hands were wound up in a fringe of the coverlet which she had been twisting, either from mental or physical anguish. Frances held a hand out in sympathy.

'Frances,' she exclaimed weakly. 'I am glad to see you. I've had a fever for several days, but I think I'm over the worst now. John wouldn't call anyone else to help in the house and look after me when I was ill.' She reached out and grasped Frances' hand. 'You are just the person to give me some comfort. John has been very helpful, coming up and down the stairs whenever I need anything. But there has not been much that he could do for me except give me water and a little broth occasionally. I haven't wanted to eat, only drink. For several days he has only felt able to attend work briefly, and he worries that his men are not fulfilling their duties in his absence. He did go to church yesterday, but only because my great uncle Josiah called in.' She rested her head back on the pillow, obviously tired by the talking.

Then she unburdened herself of her real concern. 'What worries me is that the fever may have caused other complications. I have missed my monthly time for the past several weeks, and I believed that I might have been pregnant. But because of what's happened during the fever it's possible

I might have had a miscarriage. I hope it might just be the illness. I haven't dared to tell John, just in case it's a false alarm. I don't think he suspects anything yet as he has been sleeping in the other room to give me some peace at night. But I've managed to persuade him to call the doctor, and he should be here soon.' Tears came into her eyes again. 'I will be so disappointed if it is true. I hope that all our prayers have been answered, and that we will have a baby.'

Frances pulled the chair up to the bedside and sat down, still with Sarah's hand in hers. She stroked it comfortingly, not knowing really whether to say something encouraging or not. She took a middle route. 'With these things I feel it is best to trust in the Lord and His plan for you. If it is meant to be, it will be. And if not, there will be an appointed time when your hopes will be realised. Both you and John are young and appear fit and healthy. I think that your John is about the same age as my John, though you are probably a few years older than I. There is plenty of time yet for you to have your family and still be young enough to enjoy them. But first of all you need to get better, and I am sure the doctor will be able to recommend a regime or a tonic to help. Summer will shortly be here, and the sunshine will help you recuperate quickly.' Frances dared not say how easy it had been for her to fall pregnant, especially as she felt that she would soon have to tell her husband that there was probably another baby on the way.

Sarah's face softened with the reassuring words, and her whole body seemed to relax. Her eyes closed, and after a few minutes she seemed to be much happier and more content. Her lips moved as if she was saying a silent prayer, but her eyes flickered open at the sound of a heavy footfall on the stairs. Frances withdrew her hand and stayed sitting primly as the Lieutenant came into the room. He had brushed his hair and straightened his clothes so that his appearance had improved. He was closely followed by a gentleman dressed in a heavy riding coat and boots, and carrying a large, black medical bag. His bright blue eyes, deeply set under long shaggy eyebrows, flickered glances round the room, taking in and assessing the scene. There was a smile of recognition and a bow of the head when he saw Frances, as he had treated Lottie for whooping cough some time before. She stood and bobbed a little curtsey in reply to his unspoken greeting. Without a word the doctor moved over to the bed and peered closely into Sarah's eyes.

'Good morning, Mrs. Bulley,' he said. 'I am Dr Williams from Newport. I gather you have had a fever. What have been your symptoms? What can you tell me?'

Frances rose, edged round the bed, and made for the door, knowing that she would not be wanted any longer. 'Please excuse me, I must go now,' she said.

The Lieutenant stood to one side so that she could leave, and with all the grace that he could muster said, 'Thank you for coming. I know Sarah has appreciated it.' Sarah raised her hand in a wave of thanks, but didn't speak, being too preoccupied with the doctor's hands pressing the glands under her chin and feeling round her neck.

'I am glad to come,' Frances replied. 'Please let me know if there is more that I can do, or anything that Sarah wants. I can always arrange to sit with her if you have to go out and work.

Don't worry, I can find my own way out,' she added as he made as if to follow her down the stairs. He said nothing more.

In the lane outside was the doctor's dog-cart, with a sleek and sweating chestnut pony standing docile between the shafts recovering from the long trot. Frances went up to it with a handful of grass that she pulled from the hedgerow, gave it a pat on the neck, and whispered in its ear; the pony snuffled in return as it chewed on the succulent mouthful. As she turned to walk home, Frances looked up at the cottage. The Lieutenant was watching her out of the bedroom window, frowning thoughtfully. She shivered as if a breath of cold air blew over her neck.

Chapter 13

John was getting both worried and excited. He was worried because his father had been in prison for nearly the year of his sentence, none of the family had seen him in that time, and despite letters and messages that said he was well and fit, John was concerned about how much he might have suffered in incarceration. The excitement was because he was due to leave the prison in Winchester the following day, and John was going to fetch him; not directly from the prison, but from the quay at Southampton. Jack had refused to accept John going to the prison, insisting that he would be quite alright and wanted the short period of travelling to help him adjust to the shock of life outside. He had even suggested that he could take the steam packet over to Cowes; he had enough money left to pay for the coach ride, the boat fare and a good meal on the way. But it was obvious to John that his father would prefer to feel his feet back on the moving deck of a familiar boat, and feel the healing wind and the sea air on his face again. So John, Robert and their Uncle James were to sail the *Sweet Frances* from Newtown to Southampton and back again, and walk the rest of the way home or find a carriage.

To help pay for the voyage the smack had been loaded by a carter the previous evening with fish and shellfish from the Wheelers and other Chale families, to be sold either directly off the boat at the quay or to the ever attendant merchants.

They were making very good progress. It was a lovely spring day. The sky was blue without a cloud to be seen, and a light wind was blowing from the west; it looked as if it was set fair for several days. They had left Chale before sunrise, and were aboard the smack by eight o'clock. By ten they were past Calshot Spit and well into the broad reaches of Southampton Water, slowly gliding up the wide waterway in company with several other vessels of various sizes heading for the Thursday market. It was some time since John and Robert had been there, and it had been several years since James had last visited Southampton too. He reckoned it might have changed a great deal in the meantime. They relaxed and admired the unfamiliar coastline.

On their port hand side dense woodland, at the edge of the New Forest, stretched down as far as the fringing reed-beds. Then, between the reeds and the water, was a wide area of very soft and treacherous mud, which could easily strip the boots off anyone trying to walk on it. The blackened skeletons of several long abandoned and rotting boats stuck out of the mud; resting places for cormorants wanting to dry their wings. On their starboard hand was the narrow tributary channel of the Hamble River, home of a number of trading boats that plied the Solent and beyond, and increasingly of yachts belonging to the wealthy. Above the Hamble, off an area locally known as Spike Island, there was a small fleet of oyster boats working the extensive shell beds in the shallows. The scene was peaceful and rather idyllic in the early spring sunshine.

However, they could already hear the clamour of Southampton, and the smell of the town and its activities assailed their nostrils. They could see the cloud of smoke arising from the town as cooking fires were always alight. In front of the town was a small forest of masts, and a steam ferry chugged across the water to Hythe on the other shore.

Before they reached the busy port, another estuary, the River Itchen, branched off to the right. Though this estuary was still largely natural and surrounded by farmland, it was increasingly fringed by boatyards, carpenters' shops, sail-makers, chandlers, and mean houses along the waterside. They could see the recently opened floating bridge crossing the river between Southampton and the small village of Woolston which provided a vital link in a new road leading east to Portsmouth. Between the Itchen and Southampton some wharves and quays were being demolished, and a start was being made on reclaiming the tidal marshes and dredging and extending the docks to make a new dock for ocean-going vessels, and the anticipated new generation of large steam cargo ships; but it would take several years more for what would become known as the Eastern Docks to be completed.

The industrial expansion happening in the north of England was beginning to be felt throughout the country. Southampton was rapidly growing in size and in wealth, and trade was increasing with the colonies overseas. This was evident from the large number of ships of all sizes that were moored up the sides of the channel, some with lighters alongside, into which their cargos were being unloaded. There was a busy traffic of small boats moving between them.

John compared the atmosphere with that at Portsmouth, where he went much more often to sell fish and shellfish. Portsmouth was suffering from the run-down of the Navy and the channels were lined with hulks and ships not in commission. Though a vibrant town during the war, at the moment it had lost that immediacy and appeared to be rather depressed, gloomy and shabby. Southampton, on the other hand, appeared to be thriving with active trade and commerce, which was leading to the need for development of new facilities, docks and buildings. Work was already anticipated on a railway from London, and it was hoped that the combination of the sheltered deep water estuary, and the new docks would lead to regular transatlantic shipping. John suggested to Robert that if the market was good perhaps they should come here more often to sell their fish and shellfish.

Straight ahead of them the old town walls came nearly down to the water's edge, with the Watergate giving access to the town. The walls were a pleasant cream-coloured limestone, about twenty or so feet high, unused for several centuries, but still largely intact. Beyond, the roofs and spires of the town could be seen, though the town had outgrown the walls, and spread into the fields behind. Against the walls was a line of shacks, stores, cargo sheds and lean-tos. However, there were a number of more recent buildings being used as stores, offices and businesses – a sign of the burgeoning trade – but much of the business was still carried out within the town walls. Most of the cargos were unloaded on the short jetty of Town Quay, which stretched out far enough to give access to water at all states of the tide, and those wharves were full and even double banked in places. But, as one of the unique characteristics of the area was that high tide lasted for about two hours, rather than quickly turning and ebbing, there was generally plenty of time for loading and unloading small boats.

Left of Town Quay was the Royal Pier, opened only three years before by the Duchess of Kent and her daughter Princess Victoria, destined to eventually become Queen. It was the longest pleasure pier in the south of England, with a concert pavilion at the end and a horse-drawn tramway along it. Of course it attracted many visitors, for it was fashionable to walk out over the water, admire the sights, and revel in the novelties. Moored at the end of the pier were several steam packet boats, one destined to Cowes and another to the Channel Islands. The latter was just about to depart, and clouds of smoke and steam belched from its tall funnel and wreathed around the masts and shrouds. A plume of steam issued from the whistle, and a moment later the shrill sound echoed from the town walls, signalling its departure. The ropes were cast off from the bollards, its paddles began to thresh the water into foam and spray, and she moved away to cheers and shouts of goodbye. Once well under way and clear of any hazard, the sails would be unfurled and wind would be the main propulsion. As the *Sweet Frances* passed her, John could see many people on the pier waving handkerchiefs and calling to those on board.

Their destination was a little further along, near the monument which celebrated the departure of the Mayflower pilgrims to America in the 1620s. Just in front of it was the area of wharves given over to the fish quay, crowded with dirty working boats, smelling badly of salt, fish and seaweed. They searched in vain for a gap they could move into, to moor against the wharf. As John didn't want to have to use the oars or moor outside another vessel, except as a last resort, they were forced to complete a wide circle while they waited for a space.

Finally, Robert, who was ahead in the bows, pointed to a boat just about to leave, and they were able to creep in with flapping sails. Robert threw a line to a small boy standing on the quay, who adroitly looped it round a bollard, expecting to earn himself a halfpenny, or more.

After the boat was made fast, a small crowd of youngsters very quickly gathered. They avidly watched what was going on, and probably speculated about where the boat had come from and dreamt of the excitements it might have been through. Some of the smaller urchins had grimy pock-marked faces, runny noses and bare feet. Their dirty legs were exposed by short and ragged trousers – hand-downs from older brothers, or taken from the garbage heaps. Some of the larger lads were slightly better dressed, with caps or straw hats on their heads. Though they may have been just curious, they could have been looking to see whether there was anything they could thieve. John was mindful that he would always have to leave a look-out on board to deter them.

Robert climbed down into the hold and was about to pass up one of the creels of crabs, when an official in uniform came elbowing through the crowd. 'Wait,' he shouted. 'Where are you from? And what is your cargo?'

John's heart sank, for he was a Customs officer, capable of causing them all sorts of trouble. He looked like an officious type as well, with a florid face, well trimmed red beard, and a smart uniform; he could be a real nit-picker.

John answered. 'We have come from Newtown, in the Wight, with a load of fish and shellfish for the market.' In case the officer might be thinking they had contraband on board, bought from a French boat in mid-Channel, a fairly common practice, he added, 'You can come on board if you want and inspect them.'

The official looked rather dubious, but decided. 'I'm coming aboard,' he said.

John didn't want him to rummage the smack; it could delay them for hours and result in them missing the market. He replied, 'Come if you want, but the deck is slippery and covered with fish guts. Why don't you stay there and inspect the baskets as we unload? Then, when we are clear, you can board and satisfy yourself we haven't anything dutiable hidden away.'

The officer acquiesced, and stood on the quay while they started bringing the creels ashore. He poked with his cane rather ineffectually at the first two, with an expression of distaste on his face, particularly when one of the live crabs grabbed his cane and he had to shake it vigorously loose. John saw it might be a good time to leave him, and said deferentially that he would have to go and find a fish merchant or two to bargain with. With the officer's agreement he went off, fully anticipating that the man would have become bored and left by the time he returned.

John walked further along the quay, heading for the

building where he knew a merchant was likely to be. On the way he had to dodge busy porters pushing laden barrows, and lighter-men carrying sacks and boxes, as well as the inevitable carts and drays. He stepped over horse dung and piles of rubbish, stinking in the warm sunshine. All the while he kept his eyes peeled, looking out for his father.

He found a merchant who frowned and said that the market was not very good for shellfish at that time. This was the anticipated response; he was obviously trying to keep the prices down, and get himself an easy profit. But he said he would have a look. Together they returned to the *Sweet Frances*, where they found all of the creels had been unloaded, and another fish merchant had appeared. Under Robert's watchful eye, he was already looking through the catch, making notes in a small book. Seeing the approach of a competitor, he immediately offered a price for the whole cargo at twenty shillings a creel. The rival looked a little uncertain whether to best that price, but, after a quick look at the plump crabs and large lobsters, he offered more. John stood passively gazing at them with a raised eyebrow, waiting for them to reach their top bids, thinking how unusual it was to have merchants arguing between themselves, and competing for the purchase; often it was difficult to get any realistic offer. Perhaps they should come more often to Southampton to trade.

Just then, a tall, gaunt, rather stooping man, with a long, unkempt grey beard and worn old clothing, appeared through the crowd of busy workers and onlooking children. John had to look twice to recognise the man he had last seen in court a year before; it was his father, older, greyer, and thinner.

'Hullo, my boy,' he said, and uncharacteristically put his arms round John, pounding him with a hand on his back. Tears started rolling down his face. He then turned to Robert and did exactly the same, and then to his brother, James. John, with a lump in his throat and tears in his eyes too, was surprised at such a show of emotion, as his father was normally a taciturn man who kept his emotions well under control.

'It's very good to see you again, Father. You look as if you've survived Winchester pretty well. We'll be away from here soon, just when we've sold the catch we brought with us.' John looked at the others and asked, 'While we are here does anyone want to buy anything or look around?' He got shakes of the head in response; they were obviously keen to get away from the noise and the smells, and be off home.

While their attention was diverted, one of the fish merchants had walked off, leaving the other as the victor, with a stated price of twenty-two shillings a creel. John accepted that price with a handshake, and followed the man to his office to receive payment.

When he returned to the boat, his father was on board watching while the other two prepared to set sail. John released the mooring ropes and leapt down onto the deck, and prepared to take the tiller. As the tide was now ebbing they would have the benefit of the current with them all the way back. They moved away from the wharf and out into the channel, John steering and Jack standing beside him. The other two sat on the gunwale talking, waving as they passed other boats, and looking at a newspaper that Robert had bought on the quay. They read out parts of the leading report of hearings in the House of Commons about the bill for a railway between London and Bristol. John was interested because Andrew had bought shares in the scheme, and was hoping it was going to be a good investment. There was a mania for purchasing railway shares at the time, though Jack said he had had a discussion with a debtor in the jail who didn't think that all of them could be successful, and predicted there would be many bankruptcies.

When they were a mile or so down the channel John turned to his father and asked if he would like to steer. Jack nodded, smiled and placed a hand on the tiller, smoothing it up and down, as if welcoming an old friend. He peered up at the sails, taking deep breaths of the clean, salty air. John could see him making an effort to relax. A contented smile stayed on his face. He flexed his shoulders and obviously began to enjoy himself, probably the first time for a year.

While he was occupied John was able to have a good look at his father. The hand on the tiller was thinner, with the veins showing and the flesh loose over the joints; previously he remembered it as being firm and muscled, with fingers like sausages. He noticed the weariness and strain around Jack's eyes, which were much deeper sunk and sadder than they used to be. His skin was more lined and was much paler, having lost the perpetual tan of sun and wind that used to be a fact of life. His hair now had broad streaks of grey, rather than the occasional dusting at the temples, and he was stooped, instead of being upright and square. John was saddened that he had aged such a great deal in the year.

However, during the voyage there was a gradual return of the old sparkle in his eyes. He stood more upright, with his legs braced against the boat's motion. Determination replaced the contemplation and introspection, as the fresh air cleared his lungs and his mind of the year's trials. John could see the steel within his character surfacing anew. He started to ask about Hannah, the family and home, obviously anticipating the pleasures of arrival.

He had heard about the Dornford inquiry, as it was a common topic of conversation within the prison. And he had read a report of the proceedings in a newspaper, but avidly listened to John's impressions, once he realised John had attended part of it. In a reflective tone he said he was disappointed that Dornford was to leave the Island, as he had a great deal of respect for the Lieutenant; he was a good man who understood the sea, and besides that, he also had respect for those who might not have been so fortunate in life. Reminiscing, Jack commented that he hadn't seen those qualities in the other man, Bulley, the one who had arrested him. This was said without any visible rancour, which surprised John who thought he would have brooded in prison and built up resentment about it. However, John could only agree, for he felt the same way.

They were well on the way back down the Solent, it was late in the afternoon, and John had persuaded his father to give up the tiller to James. John asked his father whether he was up to walking all the way from Newtown to Chale in the evening twilight. Jack replied that he would enjoy the exercise, but could do with a square meal first. John could see that he was getting tired, and suggested they should walk as far as Shalfleet where they could obtain a meal in the New Inn, and find a cart or a wagon to take them the rest of the way. Robert and James were happy to acquiesce to the plan, but had to put pressure on Jack to agree.

The talk of hunger led John to ask whether the food had been tolerable in the prison. Jack replied, 'It wouldn't have been enough without the extra I was able to buy with the money I had with me, or that you sent in. But I suspect that the warders kept a lot of it for themselves. Without the money I'm sure the cell would have been a damper one too.' He then went on to detail what the normal food ration had been.

'Every day there was a half a loaf of bread and about a pint and a half of broth for breakfast. On Saturdays, Sundays and Tuesdays there was the same amount of bread, with a couple of ounces of cheese for dinner, and the same again for supper. On Mondays, Wednesdays and Fridays there was a real treat for dinner, about a quarter of a pound of meat, normally tough, fatty and gristly stuff, with vegetables, potatoes, and either turnips, cabbage, carrots or swedes, all overcooked. Those days there would only be bread for supper. Thursdays was the worst day, as there was only peas for dinner; nothing else. The bread was normally stale, and the cheese was what the mice left. The routine was so monotonous, it will be unforgettable. Despite paying for better quality and quantity food, it isn't surprising that I've lost weight. I'm looking forward to a good plateful of fish, with some fried potatoes,' he added with relish.

After this revelation, everyone fell quiet, thinking how

awful it must have been for a fit and energetic man to endure the privations of being shut in all day. They were surprised that he managed to survive without losing his sanity, or sense of humour.

It was only about two miles from Newtown to the inn, but the sun was setting by the time they arrived. The walk had been cheerful, with chatter going on between them all to start with. But Jack had gradually become quieter, taking less and less part in the banter. He had become tired, his footsteps were less firm, and his shoulders more bowed. John thought he looked near the end of his tether. They trudged down the hill into Shalfleet and across the bridge over the Caulborne, the stream flowing into one of the branches of Newtown Creek. As they approached the low, thatched Inn building abutting the road on the right, Jack looked up at the stubby tower of the church on the hill just above them, capped with a stunted wooden spire, and muttered a brief verse:

'The Shalfleet poor and simple people,

Sold the bells to build the steeple.'

This raised a laugh from the two brothers, who hadn't heard it before. Jack had to explain that the funds to build the steeple had been provided about twenty years before by sale of the bells and the village gun, thought by the villagers not to be necessary after the defeat of Napoleon Bonaparte; it had obviously made them victims of ridicule.

They entered the inn in a brighter mood. The landlord welcomed them, recognising their thirst. Soon, four pints of beer were drawn from the barrel racked in the corner, and set on a table. Luckily, the local carter was already in the bar, and he was more than willing to carry them to Chale once they had offered an acceptable fare.

After a simple meal of fish soup, bread and cold meat, they paid the landlord and departed. In the meantime the carter had fetched a large pony trap that could take the four of them, and harnessed up a pair of spirited looking geldings. He would have to get to Chale and back before starting his normal day's work, but the extra shillings he would earn would make it worthwhile.

It was an uncomfortable ride. The motion was not as smooth and steady as that of the boat, and to the fishermen the rattling, jerking, bouncing motion was tiring, especially when they crossed the rough tracks on the downs. They had to hang on to the armrests to ease their backsides. But Jack went off to sleep in no time, unaccustomed as he was to the fresh air and the exercise; he was held in place by the men on either side. The others may have nodded off from time to time, but otherwise enjoyed the cool, breezy night with a fitful moon shining between ghostly ships of cloud that passed across it in stately progression.

It was almost two hours later, and it must have been about midnight, that they were approaching Stroud Green, and were about to take the lane to Atherfield. They would take Jack to Under South Down first, and then take the others on to Chale. They were looking forward to being able to roll into a warm bed and sleep properly for a few hours; at least till daybreak. They had seen no one, until in front of them a horse and rider suddenly appeared out of the darkness. Their own horses stopped, snorting and stamping, as the startled carter pulled on the reins.

'Ho there! What are you about at this time of the night?' demanded the rider. John's heart sank for he recognised the voice. It was Lieutenant Bulley out on his rounds. This was the last person he wanted his father to confront at that moment. He dropped his head down, letting the carter do the talking.

'I am taking these gentlemen back to Chale from Shalfleet. And who are you to ask?'

'I am a Revenue Officer, and I have every right to ask, to find out whether you have legitimate business, and if you are carrying contraband.' He came closer, with his hand on his cutlass, peering in the semi-darkness at the occupants of the trap.

Seeing and recognising John and Robert he became even more suspicious. 'Ah! The Wheeler brothers, and their uncle too! This is an unusual style of transport for you, one I wouldn't normally expect to see you in.'

Their father, who had been woken by the voices, sat up and broke in, 'Young man. I would be obliged if you allow us to get on. It's a long time since I've seen my home, and it's not likely I have any contraband, seeing where I have come from.'

The Lieutenant was taken aback by the abrupt tone, but after a few seconds realised what the situation was and his voice changed its tone, and surprisingly became much warmer. 'Ah! Mr. Wheeler. I had heard you were due home soon. I appreciate your haste to get there, now you are so close. May I welcome you back and I hope that you and your family will enjoy lasting peace and good health. I am sure you will again act as an upright example to the rest of the community, as one of its leaders.' The latter was said without a trace of sarcasm.

He could have been scathing and spiteful. He could have set out to demean his old adversary, but John was struck by the tone of the Lieutenant's voice, despite the formality. It certainly sounded as if he was genuinely pleased to welcome Jack home, and carried no continuing rancour or resentment about their last encounter, or the illegal activities; perhaps it was now considered as water under the bridge, paid for and best forgiven and forgotten. 'I will delay you no longer.' With a slight inclination of his head the Lieutenant pulled on his reins and drew the horse back off the lane, allowing them to go on.

When they were clear of him and out of earshot Jack said quietly, 'I had a hard time for the first few months in jail, trying to suppress my dislike of that officer. But, he was only doing his duty, and I was caught. If I had been in his shoes, would I have done any different? I think not! I've got over it now, and though I regret losing a year of my life, I could have lost much more. It was certainly better than being transported to Australia and not seeing any of my family again. Many don't even get there, they are lost on the way.' He paused and looked intently at them in turn.

'Don't you ever look to revenge what I have lost, or harbour any resentment of the Lieutenant. Life is too short. I must get on with my life and make the best of it, and you must get on with yours. I don't want to hear any more of hatred, or retribution, especially in the hearing of your mother. We must pick up where we left off.'

This was the longest and most heartfelt speech that John had ever heard his father make, for he was normally a man of few words. As he thought about the sentiments later he resolved to heed his father's advice, and try to come to terms with the conflict in his feelings. Certainly, Jack had changed. His character had become much warmer and more emotional, and he was outwardly more cheerful and forgiving than before.

They pressed on to their homes; Jack to a warm and tearful welcome from Hannah, who had been waiting impatiently for his return.

Chapter 14

During the periods between fishing trips, when he couldn't abide mending nets and pots any longer, and needed a rest, John walked on the cliffs and the beach; the change was both relaxing and reinvigorating. He particularly enjoyed it in the early summer when he could inspect the new rock falls brought down by the rain and the action of the waves. The fallen rocks always provided opportunities for finding fossils and prising the fragments open to discover what might be within; though it was always more satisfying if he could feel the sun warm on his back at the same time. He delighted in cracking open a hard concretion with the prospect of seeing an ammonite within, or a cavity full of crystals he could then take to show Andrew and try to name. He also had a hidden agenda which gave an added interest, not that it would necessarily be of any value. He was innocently able to keep an eye on the Coastguard's movements, and try to work out their watches and lookout timetables. His was therefore a familiar figure to be seen poking about, much to the amusement of the other villagers.

Some people cleaned up fossils and sold them to the

visitors in the summer. It was a very useful way of earning additional money; some people even made their living in this way. John was aware, because it had been reported in the newspapers, that Mary Anning, a woman living in Lyme Regis, had found many complete skeletons of dinosaurs, exciting the curiosity of scientists and collectors. They vied to buy them for considerable sums, and some of the best fossils even ended up in museums. Some dinosaur remains had also been found along the coast near Brook.

But the best ones John found, he kept, to admire and to think about. He did it hoping to resolve a major religious and philosophical problem he had. The difficulty was in equating the biblical statement that creation of the earth and all living things occurred in seven days, with the, to him, apparently immense timescales of the formation of the rocks, the layering of the strata, and the development of life in its multiplicity of forms. It was an enigma that puzzled and worried him. Similarly, it was the source of much wonder and interest to Andrew, as well as to many others of the educated gentry. Collecting fossils, pressing and drawing flowers and plants, preserving butterflies, and examining and describing minute creatures using microscopes, were common intellectual hobbies for the wealthy, having no need to spend their time occupied in anything other than satisfying their curiosity. In particular the science of geology was developing rapidly.

John's interest had been recently sharpened by further acquaintance with Joshua Haygarth, who had reappeared in the area in June to collect more fossils and carry out further study of the strata. John came across his portly figure on the beach crouching, red-faced and sweating, belabouring fallen rocks with his hammer. When John appeared he looked up, wiped his brow with a gaudy red handkerchief, and cleaned his glasses. They then started an intense discussion which went into realms that John had only a vague knowledge of. He concluded that he needed the help of a trained mind and one with a religious viewpoint, so he decided to introduce the geologist to Andrew.

This turned out to be a good move. Joshua had long been missing the questioning attitude of an intelligent audience for his results and theories, and their meeting led to several vigorous arguments in which they tried to reconcile the findings of geology with the beliefs of religion, unfortunately without reaching a conclusion acceptable to all parties.

Andrew had already told John of a calculation that had been made by Archbishop Usher in the mid-seventeenth century of the age of the earth. Based on intensive studies of the Bible, he had decided that Creation occurred at 9 a.m. on 26th October in 4004 BC, making the earth less than 6,000 years old. Despite the eminence of the Archbishop, Andrew and John had both found it difficult to believe he could be so precise, especially considering the problems with summing up the duration of the lives of those appearing in the lists in the Bible of who begat whom. Nevertheless, ever since he made this pronouncement the widespread belief was that, as a consequence, the rocks were formed as a result of Noah's great flood. This belief formed the basis of a theory known as catastrophism; that the earth had undergone a series of events or disasters which had suddenly created the mountains and the seas in the comparatively recent past.

Andrew also brought into the discussion the publications of a Scottish geologist, James Hutton, well thumbed copies of which he had in his collection. John had poured over them, and tried hard to understand their implications. The books presented an alternative view, proposing that the earth surface landforms developed slowly, at the same rate as they were changing now. Hutton thought that most rocks were formed beneath the sea from sediments derived from even older rocks, and incorporated the fossilised sea creatures, as well as remnants of land creatures, that lived at the time. His idea could be simplified as a statement that the present was the key to the past, and he was of the opinion that there was no vestige of a beginning, and no prospect of an end. This led to a theory of uniformitarianism, leading to obvious conflict with the catastrophists over the age of the earth, the development of life and ultimately with the biblical story of Creation. Hutton accepted that life arose from miraculous intervention, but that thereafter creatures could have adapted to changes in their environment, and could with time evolve from simple to more complex forms. However, this principle of variation was used to explain the development of varieties, rather than evolution creating new species from others.

To add further to the discussion Andrew and John were having, Joshua Haygarth introduced a book that he had been reading intently and thinking about. It had been published by Charles Lyell only a couple of years before. The author supported Hutton's ideas, and from his own study of the development of molluscs in different strata had estimated that the age of the earth must be much longer than the Archbishop had estimated. To explain the diversity of the animal species, and their territorial distribution, Lyell suggested that creation had occurred at a series of centres, rather than at one place, thus allowing for competition, eradication of species, and simultaneous development of others. Nevertheless, miraculous processes were believed to have been required for their initial appearance. He estimated that the age of the earth would have to be many millions of years to allow it all to happen.

Joshua's and Andrew's discussions, with John demanding explanations and asking simple but difficult questions, revolved around whether it was possible that new species could have arisen naturally, or whether they had all been created at the same time for the use of mankind. These were difficult ideas, especially as mankind appeared long after many of the species had disappeared. How was it possible to resolve the apparent facts that dinosaurs appeared to rule the earth for vast sections of the geological record, and then disappeared before man was present? Also, there were life forms, such as trilobites, in older rocks, which were not living when the dinosaurs were. Lyell's theory of centred-creation would allow for this, if the Creation occurred not once, but many times, separated by millions of years. But this was not what the Bible said.

Additionally, ice ages appeared to have covered huge tracts of the earth, with a tremendous impact on the landscape, and had then virtually disappeared. Coasts were gradually eroding in some places and building out in others, thereby further changing the shape of the land. Nothing appeared to be constant; everything was gradually changing. Obviously they had to accept that it was all part of God's plan for the world, but how did it start, how did it all fit together, what was the plan, or was it just a celestial game? The fundamental beliefs and Christian teachings seemed to be in conflict with what they and others were observing. These were questions that plagued them, they found it worrying and upsetting, and John found it undermined his belief in the Bible as a true statement of Creation. He had to ask himself, if the Bible was untrue on those details of Creation, what of all the other teachings? Andrew and Frances were more pragmatic about it, and accepted that there were very many things that they did not or could not expect to understand, and possibly never would. They believed that the Bible expressed the Lord's plan and teachings, and that those with faith should not question every word in too much detail, but should accept the overall principles.

Joshua, being an intelligent man and a very educated scientist, believed in the power of visual evidence and proven facts. He thought the statements in the Bible, which were often open to many different interpretations, combined with the scientifically arrived at facts would show the route to the correct version of the Lord's teachings. He told them he could not believe the earth, in the form that he could see it, was created quickly. He was convinced the Bible had to present a simplified version, understandable by simple people. A lot of detail had to be left out, and the complex system that was God's world had to be presented in terms that the normal man would readily believe and accept. The seven days of Creation must in fact have covered eons; but that was a concept of time that would be incomprehensible to most.

John found himself being more and more persuaded of the

justification for this approach, and the more he heard Joshua talk, the easier he found it to believe the immense times it would take to create the rocks that he saw in the cliffs. Joshua tried to convince him with a simple sum: if the 300 feet of sandstone they could see in the cliffs was formed at the rate of one inch per 100 years, the total time would be 360,000 years, a third of a million years. In the whole of the geological column there were thousands of feet of sediments, meaning many millions of years would have to be involved. But without proof John didn't know whether the rate of deposition on which this supposition was based was realistic. He did not know which way to turn. In an attempt to further convince him, Joshua offered to show him some of the evidence that he had been investigating, revealed in the cliffs between Blackgang and Brook.

During their discussions the three men started using their Christian names to address each other. Of course John and Andrew had been doing this for years, but it gave John a tremendous thrill to feel that he was accepted as an equal to someone as highly educated and intelligent as Joshua. He felt honoured to have the familiarity of being called 'John', rather than 'Wheeler'.

* * * * * *

It was several weeks before John and Joshua met to try and resolve John's dilemma. They arranged to meet at the foot of Blackgang Chine. It was a fine summer day with a cool wind from the north-west, and fluffy white clouds sending shadows scudding across the sea and along the cliffs. The stunted trees which cowered in the clefts and crevices were showing green, bright and hopeful with renewed growth. The waves curled and broke on the beach giving a soft susurration, the sound rising and falling with the size of the waves and the strength of the breeze. John really should have been fishing, but as he and the other crew had been out the day before with resounding success, they felt that a day without the hard labour was justified; not that it was really a rest day when all except John were either taking the catch to market, or tending their gardens and digging the first potatoes.

When John arrived at the beach Joshua was already there, eager to start. Brandy, wagging his tail wildly, jumped up at the portly man; the dog was always glad to see him because he smelled so nicely of the open air and the country, mixed with the exotic aroma of tobacco. As normal, the geologist was dressed in well worn but stout hob nailed boots, tough cord trousers and a coarse woven jacket. A small knapsack on his back held his hammer and chisel, with plenty of paper to wrap specimens in, and a sandwich or two. John had only a bottle of beer and some bread and cheese stuffed in the capacious pockets of his fishing coat. The two of them trudged along the shingle, side by side, on their way to the site Joshua wanted to show John. They both had their heads down while they talked. Nevertheless, the occasional glance by John was enough to scan the flotsam at high tide mark, along which Brandy sniffed; John could be sure that the little terrier would find anything that might be worthy of use. Joshua in his turn scanned the cliffs above to ensure they missed nothing of interest.

Joshua excitedly told John about a raft of fossilised trees that were exposed at low water near Brook Point. Associated with them he had found fossilised fir cones which looked exactly like those growing on the trees in the groves beyond Shorwell. This 'pine raft' was in the Wealden beds, older beds lying beneath those that formed the sandstone cliffs in front of them. The Wealden clays also contained fragments of dinosaur bones, and there was always the hope that a complete skeleton might be exposed by cliff falls.

Together they stood and tried to estimate the total thickness of rocks they could see, including the chalk of the downs above, and concluded there must be several thousands of feet of sediment accumulated, equivalent to many hundreds of thousands or even millions of years of deposition. And this was only a part of the geological column.

Joshua now lapsed into his most pompous lecturing style, describing how the rocks of the Wealden Beds had been formed in a vast estuary or shallow brackish sea into which the tree trunks had been washed down from the adjacent land mass, together with sand, silt and clay. The whole mass gradually accumulated, being slowly squashed by the weight of sediment above. The water deepened, with dominant sandy deposits, as were visible in front of them, being laid down above; the estuarine creatures disappeared and salt water ones replaced them. Eventually the water became clearer, and a little sand came from the land. The water was warmer and chalk, which was made of the calcareous remains of innumerable tiny creatures, settled to the seabed.

John asked Joshua to explain why the chalk rocks they could see in the distance at Freshwater and at the Needles were vertical, when what appeared to be the same chalk rested almost horizontally in St. Catherine's Down, the downs above them. Andrew and he had puzzled over the explanation, and had come to the conclusion that there must have been a fold in the rocks, and the chalk disappeared beneath Hampshire, only to reappear further north around Salisbury.

Joshua laughed, and revealed that John had deduced correctly; he then went into detail. Long after the chalk had been laid down there were movements of the earth that caused a compression of the rocks from the side, not from above. These forces rucked the rocks up, and pushed them into great folds, with the result that some areas were raised high up, and others thrust downwards. Joshua said the fold John had defined was called a monocline, a fold where one limb took the chalk deep beneath younger rocks to the north. The other part of the fold, at one time, was high in the air, and almost horizontal. But it had been largely eroded away, exposing the older rocks beneath. He said that near Brook Point the axis of the monocline could be seen in the cliff, with rocks to the north dipping steeply towards the north, and to the south the rocks dipping more gently the other way. During the folding the rocks in the vertical limb had been squashed and made harder and all the fossils within had been deformed. Joshua said he had found some of the fossilised shells and sea urchins that had been misshapen by the forces, quite recognisable but flattened.

Conversation ceased when they arrived at a particular spot of interest. At the base of the cliff was a bed of brown, gritty sand that John and the other fisherman called 'The Crackers'. Joshua had found the remains of lobster-like creatures within nodules appearing as bands within it. John knew them well as they had been long called 'fossil prawns' by the fishermen. Part of the stratum was formed of long, tabular slabs, about a foot or so thick, within which many of the fossils could be seen. Often the sands beneath the slabs were eroded by the waves to form large cavities or caverns, with the slabs as a temporary roof. John explained that children had played in them until, during a collapse, one child had been trapped and almost suffocated by the fallen rocks before it was rescued. After that their parents had forbidden them to play there; not that this prevented the adventurous ones from still risking it.

Though the two men searched for many minutes they couldn't find good specimens, so they walked on further towards Atherfield Point, to the spot where the underlying massive, dark grey clay began to be exposed beneath the sandstone. The cliff there was deformed by landslips, where the clay had fallen or slid, often bringing down the sandstone above to form a terrain of jumbled lumps or wedges of the clay, sometimes with sandstone, soil and grass still on top, often separated by fissures and cavities. The grassy areas, which at one time must have been at the top of the cliff, were sometimes horizontal platforms, and sometimes contorted at very great angles, and they varied in size from individual table-sized tussocks to segments the size of a small field, bounded by steep faces of fissured clay. With some effort a person could climb to the top of the cliff using the slips as huge irregular steps, and if they did, they would appear more or less at the position of the Coastguard lookout.

Though the whole area of these slips was continually being eroded by the sea, it nevertheless stuck out as Atherfield Point, having the added protection of the thin, hard band of ferruginous grit at its base. This formed the notorious ledge stretching far out to sea.

Joshua started clambering up the slope, trying to find fragments of the upper part of the clay in which, he said, there were many distorted and water-worn fossils, indicating that they had been transported from elsewhere to their final site of deposition. John and Brandy followed slowly behind, John looking with interest at the transition between the clay and the firmer sandstone above, while Brandy dug a few exploratory holes.

Suddenly, John heard a shout of pain from above. Joshua was out of sight. 'Are you alright, Joshua?' John called. As he heard no reply he told Brandy to go and find him. The dog scurried off, and John climbed up as fast as he could, jumping from one platform to another, and scrabbling over the slippery clay between, upon which he could see the imprints of Joshua's boots and of the dog's paws. He couldn't see Joshua, but was sure that he couldn't be any further up the cliff. He stopped and shouted again. He listened. Then he heard a loud, urgent barking over to the right. Brandy had obviously found Joshua, and was leading his master to him.

John found Brandy barking, it seemed, at a tussock of grass. 'Brandy, where is he?' John demanded of the dog. Brandy renewed his barking, looked at John and then at the ground, wagging his tail. Then faintly John heard a noise that sounded like his name being called. The call, it seemed, came almost from his feet.

John realised that hidden behind a row of grassy tussocks, and almost covered by them, was a fissure created by the slab of slipped clay on which he stood, pulling away from the body of the cliff behind. He called again, and leant over the fissure, peering down.

'Joshua, are you down there?'

The answer came as a weak voice from within the earth. 'John, I am stuck fast, and I think I have sprained my ankle. I can't move.'

Moving along a little, John soon found the place where Joshua had fallen in. The fissure was only about two feet wide, and had been covered with long grass. He could see the marks in the clay where Joshua had gone through. He parted the grass and peered down. About five or six feet below he could see the top of Joshua's balding head.

'Joshua, can you raise your arms?' he called. 'If you can, I can probably reach to pull you out.' Joshua writhed and squirmed, managing to release one arm which he held above his head. It was covered in dark grey mud and was very slimy. Though John could just reach his hand, he couldn't get enough of a grip to pull; it kept sliding through his fingers even though he wiped his hand dry on his trousers. He was afraid that Joshua might become more tightly jammed if he struggled too much.

'Oh dear!' Joshua said. 'I think I've slipped a bit further

down. I daren't move anymore.' He seemed remarkably calm considering the predicament he was in.

John found he now couldn't even touch Joshua's finger tips, and realised he would have to go for help. 'Do you think you can stay there without slipping again? I can't do anything by myself. I will have to get some help and a good rope to pull you out.'

'I think I'll be alright, John. At least I can feel something under my feet. I don't think I'll slip any further. Go, but please hurry, John.'

'I'll go to the Coastguard station just above us. There's bound to be someone there, Joshua.' John replied. 'I'll leave Brandy here to keep you company.' Then he told the dog to stay. Brandy immediately sat down, gazing fixedly at the tussock of grass, knowing precisely what he was being ordered to do.

John straightened up and looked at the cliff above him. He could see a way up by going to the end of the grassy platform he was on, over a steep slope of clay and over some further slips. It was about fifty feet to the top, he thought.

It was not an easy climb. Several times he lost his footing in the slippery clay and slid back down himself, becoming covered in mud. But eventually he reached the firm ground at the cliff top. It was only fifty yards to the station, and he could see a person within it, looking out to sea. He ran over, waving his arms and shouting to attract the Coastguard's attention.

The man looked across, and immediately came to the door. It was Lieutenant Bulley. John cursed inwardly. It would have to be him. 'Lieutenant!' he called out. 'Mr. Haygarth is down the cliff, stuck in a crevasse. I need some help and a good rope to pull him out.'

Without a word the Lieutenant turned back into the station, but quickly reappeared with a stout rope slung over his shoulder. 'Is he far down? Will this be long enough?'

'Yes. That should do very well,' John replied, and led the way back to the cliff edge. 'This is the best way down.' While they descended John was questioned about how the accident came about, and the situation Joshua was in. John thought that it would be fairly easy to get the rope round Joshua's armpits and haul him up, once they could break the suction caused by the cohesion of the wet clay.

Only a few minutes later they found Brandy still guarding his trapped friend. Joshua was in the same position as when John left, but he was coughing painfully and wheezing badly; he was obviously becoming choked by the smell of the mud and stressed by the pressure on his chest holding him wedged.

The Lieutenant peered over the crevasse, and called, 'We'll soon get you out of there, once we get this rope over you.' He took the rope off his shoulder and made a large bowline in one end to pass over Joshua's head and arms. John lay down on the grass and managed to drop the loop over Joshua's free arm and over his head, but couldn't do anything about getting it under his other arm.

'Joshua, can you get your other arm free?'

Joshua wriggled, but the arm was trapped by the strap of his knapsack. 'No, and I can't even get my free hand under my armpit to pass the rope round.'

'Well, you will just have to hang on while we pull. Try and

clamp the rope under your arm, otherwise you might find it cutting into your neck.'

John stood up, and with the Lieutenant they took the strain on the rope. But when they pulled all that seemed to happen was the rope cut into the earth rather than transmitting any lift on the geologist. 'This is no good. We need something for the rope to run over.'

'I know,' said the Lieutenant. 'I saw a fence post in the turf above us. That'll do. I'll go and fetch it. Stay here,' he said unnecessarily.

Within a couple of minutes he was back and kneeling down he slipped the post under the rope at the edge of the crevasse. There was now a good solid base for the leverage they needed. When they pulled again there was a groan from Joshua as the strain came upon him. 'I'm not moving yet,' he sighed.

'If we keep a steady pressure on the rope, can you try and ease yourself out by moving a bit?' shouted the Lieutenant. John and the Lieutenant took the rope anew in their horny hands, adjusted their grip and leant back on the rope to use their weight to keep a continual pull. But their feet kept slipping on the muddy grass. The trapped man wriggled to try and help break the suction of the clay, but little happened.

They kept this up for several minutes with Joshua groaning under the effort of fighting the mud, the rope cutting painfully into his chest. But then he shouted with joy. 'I think I'm moving. Yes, I am. I've managed to free my other arm.'

John immediately dropped the rope and flung himself on the grass to pass the loop properly over Joshua's upper torso. This would now give them a better lift on his dead weight.

They returned to pulling steadily and were able to take a step backwards to a new foothold. The clay gradually gave up its grip. Having raised him by about a foot, John thought they could now lift him bodily. He and John Bulley crouched down and managed to get their hands beneath Joshua's arms, grasp his jacket and give a straight lift. There was a loud sucking noise and Joshua's head appeared above the level of the grass, with his hands scrabbling frantically at the clay in front of him. He was free.

Once they got him out of the fissure and rolled him over onto the grass, John burst into laughter. Partly it was relief at the rescue, but mostly it was at Joshua's comical appearance. He was plastered head to foot with sticky, grey clay. It was over his face and in his hair, which was firmly caked to his head. Brandy busily licked the mud off his face until he decided that he didn't like the taste very much. By some means Joshua had managed to retain his glasses, but could scarcely see through them, covered as they were with an opaque grey film. His clothing was thick and slippery with clay which had penetrated right through onto his skin, to which it clung. Masses of clay were wedged in the tops of his boots that prevented his ankles flexing as he struggled to sit up.

'I'm sorry, Joshua, but you really do look like a dinosaur encased in that matrix. With no disrespect, you could be taken as a fossil.'

The Lieutenant joined in the laughter, and eventually Joshua saw the funny side of the situation and laughed too. He realised what a very sorry mess he must look as he sat on the turf, with the dog prancing round him excitedly. But he thought that neither John nor the Lieutenant looked much better, for they too had become fairly comprehensively covered with mud during their exertions. He laughed so much that tears came to his eyes, making him even more clown-like as they ran down his face and streaked his dirty cheeks.

Together they tried to clean him up with handfuls of grass, but it just seemed to make it worse by spreading the mud about. As they helped him haul himself to his feet, he winced as he put weight on his injured ankle, and he almost fell down again. 'I don't think I'll be able to climb up there,' he said, looking at the cliffs above.

John glanced at the Lieutenant. 'The only solution is we'll have to carry him up.' They looked at the dishevelled figure with dismay; though shorter than either of them, he was fatter and must have weighed more.

'Never mind,' said the Lieutenant. 'Let's see if we can organise a bosun's seat with the rope so that we can carry him between us, like a pail of milk.' He took the rope, wound it into a cradle and knotted the ends into loops that would fit over their shoulders; quite a seamanlike job he made of it too. John and he tried it, but it was rather small to have the large geologist seated between them.

'If we put our arms on each other's shoulders, we could shorten the loops,' suggested John, and with a few deft manipulations altered the seat. 'Try that.' They held the seat and took the strain, gripping each other's shoulders, while Joshua placed his weight on it. They decided it would suffice, provided Joshua took some of his weight on his good leg.

They set off up the cliff. It was very hard for John and the Lieutenant as they couldn't walk side by side, the pathway was too narrow. Also they kept slipping and sliding on the wet clay. Sometimes they had to support each other as well as their cargo, and sometimes it seemed they were dragging each other down and the geologist was dumped on the ground. Their legs soon ached and their breath became laboured. Brandy didn't help by occasionally standing in front of them with a quizzical expression on his face, and getting in their way. He appeared to be laughing at their antics.

It took them about half an hour to reach the top, when singly it would have only taken less than five minutes, and they were exhausted and filthy. All three sat down to regain their breaths. Brandy flopped out panting heavily, desperately wanting a drink. John, being probably the fittest of the three, recovered quickest. 'Now we need to get you to your lodgings, and medical attention. I think you are staying at the Blackgang Hotel, Joshua. Is that right?' Joshua, still out of breath, and in some pain, nodded.

'I have my pony over there at the watch house,' said the Lieutenant. 'If we can get you up on her, you can ride while we support you.'

'Does it need both of us to do it?' countered John. 'I could take him. It's on my way home, and you probably have more duties to perform yet. I can return your pony later.'

John Bulley agreed to John's proposal and quickly walked over to the station, returning with the grey mare, over which he had thrown an old blanket; he obviously didn't want the saddle spoilt and the pony caked in muddy grey clay. As they struggled to get Joshua onto the pony, clouds of the now drying clay flaked and powdered off his clothing, forming a haze that got into their eyes and up their noses, making them sneeze.

The strain of Joshua's injured ankle was obviously now telling on him as he looked pale and drawn. He would certainly need someone to guide him home; he couldn't be trusted to ride all the way without assistance. Even though the pony was a calm and steady mount, unlikely to buck or canter off, John would have to walk alongside to help keep Joshua awake, and prevent him falling off.

Joshua was effusive in his thanks as he shook the Lieutenant's hand. 'I could have been stuck there all night without your help,' he gushed. 'I will have to invite you and Mrs. Bulley to join me at the hotel for dinner, as compensation.'

The Lieutenant made a deprecating gesture, 'I am only glad to have been of assistance,' he replied, and raised a hand in salute as they started on their way. Then he stood with a thoughtful expression on his face and watched them go a little way before returning to the station to write his report of the activity and finish his duty. He would then have to walk home stiff in his drying uniform, but it was only half a mile or so.

As the mare with its unlikely burden plodded up the lane, accompanied by a muddy dog, Joshua was unusually subdued, being tired and in pain from his ankle. John turned over in his mind his reaction to working alongside the Lieutenant that he disliked, and even having to virtually embrace him in carrying the geologist in the seaman's sling. He had felt no animosity coming from him, no unwillingness to cooperate, no disdain at having to get his hands dirty; only a willingness to do whatever was necessary to rescue Joshua from his predicament. John came to the conclusion that maybe the man wasn't quite as officious, unhelpful and ungentlemanly as he thought. Bulley had certainly done his job effectively, solved the problem of getting the injured man up the cliff, and really put his back into his share of the hard work in doing it. John realised that he might even be able to concede that Frances could have been right in saying 'live and let live' over his father's arrest.

Eventually, at the hotel, the landlady, Jane Rose, appeared at the door just as they arrived. She stood, hands on hips, and it was several seconds before she realised who the dishevelled and filthy people in front of her were. Her mouth dropped open in surprise, and she came fussing down the steps, clucking like a mother hen, asking what on earth had happened to her guest, the dear Mr. Haygarth. While John helped him dismount, she shouted for the maid to put on extra hot water so that Mr. Haygarth could have a bath and clean himself up.

Joshua cheered up by being fussed over, and the prospect of comfort and relief. He thanked John generously for all his help, saying that he actually had enjoyed John's company for the day, and was sorry that it had ended so badly. He was exceedingly grateful for John's and the Lieutenant's help in getting him out of the difficulty he had so inadvertently got himself into. He took all of the blame on himself for the problems that his over-exuberance had caused. John responded that he was pleased the escapade had not resulted in serious injury, which it could have done. He helped Joshua up the steps and into the hotel where a pot-boy took over assisting the hobbling man.

John, whose legs had been rubbed sore by his now stiff and prickly muddy trousers, mounted the Lieutenant's pony and trotted back down the hill towards Chale, wondering whether to take the pony directly back to the Bulleys' home, or whether to stop at his own cottage to clean up first. If he did the latter it would be late before he returned the mare, because it would take a long time for him to wash and tell Frances the saga. He decided to go straight to the Lieutenant's home. By doing so he might avoid further contact with the Lieutenant, not that it was a serious problem, for they now at least had something in common. But he wanted to have some time to mull over the implications the day might have on their future relationship, before they met again.

When he reached the Bulleys' cottage he dismounted and hitched the reins to the fence while he knocked on the door. Sarah Bulley answered almost immediately, as if she had seen him arriving. 'Good afternoon, Mr. Wheeler,' she said as she curtseyed.

He inclined his head briefly. 'Please excuse my muddy state, Mrs. Bulley. But I have been involved with your husband in rescuing Mr. Haygarth from the cliff. As he couldn't walk I had to take the Lieutenant's pony and escort him to his hotel.'

Her hands immediately flew to her face. 'Is my husband alright?' she asked in alarm.

'Don't worry yourself. There is no cause for alarm. He had duties to complete. He will be here directly, but I'm afraid he will be as dirty as I am.'

She looked relieved, opened the door wider, and with a gesture invited him in. 'Please, I insist you come in and tell me all about it.' Even as she said this she wondered whether it was wise to invite a barely known man into her home without her husband or a chaperone present. But she was sure that the husband of her friend, Frances, would be accepted as he had been working with her husband that day, and was returning a favour.

Though much against his inclination, he felt it would be churlish to refuse. 'Is there somewhere I can stable the pony first,' he asked with a slight bow of the head.

'She normally goes in the shed round the back. If you shut her in and take her saddle off, there should already be water and some hay hanging up. John will deal with her later.' She stood and watched while John led the pony round the cottage, thinking what a fine looking, strong young man he was, and how lucky Frances was.

Inside, Sarah insisted John took a cup of tea from the pot she had set on the stove. He held the cup gratefully in his hands, thankful for the warmth; he was now feeling a little chilled as the evening was drawing in. He refused to sit on the nice clean chairs, because of the condition of his clothes, and stood awkwardly before her while he recounted the day's events. Sarah listened wide-eyed.

Just then there was a noise outside, and a dirty John Bulley burst into the room with a smile on his face, obviously pleased to see his wife, and have something amusing to tell her. He started on seeing John there, and his expression changed and became a little more wary. Sarah rushed to him and gave him a peck of a kiss on the cheek. 'Mr. Wheeler has just kindly returned The Duchess, my dear. She is in the stable. And he has been telling me of your escapades. What a state you are both in,' she laughed as the two men stood rather sheepishly before her in their muddy clothes. 'I hope Mr. Haygarth will be alright after his accident.'

John turned to the Lieutenant, saying, 'I left him at the hotel getting ready for a hot bath. His ankle was still troubling him, but with rest I imagine he will be fine in a couple of days. I will call on him tomorrow to see how he is.' Then to Sarah he said, 'If you will excuse me, Mrs. Bulley, I must go home and change my dirty clothes and clean myself up, and I am sure the Lieutenant here will want to do the same.'

Sarah expressed surprise and looked at her husband as she said, 'Surely you can call me and my husband by our given names. Your wife, Frances, calls me Sarah. I think your name is also John.' Then she laughed again, 'But that could be confusing.'

John smiled, enjoying her frank openness, thinking it was not surprising that she and Frances were so friendly; they were very like-minded in many ways. But he thought Sarah was attempting to force a friendship between the two men before they had reached a state where of their own volition they could accept they were equals; there were still too many barriers between them, barriers of class, education and occupation. However, he couldn't throw the suggestion back in her face too abruptly. It would be insulting. He dissimulated, leaving the first response to the Lieutenant. 'My family generally call me John. My father was christened John also, but he is normally called Jack. It is a common alternative form to John round here, and we needed something to distinguish between us. But you can continue calling me by my surname, if you wish. I don't have a problem with that.'

The Lieutenant had also looked a little taken aback at his wife's presumption. If it was his wife's opinion that they were equals, then he would need to consider John Wheeler with fresh eyes. He would have to ask himself whether this common fisherman was his equal; his father was a fisherman, his grandfather was a fisherman, as were most of his relations, and he was probably a smuggler to boot, whereas he was a Lieutenant, with a family of minor gentry, and a status acceptable in society. Admittedly the fisherman had wooed and won a lady outside his class, but that didn't necessarily give him immediate access to familiarity with the gentry. But to refuse would be seen as a snub by his wife. He had to put a good face on it, and do what he thought was right. Whether he agreed or not, he didn't want to lose face by appearing churlish, so he took refuge in his position. He had no alternative to refusing, even if it were to upset Sarah and appear snobbish or patronising.

'I'm sorry, my dear, but I think you may be presuming a bit too much. As a Naval Officer, and Chief Officer in the Customs Service I cannot be seen to favour one person above another. At the moment, I think it's inappropriate to call any of the village people by anything other than their family name.' Then to John he said, 'I'm sure you would agree. It would make it difficult for me to carry out my duties and exercise necessary authority if it were otherwise.' But he held out his hand to

John, saying rather stiffly, 'We did a good job today in rescuing Mr. Haygarth, and I was glad to be of assistance. I have written an account of the whole affair in my report, as is required.' Then he relaxed a little. 'Contrary to what I have said before, your wife will be welcome to visit Sarah. Her kind attention is appreciated.'

John took his hand, finding the grasp was firm. He squeezed to see what reaction he got, and found strong fingers responding; it was not the limp 'cold-fish' handshake that gave the feeling of an insincere and weak character. He understood what the Lieutenant implied, that Frances was of an acceptable class, despite having married beneath her, but he wasn't. This didn't upset him because he had no real aspirations to climb into a class where styles of behaviour, attitude and responsibility were expected of him that he wouldn't be comfortable with. To him it was the manner and character of the man that was important; what he was, not what his family was, or possessed.

He thought he had seen some traits in the Lieutenant that appealed; he appeared to be hard working, conscientious, loyal, upright, and with a sincere Christian attitude. But John still had serious concerns about his possible mistreatment of his wife a few months before, and his possible drinking habits. A major concern was the Lieutenant's attitude to the welfare and wellbeing of the people within his purview, and the way he should consider his responsibilities. To be inflexible and arrogant could easily be considered as vindictive and spiteful; it wasn't like being in the Navy where discipline and strict obedience to the rules were paramount and essential. These outstanding questions remained to be resolved. As far as John was concerned, the Lieutenant was still on probation. Was he a man to be trusted and respected, one who, like Dornford, fitted into the pattern of Island life?

John felt very awkward having to talk about and express these feelings without being too explicit. He was aware that the Lieutenant probably felt the same. 'I agree. It would not be wise for me to use anything but your title in public. As you probably appreciate, having now lived amongst us for several years, it is a very close community. Outsiders take a long time to be accepted, but when they are it has to be with no reservations on either side.' Then he looked at Sarah. 'You will have found that it's rather easier for the womenfolk. As a friend of my wife I will be quite happy to address you by your Christian name, if that is your wish, and it is acceptable to your husband.'

Both men obviously were of the same opinion. They couldn't accept Sarah's suggestion. It would mean too quickly crossing the line between two different, clashing backgrounds, lives and cultures. Carrying on as they were was quite acceptable to John. He felt comfortable with accepting an officer-fisherman role. He accepted it when he was in the Navy, but he preferred to retain the respect of his village friends rather than try to become anything other than a born and bred Islander.

Sarah looked rather sad at the response, and the failure of her initiative. But she realised that men reacted differently from women. They were much more inflexible in their attitudes, more reserved in their relationships with others, and more stubborn in their adherence to the disciplines of their work.

She considered her best plan was to leave the thought to gestate in the men, and develop her friendship further with Frances, hoping that the two Johns would gradually accept that they also could be friends. Realising that John needed to go home to clean up and get out of his filthy clothes, she rose.

John took this movement as his dismissal, bowed to Sarah and said, 'I will take my leave now, Sarah. I am sure Frances will be calling on you soon.' Turning towards the door, which was being opened by the Lieutenant, he said, 'Thank you for your assistance today, Lieutenant. I am sure that Joshua will be adequately grateful.' He received no response, except for a momentary inclination of the head, as the Lieutenant was a little irritated at the familiarity with his wife. However, the Lieutenant didn't miss the implication that the eminent geologist considered John as an equal. That gave him food for thought – that someone as intelligent, educated, and eminent should consider a humble fisherman his equal.

When John was outside, he breathed a sigh of relief, not having appreciated how tense the interchange with the Lieutenant had made him. It wasn't that he felt vulnerable or patronised, it was just the stress that the constraints of society imposed on those not familiar with it as part of their upbringing and their everyday life. However, he did feel that he had in some way cleared a hurdle that had been worrying him.

* * * * * *

It was only a few days later, when Joshua had recovered from his accident and could walk reasonably well again, that invitations were received at both the Wheeler and Bulley households. Both men, together with their wives, were invited to lunch at Joshua's hotel in Blackgang. This was obviously a 'thank you' for their assistance, and it was understood that no refusal would be accepted.

When they discussed it, Frances and Sarah agreed that it was the ideal situation to further break the ice between the two families, and bring the men onto common ground upon which Joshua was likely to provide a splendid catalyst. Frances knew from having met him several times that he had the character and the social skills to make it a pleasant lunch, whoever was there. Despite his fixation on geology, he was widely travelled with a fund of good stories and reminiscences which he could deliver in an amusing and non-patronising way.

The women immediately started to think about what they would wear for the occasion. Frances was clear that she would wear the dress that John had brought from France for her the previous year; it had only had one outing and had been put away carefully for just such an occasion as this. But what concerned her more was what John would wear, as he had no clothing that was suitable for a social function. He had his Sunday best suit, also used for weddings and funerals, and he insisted that he would wear that. He presumed the Lieutenant would be in his uniform, so there was no need for any flamboyance, not that that would have been within John's character anyway. They would leave the glamour to their wives.

However, both the men felt concerned that the lunch could show up the gulf in background and attitudes that separated the two families, and looked forward to it with a degree of trepidation. In particular John was aware of the broad Island accent that he had been bred with. He had experienced problems when he was in the Navy and when sailing at Cowes, with the officers and other men not being able to understanding his dialect. Also Frances' way of speaking was much more refined, and she often teased him about some of the words he used. Consequently, he had learned to moderate his speech to a certain extent, by leaving out the local dialect words, and replacing them with the mainland alternatives, by using shorter vowel sounds, and pronouncing the 'h' at the beginning of words. As a result he spoke in a different manner depending on whom he was talking to. When he was with Frances, Andrew and Anne, Joshua, and their like, he moderated his dialect, but reverted to his normal speech when with the other villagers. To him it wasn't really a problem, but he would have to be careful not to get emotional or worked up about anything, otherwise he would naturally break down into the broader speech.

As it was, the lunch was a very gracious and memorable occasion. Joshua was on his best form, playing up to the ladies, to the extent that Frances wondered why he had never married. He quickly put both men at ease by making them feel that they were his intellectual equals, valuing their opinions on a wide range of difficult topics, from the industrialisation of the cities, and the state of the King's health, to the growth of railways, and repeal of the Corn Laws. John was relieved, because many of these subjects were those he had long discussed with Andrew, and Frances had robust opinions on them too. He found that he quickly relaxed, and the tension went out of John Bulley's demeanour as well. They found themselves enjoying the company more than they ever thought they would.

But it was obvious that Sarah was not as familiar or as comfortable with this level of discussion as the others seemed to be. But Joshua interspersed the discussion with amusing anecdotes and stories, and involved her in revealing more about her family, her siblings, and life as a Coastguard's wife. Astutely, Joshua made sure that smuggling and children were not mentioned, or if they were, were glossed over, or the subject rapidly changed with a laugh.

The food was good. Jane Rose had worked hard to ensure that only the best was placed before them. Also the wine and liquor helped to impart a relaxed benevolence over them all. When they parted it was late in the afternoon, and they all felt that it had been a memorable occasion. Certainly the reserve between the two men had been severely eroded, to the extent that the beginnings of mutual respect had been established.

Chapter 15

It was on Tuesday, 11th October 1836, that the full rigged West Indiaman, the *Clarendon*, was trapped in Chale Bay under a lee shore. This was to be one of the most momentous events that occurred on the Isle of Wight. Not only did it affect John Wheeler's life and those of the other inhabitants of the coast, but it resounded across England, and the resultant public outcry led to an increase in measures to try to prevent shipwrecks and reduce the loss of life of those wrecked at sea. It was also significant as part of the changing role of the Coastguard from prevention of smuggling to the saving of lives. It was consequently to have a salutary effect on the life of John Bulley and his fellows.

It transpired that the ship had left Basseterre Roads, St. Kitts in the West Indies on 28th August and consequently had been at sea for almost six weeks. She was a three-masted ship of 345 tons, owned by Messrs. Manning and Henderson of Lothbury. She sailed with a crew of sixteen under Captain Samuel Walker, an experienced Atlantic sailor. She was laden with a valuable cargo of rum, sugar, coconuts, cedar, arrowroot, pimento and turtles, all produce of that tropical island. She also carried a full complement of eleven passengers. These comprised: Lieutenant Shore (though some reports spell his family name as Shaw), an adjutant in the 14th Regiment, the Buckinghamshire Regiment, at that time stationed in the West Indies. He was returning on leave with Mrs. Shore and their four daughters, one being three or four years old, another a baby, only eight months old; a corporal George Higginbottom; a planter, Walter Pemberton, returning to England for his health, and his twelve-year-old Creole daughter, Ann, coming for her education; a Nevis man, Robert Shepherd, with relatives in Exeter; and a Miss Gourlay, daughter of Captain Gourlay R.N., whose widow lived at Southsea.

They had had a rough voyage and made the Lizard Lights, on the coast of Cornwall, on 6th October. They endeavoured to get into the protected waters of Plymouth Sound, only to be denied access by strong north-westerly gales. Instead, they were forced to head for Portsmouth to seek respite, under severely reduced sail. They could only mount a close-reefed foresail and a storm trysail.

During 10th October the wind had been increasing all day, and by the evening the gale had increased even further and had reached storm force. All that night the master and crew had fought to keep the ship safe as they thrashed up the Channel, shipping immense quantities of water. The passengers had had to endure being entombed below decks listening to the cacophony of noise above decks, the shrieking of the wind, the thunder of the waves, the creaking and groaning of the ship's timbers moving under the stress, the thuds, the bangs, the shouts, the clanking of the pumps, and the horrendous motion of the ship. They were being thrown all over their cabins, and the only relief was to strap themselves into their bunks. All they could do then was pray; and they did.

Because of the very dark and rainy conditions, visibility was terrible. They didn't know where they were, even though the helmsman had tried to maintain an easterly compass course during the awful night. They thought they had seen the light at the Needles at about midnight on the Monday night, but this must have really been that at Portland. This mistake is likely to have cost them dear. Soon after four o'clock on the Tuesday morning they discovered land close by on the larboard bow. At the first flush of a terrible, wild dawn a frightening sight met their eyes. All they could see through the spray, the rain and the mist, were the stark, looming cliffs of the Wight hard on their port bow, rising right up into the darkness of the wreathing rain-laden clouds. With horror they realised they were embayed, unless they could claw their way to the south-east out of the trap. They immediately tried to set the mainsail in order to obtain an offing, but the fury of the wind made it impossible, the squalls made it too dangerous for the crew to try and man the spars.

The passengers had been petrified for so long, and the seamen so exhausted, they felt their chances were slim. They all contemplated their fate with sinking hearts. Nevertheless, Captain Walker was confident they could weather Rocken End and escape. That was, until the wind suddenly backed towards the south and increased in fury to hurricane force. The Captain then gave up all chance of saving the ship and distress signals were made. At that time the men were all on deck, and the ladies and children were crouching in the companion ways. He called for the men to save themselves and the ladies, and he took a rope to lash Mrs. Shore to something substantial.

In view of the bad weather and the possibility of shipwreck, watchers had been out on the cliffs all night ready to call for help should a ship be seen in distress. It was a routine they had grown accustomed to over the years, unpleasant as it was. In the hazy twilight before dawn the *Clarendon* could be seen through the rain squalls, battling against the wind and the awful seas to keep off the dreaded lee shore. She had little canvas left on her spars, and relied solely on the fore-and-aft sails to fight for her life. But she was being blown sideways towards the shore rather than making headway across the wind. To the watchers it was inevitable she would come ashore.

As soon as she was sighted a runner was sent to the village to spread the bad news and call for helpers. Quickly, a knot of longshoremen and other hardy souls assembled on the cliff above Cliff Terrace watching and waiting. They were eventually joined by further men from Ladder Chine who followed the progress of the ship along the coast as she managed to survive passing through the seas off Atherfield Ledge. The conditions were so bad that there was no chance of putting a boat out off the shore to help, and the rocket apparatus would have no chance against such a wind.

John had gone to bed with a premonition that a disaster was in the making. He slept only intermittently, having been kept awake most of the night by the roaring of the wind around the house and the lashing of rain against the windows.

The rattling of the slates made him worry that the roof might blow off. Eventually, thinking that his tossing and turning might disturb Frances, who slept innocently beside him, he decided to get up and go to the cliff to see for himself. He was already pulling on his oilskins and boots preparatory to going out, when he heard shouting in the lane outside. His heart sank, knowing that the village was going to have to endure another calamity.

When he reached the cliff edge he could see in the gloom the plight the ship was in. He knew that with the wind backing she would eventually be doomed. The sea was running mountains high in the Bay, and the ship was being held over almost on her beam ends by the strength of the wind. It was only a question of when and where she would come ashore. He didn't think it would be much longer before she hit. Just then the distress signal rockets were visible rising from the stricken vessel.

As soon as it was obvious that the ship could not weather Rocken End and the signals were seen, John and a number of others started running down to the beach, fighting against the wind and rain, their hearts beating wildly, and their boots slipping on the wet path. As he ran, John realised he would need a rope if he were to help save those on board. He ran along the track to one of the nearby huts, the one in which a few months before they had buried their tubs. The door was as usual unlocked, and luckily he could see in the half-light a long coil of flexible, but light and strong manila rope hung on a peg. He grabbed it and dashed out and down the last flight of steps to the beach.

Slowly and surely the ship was driven landwards despite the efforts of the crew and the prayers of the passengers. It was close to high tide, and if she were to hit close to Blackgang, where the cliffs were fronted by a good width of beach, there would be some chance of the passengers and crew surviving; elsewhere, where the cliffs came right to the water's edge, they stood little chance. But surely, even close to Blackgang, the ship couldn't withstand for long the immense curling breakers thundering onto the beach, creating columns of spray laced with shingle and sand, the spray blowing across the beach and up the cliffs. The ship would quickly be destroyed.

By the time John had reached the beach, the vessel was only a couple of ship-lengths away from striking. She was broadside on to the waves, and almost on her beam-ends. The masts adorned with blown out or furled sails, flapping like gunshots in the wind, were leaning over towards the beach, almost over the heads of those waiting on the shingle. Passengers and crew could be seen clinging white-faced to the rail and the shrouds, and huddling in the sparse shelter of the poop. The screams of the children could be heard on the wind. John ran along to the point where he reckoned the ship would ground, stripping off his oilskin jacket, and tying an end of the rope into a bowline around his waist. He felt sick with anticipation.

A huge wave appeared out of the blackness, determined to crush the ship against the boundaries of its universe. It pushed the ship onwards, and with a thunderous ear-splitting explosion that was even heard in Chale, she struck. The masts canted even further over, and with the impact two of them broke off near the deck and fell into the surf, with a tangle of spars, yards, shrouds and sails. The hull squealed, grinding, crunching and cracking on the shingle as she was pushed up the beach, digging well into the stones. There was a cry of desperation from those watching.

The next wave, angry with destructive malevolence, exploded with a roar against the far side of the hull, sending a plume of spray high into the air, and a torrent of foaming, cold green water cascading over the rail and across the deck. Some of the people were washed into scuppers and others into the raging sea. Their screams were lost in the tumult and the cacophony of noise. As the ship had driven bows-on to the beach, the poop took the main impact and largely disintegrated. The force twisted the ship round so she would be broadside on to the next wave. The wind sent the spray whipping across the beach, the drops stinging the faces and hands of the onlookers like hailstones. On deck there was a scurry of activity as the figures tried to regain their feet and shelter from the torment. For a moment in the lee of the damaged ship there was relative calm as the wave retreated and the next wave gathered itself to inflict further punishment. But the trough gave little respite to those in the water as it sucked them, entangled in a mass of wreckage, under or around the hull.

Once the ship hit, John knew that he had to do something; it was now or never. He thrust the loose end of the rope into the hands of the man next to him, and strode down the beach at least twenty yards with the retreating wave. 'Jump! Come on! Jump!' he bellowed, his words being whipped away by the wind. He waved his arms, signalling, making it plain what he wanted them to do. But seamen did not learn to swim on purpose, as it was thought better to drown quickly than slowly, and most of the passengers were probably too scared to trust themselves to the maelstrom in front of them, even though solid ground was only a few yards away. Nevertheless, one or two figures were seen to take a running jump into the foam, to clutch at pieces of floating timber, and flail at the water, hoping to be carried ashore.

John took a deep breath and braced himself for the impact of the incoming wave. The force of the blow which hit him drove the breath out of his body. It lifted him and carried him several paces back up the beach, almost knocking him off his feet. Water flooded over him, penetrating his nostrils, into his ears, and pouring cold down his neck and into his boots. Almost immediately he was wetted to the skin, and his muscles started to contract and stiffen with the cold. He could feel the loose shingle being washed away from under his boots, making him stagger to keep his balance as he waded further out; though he was careful not to go so far that he couldn't touch bottom. He thrashed his arms to help make headway against the drag on his clothing, and he shook his head to clear the water from his eyes.

An arm appeared from beneath the water in front of him. John instinctively grabbed it, pulling the man to the surface. He was bearded and unconscious, with water pouring from his open mouth. John caught him firmly beneath the armpits and turned against the backwash which threatened to drag them further out. He staggered two steps against the retreating water, aided by the pull of the rope, and thrust the man up the beach to the waiting arms of others. He shouted for some slack on the rope and immediately forced himself to turn and wade again into the sea. There were others on the beach also plunging into the surf, trying to rescue the unfortunates. But as they didn't have ropes, they formed human chains, desperately hanging on to one another with each hand while they staggered to keep their feet, with the end man using his free hand to fight the terrible waves and try to reach someone.

A second wave hit the ship, with an ear-deafening crash, and pushed it further up the beach, squeaking and squealing, grinding on the stones, and ploughing into the beach. The main mast broke at the deck and fell almost straight towards John. He looked up and dodged several steps to one side, frightened that it was actually going to hit him. It crashed onto the beach only feet away from him, broke into three massive lengths and added further spars and cordage to that already in the water. Part of the hull split, sending a shower of splintered wood, spars, ropes and other wreckage into the air, and across what was left of the deck into the sea. There were few people left clinging to the ship now, most had been swept into the maelstrom of water and flotsam, where they floundered or sank.

The wave curled, foaming round the stern, reforming in its lee, where it joined the water pouring over the deck, and round the bow; less in height, but still frighteningly high and vicious. The wave hit John and knocked him off his feet. He was completely under water, the noise of it roaring in his ears.

He opened his eyes in an attempt to see and avoid the debris, but all he could see was a green translucent glow, and a froth of rising bubbles. He struggled to regain his feet as he felt the strain on his lungs demanding air. The tug of the rope at his waist pulled him back to the surface. He regained his feet and took a quick gasp of air, coughing at the stinging saltiness of the water which poured down his face, and off his beard. He winced and stifled a groan as a chunk of splintered wood hit him in the face. Though he took little notice of it at the time, it hurt. Clearing the water from his eyes he glimpsed a man close by, thrashing his arms in an attempt to stay afloat. The frightened man caught hold of him with desperate strength and struggled so much that John had to knock him out with a lucky blow, before being hauled back towards the beach with his load by the men on the end of the rope.

John unceremoniously dumped the man onto the beach, for others to carry out of harm's way, and adjusted the rope round his waist. Even though already exhausted, and wanting to sit and rest, he turned without a second thought to face another effort to reach the wreck, driven by his sense of humanity; he simply could not stand by and watch people dying without making every effort to help them. He staggered down the beach to plunge into the surf again, just when the third wave hit with a crash. The hull seemed to explode and fall apart, no longer bearing any real resemblance to a ship. The hull must have been holed on the far side as water burst out through the deck carrying with it a load of personal possessions, more timber and some of the cargo. Deck planking shot into the air, twisting in the wind and splashing into the seething water, hitting those struggling for their lives and shouting for help in the mass of debris wallowing in the lee of the wreck. The wave reformed and travelled on towards the beach, submerging the flotsam and pulling under feebly moving bodies.

John hardly saw this as he was again engulfed in the water as he waded out. He felt drained of energy, sapped out of him by the effort and the cold. But he fought on, trying to save another soul. He struggled to stand against the weight of his sodden clothing and the wreckage the water thrust at him. He fought against a tangle of writhing ropes that grabbed at him like a live octopus, and wallowing timbers that threatened to push him under. A massive blow from one of them hit him in the chest, the sudden, stabbing pain making him grit his teeth in agony, keeping his mouth tight shut against the press of water. Despite this he managed to grab a third man, but this time he would have to rely on those on the shore to pull them up the beach out of the surf; he had reached the end of his tether. His strength had gone.

The third wave hit them and knocked John off his feet. Burdened by the limp body he couldn't regain his feet and became trapped by tangled rope which held him under. He held his breath, kicking his feet and trying to fight his way upright and keep his head above the surface. He needed to escape the dreaded undertow which threatened to hold him under, drag him along the seabed out to sea, and drown him. The pressure on his lungs was becoming unbearable and darkness was creeping over him. He was aware of the feel of salty water in his throat, and he gagged, drawing more water down. Everything was becoming dark, but, nevertheless, he was aware of the pull of the rope around his waist. He was losing consciousness, but still kept a tight hold on the man in his arms. His last thought was the worry of how Frances would cope without him.

The rope pulled him back to the beach, and hands helped drag him and his burden above the reach of the waves. They were both rolled separately over onto their chests, and several men lifted their legs high to drain their lungs, and pressed rhythmically on their backs to help them breathe. John spluttered, retching and coughing out water, aware of the acute pain in his chest. He struggled and moaned as he was turned onto his back. The cold neck of a bottle was thrust against his lips and brandy poured into his mouth and down his chin. He choked anew, but felt the warmth of the liquor burning down his gullet into his body carrying a renewal of energy and a resurgence of life. It was only seconds later when he sat up and looked at the fellow beside him, the man he had brought ashore. Several people were bending over him, trying to revive him. But he was stirring and coughing too. He should become another survivor. John thanked the Lord for their deliverance, and struggled to get to his feet, determined to try and save more despite the pain in his chest. But many restraining hands prevented him from dashing again into the fray, and a voice shouted in his ear, 'It's too late now, John. She's gone.'

He looked. There was no sign of the vessel as such. The fourth wave had almost completely destroyed her. There was little left that could be recognisable as a ship, only part of the fore deck and the aft accommodation remained intact, and that was rapidly being broken into matchwood. A few of the ribs stuck up rather like the remains of a skeleton, but with occasional timbers still attached. All the rest remained as a heaving mass of planks, broken timbers, spars, sails, bodies, ropes, boxes, barrels, clothing, and masses of debris. Waves that were breaking against the remnants of the hull curled into the mass, but failed to continue breaking. Instead they made the mass of wreckage heave up and down by eight or ten feet, everything grinding and groaning, piece against piece, rolling over, disappearing and reappearing. Bodies could be seen sometimes, just to become hidden or re-submerged; too far out to yet be reached. The tangled mess surged up and down the beach, endangering anyone that got in its way, and threatening to engulf them, entrap them, break their limbs, or drag them out to sea. Those standing on the beach were now much more wary about entering the water; they could see no signs of further survivors and were loath to gain injury for little reward. But the occasional mangled body was retrieved, when the retreating sea relented and released them. The water was starting to become distinctly tinged with patches of bloody pink, colouring the foam that blew off the waves and across the shingle.

It had taken only four waves and a steep shingle beach to turn the once proud ship to matchwood and debris; a total of about two minutes. And in the same time it killed about two dozen men, women, and children. It was still only six o'clock in the morning and the sun had hardly risen.

Looking around him John realised that the person to whom

he had given the rope's end, and who had been responsible for leading those pulling him and the three men out of the sea, was his adversary, John Bulley. The Lieutenant leant over him, put his hand on his shoulder, and said, 'That was a very brave and honourable act, John. You've rescued the only three survivors. Those left in the sea must be either drowned or otherwise dead by now. There is no point in anyone risking themselves trying to rescue any more.'

John realised his face hurt, and when he raised his hand to feel, it came away covered in blood. His chest hurt, and he suspected he had gained a broken rib or two. Undoubtedly further bruises and contusions would be apparent later. He was rubbing his hand down his frozen legs, to feel where there might be other injuries, when Brandy appeared and jumped around him, pleased to be reunited with his master. Frances followed, running down the beach as well as she could; she had seen his valiant rescues as she came uncomfortably staggering down the cliff path. She clutched him fiercely, making his ribs hurt even more. 'Oh, John,' she cried. 'Thank God you are safe. I thought you were drowned too.' She fought back tears of relief. 'Let me look at your face.'

He started shivering, both from the cutting cold of the wind on his wet body, and from the delayed shock of his exertions. She wrapped a blanket round him, one that she had brought with her, knowing it would be needed to keep survivors warm. Looking at his face she prised out a couple of large splinters, and wiped away the oozing blood; the tar laden wood and the salty water would ensure that no infection would creep in.

John could say nothing in response. He was completely exhausted as well as being totally distraught by the emotional impact of the obvious death toll. Clutching the blanket around his shoulders he stood, shivering, and surveyed the scene of the tragedy. His face was drawn and pale, his eyes sunken and staring. All around him the Islanders who had been helping on the beach were crying or cursing. The women and some of the men had tears pouring down their cheeks. Others were cursing and uttering blasphemies, railing against the cruelty of so many lives abruptly terminated. And others, like John, were dazed and stricken dumb.

Suddenly, rising above the noise of the surf and the rattle of each backwash combing down the shingle, was a discordant, musical tinkling and clanging. The ship's piano was being smashed at the hands of the waves. Many of the onlookers crossed themselves, as one was heard to say, 'It is the Devil's work, surely!' A terrible gloom descended on the spirits of everyone following the catastrophe they had witnessed. Nevertheless, talking quietly, they all laboured hard, automatically wading into the surf to pull anything they could reach above the tide line. They had to move steadily along the beach, as the tide swept the wreckage and debris away from the site of the wreck itself.

One by one the bodies were being gathered from the breakers, many of them crushed and mangled by impact with timbers, and with ropes tangled round their necks or limbs. Horrible wounds made by sharp splinters disfigured their faces, and wood impaled their bodies. Limbs were contorted and broken. Otherwise their faces were serene in death. The suck of the waves and the pull and the turbulence of the currents in the undertow had stripped the clothes off many of them, revealing their fragile, white skin, disfigured by gaping, red wounds still oozing blood, and highlighting dark body-hair. The rescuers averted their eyes as the naked bodies of the Shore girls were laid out, serene after their frightful deaths, but even the hardened fishermen began to weep at their loss.

The bodies were hauled up the beach, as reverently as possible, and covered by pieces of the ship's sail, or remnants of recovered clothing. One of the survivors, who said his name was William Byrne, swathed in a blanket, walked amongst them, recognising them, and naming them. He stood for a long while looking down at the broken and naked body of a black man, an item of vague curiosity for some of the Islanders, who had never seen a black man before, even alive and with clothes on. 'That is James Paris, the steward.' Then he continued to no-one in particular, 'He came from the island of Nevis, and had never left the island before. He didn't like the sea very much, and was seasick much of the voyage. God rest his soul.'

When he came to the Shore girls, their broken bodies laid side by side on the shingle, he looked with shock at their serene countenances, and said almost reverently, 'They were lovely and pleasant in their lives, and in death they were not divided.'

He then passed on to the next. 'Edward Rush, seaman. He came from Portsmouth. He was looking forward to getting home. He almost made it.' Then he looked at the next man. 'William Steward, Chief Mate. He was a good sailor, and would probably have been made master on his next ship.'

He paused before the next body, a dark skinned girl. 'That is Ann Pemberton. She and her father came from St. Kitts. Her mother was a native of that Isle, and it was with reluctance that she agreed her daughter could come with her father to England to be educated. Their bodies should be put together when he is found, and they should be buried together.' The litany went on for a few more bodies, but many remained to be recovered.

Frances, in despair, watched John wander distracted along the beach, Brandy following him with his tail between his legs. John was cursing that he had not been able to save more, and was inwardly seething at the injustice of cruel fate. But he tried to console himself that he had done all he could. Nevertheless, he was depressed. He had tried and even almost lost his own life in the attempt to do more. What else could a man do, but rail at the iniquity of death?

He came in front of one of the survivors he had pulled from the seething torment of water. The man was lying on the shingle being tended by two of the local women. He had a leg that was obviously broken, and his face was partially obscured by a flap of skin hanging from his scalp. They looked at each other and recognition came dawning simultaneously. They knew each other, for they had been shipmates. 'Well, now. Who have we here? Damn my eyes,' John exclaimed. 'John Thompson.'

'Good Lord. Is it you, Wheeler? Don't say that it was you who rescued me.'

'It was.'

'Well, doesn't that take the biscuit? I saved you four years ago when you fell off the *Falcon*. And here you are saving me. That is truly the hand of fate, my old shipmate.'

John and the man, one of the seamen, had served together on Lord Yarborough's yacht, the *Falcon*, and Thompson had saved John's life after an accident on board. They calmly stared into each other's eyes, remembering that incident, and grasped and shook each other's hand. Honours were even. But they could say no more. Thompson's face screwed up in agony and he lapsed into unconsciousness, overcome by the pain of his wounds. One of the women looked up. 'I'm not sure he is going to last,' she said. 'He has lost so much blood.'

John moved away, and knew that his memories of Thompson and the ship, the crew and the passengers, their lives intertwined for a brief period and parted so dramatically, would become imprinted on his mind. He would live with the past few minutes for the rest of his life, waking at night in the sweat of mentally reliving the events in nightmares. Every time he closed his eyes he would see an image of the dead girls.

Frances saw that he was approaching the end of his tether, any more and he would collapse with the strain. He needed warmth, and a hot drink, and he needed to get away from this spot and its dreadful mental burden. She took John by the arm and pulled him up the beach. 'Come on, John. We are going home to get you some dry and warm clothes. I think your friend will be looked after.'

Turning to the nearest man, who so happened to be John Bulley, she had to shout over the noise of the waves and the wind, 'Can you have some of your men help carry the three survivors up to the village? They need warmth and food. I am sure the White Mouse Inn will accommodate them.'

He agreed that the Coastguard should do this, and he went away to give orders. The men were much more interested in trying to retrieve any valuables and cargo that could be claimed for Customs or insurance reward. Nevertheless, they were obliged to help.

John let himself be led away, with Frances' arm through his to steady him. Even so, it was with a huge effort that they staggered up the steep cliff path, leaving others to finish the grim task of salvaging the rest of the bodies and collecting the wreckage, pulling what might be reusable out of reach of the waves and the tide. The bodies were wrapped in sailcloth and tied to lengths of the planking so that they could be carried up to the church and the waiting vicar by the shocked local men. Andrew reverently received the bodies into the church with solemn prayers and had them laid on the bench pews, for there were too many for the nave floor.

By the afternoon the news of the catastrophe had spread, and people had come from miles around like vultures to view the wreck, to marvel and be frightened, to stare at the dead, and watch the survivors and the rescuers. They lined the cliff, subdued by the shock of the calamity revealed before them, staring down at the tangle of timbers, ropes and cargo scattered on the beach. Some of them descended to the beach and searched for anything they could salvage, or surreptitiously carry off for themselves. The Coastguard were kept busy making sure that nothing was stolen, as well as combing the wreckage for the missing bodies.

A deep sense of extreme gloom descended on Chale, as in one way or another the whole village had been involved in attending the wreck and dealing with its aftermath. Queues formed to enter the church to gaze on the bodies. Everyone could see the row of corpses waiting for the rough coffins the carpenter was preparing, they could lift up the tattered and bloodstained shrouds, and see the wounds and awful disfiguring injuries sustained. First of all the people were filled with morbid curiosity or voyeurism, but these feelings gradually turned to reverence, as the extent of the wounds and the terrible ordeal the dead had experienced eventually affected them. They left the church in a totally different mood, one in which they had perhaps viewed their own future state, their own ultimate fate.

Chapter 16

On the afternoon of the following day, Wednesday, 12th
October, the coroner's inquest on twenty bodies was held in
Chale Church. Because of their common interest in the wreck
the coroner drove from Newport, together with the Collector
of Customs, Thomas Hastings, who assumed the role of
Receiver of Wrecks. The role of the former was to certify
officially the cause of death and issue death certificates so that
the bodies could be released for burial, and their families
relieved of their burden of grief. The latter attended to
determine the ownership of any valuable goods and cargo
salvaged and provide evidence for possible insurance claims,
or claims of 'privilege of right' in return for saving the crew.

The church, as you would expect, was full to overflowing
with villagers, local dignitaries and officials, including the three
survivors. But many had to stand in the aisles, because of the
bodies occupying the pews. Though he had not arrived early,
John took a seat that someone offered him; he didn't realise
that he was already being talked of as a hero, for the way in
which he had saved the seamen. He gratefully accepted
because he was stiff with bruises and if he moved too

carelessly his ribs hurt. He had had a very uncomfortable night, with little sleep. Every movement caused him pain, and he relived every moment of the harrowing ordeal with his mind in turmoil. He had a tremendous bruise on his cheek, and the yellow and purple colouration threatened to spread towards his eye. He sat down carefully.

The Coroner opened the proceedings by saying what a terrible tragedy it was that was to be the subject of the inquiry. He expressed his commiserations for those who had suffered, and for the distress their families and relatives would have to endure. He then went on to explain that he would ask for details of the movement of the ship in the days and hours before it was wrecked, in order to see whether any blame was to be attributed. He would then ask for identification of the bodies and details of their next of kin, should any be known. He would leave it to the Receiver of Wrecks to determine whether any part of the wreck and its cargo was salvable, and to identify goods or materials recovered to determine ownership.

He called on the second mate, James Harris, being the only surviving officer, to describe the events leading up to the wrecking. The poor man was badly injured, and was allowed to remain seated during his testimony. Even though he had received a blow to the head, he remembered well the Captain's instructions regarding their courses to be steered and believed positions. Even though he had not been on duty the whole time, he was aware from the ship's log of what transpired during other watches; unfortunately, the log had not been recovered. His voice was strong, but rather hesitant as he relived the trauma of the last few days, searching his memory for the details. Everyone hung on his every word, as it was the first they knew of the actions in the time preceding the wreck; the account written above was extracted from what he stated.

When he had finished, the other survivors were asked whether they had anything to add. William Byrne said that he thought he probably could almost have leapt from the ship onto the beach had it not been for the waves dashing over the ship and reaching so far up the beach. John Thompson still looked extremely ill, and had to be carried to the church to take part in the inquest. He had his eyes closed a lot of the time, but nodded his head in agreement when the other survivors were warm in their commendation of the Captain. They stated he was highly respected as a seaman, and they considered he did all he could under the circumstances. The Coroner concluded that there was no blame to be attached to any of the officers or crew, and that the wreck was an 'Act of God'.

He then moved on to the identification of the bodies. A total of twenty bodies had at that time been retrieved, some were already lying in coffins, but many were not, as the carpenters were still making them. One by one the bodies were uncovered and were identified and confirmed by the three survivors. The injuries sustained were terrible to behold, and it was apparent that drowning had probably not been the ultimate fate of most; many must have died instantly when the ship struck and they were violently thrown against the woodwork. They were dreadfully mangled, with broken limbs and awful wounds caused by splintered timber, together with contusions and rope burns resulting from being tangled in the rigging and the shrouds.

The Captain, Samuel Walker, and the Chief Mate, William Steward, were both recognisable by the remnants of the uniforms about their bodies. Lieutenant Shore seemed to have a smile of eternal peace on his face, and the appearance of one of his daughters wrenched the hearts of everyone with her plump and innocent face. She was aged only three or four and was still dressed in a night gown and night cap. This was surprising considering the nakedness of many of the other corpses. The appearance of Mrs. Shore and the other three daughters wrenched the hearts of all present.

Ann Pemberton, the Creole daughter of Walter Pemberton, could be distinguished from the Shore girls by her pale brown skin. However, the body of the coloured steward, James Paris, was obvious and needed no identification, as he was the only coloured man on board.

The list went on. The carpenter could only be named by his surname, Hisee, no one knowing his Christian name. But it was known that he came from London, as did Joseph Hall, the cook. Both seamen James Penny and Edward Rush came from Portsmouth, and Edmund Cousins came from Felpham, Thomas Johnson, from Deptford, and William Sherlock from Deal. It was not known where the homes of Charles Stratton, Robert Smith, or John Graham were. This was significant because otherwise it would be difficult to know where to search for their next of kin in the absence of a copy of the Ship's Articles, which they would have signed at the start of the voyage.

For each body the Coroner recorded the verdict of 'Accidental Death'. But there were still seven bodies to be found. All but one were recovered the following day. The last body, however, did not come ashore at Blackgang. Miss Gourlay, by a freak of the tides and winds, was eventually found swept up on the beach at the foot of her father's garden at Southsea.

It was clear that the inquest was about to be terminated when Lieutenant Bulley rose to his feet with an apology. 'Sir! With your permission! I would like to propose it be recorded that the rescues were carried out by a local man, John Wheeler. He has to be commended for his utmost bravery and courage in the face of the most terrible conditions.' He sat down to a chorus of approval from the whole church.

John felt an immense pride at being recognised in this way, and could feel the blood rushing to his cheeks. Yet, he was also embarrassed because he felt that he hadn't done anything any other human being wouldn't have done in the same circumstances.

The Coroner cleared his throat, and said, 'Thank you, Lieutenant, for reminding me. I was intending to say just that, myself.' Then he looked directly at John and said, 'Mr. Wheeler, your conduct has been exemplary. It will be recorded.' He looked around the church. 'And I must say the conduct of the inhabitants in general in attempting to save the passengers and crew, and assisting in the rescues and comforting the rescued exceeds all praise.' With that comment the inquiry was completed.

The proceedings continued under the Collector of Customs, as Receiver of Wrecks. He had walked out to the cliff and seen for himself the chaos on the beach. For miles in both directions the shingle was covered in wood fragments, splinters and barrel staves, broken planks and timbers, ropes, cordage, sails, remnants of cabin furniture, clothes, and pieces of the cargo. Not a whole plank or spar was to be seen. Even the mainmast was in three sections. There was little sign of the ship itself, only a few ribs sticking out of the beach, and a length of the keel with some of the bottom timbers still attached. The rest was buried deep in the shingle.

He asked what of value, if anything, had been salvaged from the wreck.

Lieutenant Bulley, as the responsible officer, stood. 'The only cargo found, Sir, was seven puncheons of rum, but only one of those was full. The others were largely run out. There were three turtles, a small quantity of arrowroot, and a few coconuts. There is a little cabin furniture and clothing. All the rest has been dashed to pieces or carried away to sea.'

'Thank you, Lieutenant.' He looked around the church. 'The ship must be declared a total wreck. You are welcome to take away any of the wreckage that might be of use. But should any valuables be found, they must be declared, as they are still the property of the passenger's next of kin, or of the insurers. To not declare any such valuables may result in criminal proceedings.'

In actual fact, many of the ship's timbers were carried away and used as building materials. Some were used in the White Mouse Inn, subsequently renamed 'The Clarendon', and also in the building of the Clarendon Hotel in Shanklin.

A couple of days later, when all of the coffins were made, the mass funeral could be carried out. Meanwhile, the sexton and many local helpers had dug a long line of graves close against the north-west wall of the churchyard. Families of some of the passengers and seamen came from afar to say their last goodbyes to their lost ones. The village was in mourning and all of the houses were decked in black. The church was again full to overflowing, and the villagers assembled in a very sombre mood. It was not possible for them to celebrate lives successfully fulfilled. But they were determined to honour the dead and mourn their passing, with regret that many of them had not even reached their prime.

According to the parish register a total of eighteen souls were buried. However, the Shore family was not interred at Chale. They were taken to Newport and the funeral of the four girls, their father and mother was held at St. Thomas's Church, where they were given a military funeral attended by representatives of the 14th Regiment.

Following the Lieutenant's assistance with the rescues, and his outburst at the inquest, the relationship between the Wheeler and Bulley families vastly improved. The two Johns realised they had much more in common than they had differences. Despite the difference in birth, upbringing and class, they had learned to respect each other. They became firm friends, and Sarah drew great joy from the Wheeler children, to the extent that the Bulleys became god-parents to the Wheelers' son, John, born in 1837.

The two men worked amicably with each other. They were still rivals, but friendly rivals, both leading the efforts to save lives from the sea. John gave up smuggling; he felt the risks were too great. He concentrated on fishing and bringing up his sons in his image, together with a certain amount of crewing in the yacht racing at Cowes which still gave him great pleasure.

* * * * *

Even though there were several hundred wrecks a year around the British Isles, the wreck of the *Clarendon*, and the awful loss of life, led to an outcry for better lighthouses and warning lights around the coast. This was added to by the loss of the *Marlborough*, another large merchant vessel, on the same dreadful night, at Torbay, with the loss of Captain Rutt and the whole crew. The appeals for improvement led to Trinity House starting work on a low-level lighthouse on St. Catherine's Point. This was commenced in 1837, and completed in 1840, to become for a time the most powerful lighthouse in the world. Though it did not entirely prevent wrecks on the Back of the Wight, it must have at least saved many lives.

Only a few months later, in February of 1837, John Wheeler repeated his rescue from the beach. He again saved three of the crew of the French lugger *Jean Marie* by the same means – at the end of a rope. For this feat he received the silver medal from the Royal National Lifeboat Institution.

To show that human characteristics and values can be inherited or learnt, the tale of the Wheeler family went on further. During a fearful gale on 1st November 1859, the *Lelia* of London bringing a cargo of sponges and other tropical produce from the West Indies went ashore between Blackgang and Rocken End. Through the gallantry of Frederick Wheeler, who was let down over the cliffs by a rope, all of the crew of seven were rescued with the exception of one poor fellow who had been disabled by the fall of a mast. The coast for many days afterwards was strewn with sponges, an unusual harvest. Frederick was born in 1843, the second son of John Wheeler, which made him sixteen years old at the time.

Typical of families in the Victorian era, John and Frances Wheeler had a large number of children born at regular intervals. Their son John was born in 1837, and Edith was born in 1840. Then Frederick (Freddie) was born in 1843, Seline in 1846, and Ellen in 1849.

Charlotte died in January 1852, aged nineteen years, and Emily died in June 1852, aged seventeen years.

John Wheeler died in 1886, and his son John died in 1889. Frances died in 1891.

******

There is no record of the Bulleys having any children. Nevertheless, John Bulley had a very distinguished career at Atherfield, from which they must have derived much satisfaction, pride and fulfilment. On 10th January 1838 he rescued nine men from the Norwegian brig *Enigheden* and a further nine on 4th March 1841 from the ship *Castor*, both wrecked at Atherfield. For both of these rescues he received silver medals.

Further to that, Bulley received a gold medal for leading the rescue of eleven men from the brig *George* on 8th February 1843. The ship bound for Grenada had struck Atherfield Ledge and the Captain and Mate were swept away. The Lieutenant organised a rocket crew, shot a line out to the vessel along which a boat was pulled to evacuate the rest of the crew.

Also on 10th February 1848 he led the rescue of all fifteen men from the ship *Lianrumney*, which drove onto the same ledge. Sadly, this was after two local fishermen had put out in one of their boats to effect a rescue, only to become overwhelmed and drowned. For this John Bulley received a bar to the gold medal.

* * * * * *

After leaving the Island under a cloud, life was obviously still eventful for Josiah Dornford in his new station at Worth, near Deal, in Kent. On 23rd December 1839 it is reported that he was attacked by a man with a loaded pistol who fired it at him. The man, William Ruck, was also in the Customs service. Dornford had sent him to Sandwich with some business. Ruck was very late returning and, as he couldn't explain his tardiness, Dornford told him he would report him to a senior officer. Upon this, Ruck drew a pistol from his belt and said, 'Will you,' and fired at him. The ball missed Dornford, but hit another man named Vallance, who was standing behind him, in the thigh. Ruck was found guilty and imprisoned. Dornford's eldest son, Josiah James, was promoted Lieutenant, R.N. in 1842, and served off Africa and in the West Indies. Dornford died sometime in the early 1850s at the Royal Hospital, Greenwich.

In 1846 the government, under Sir Robert Peel, repealed the Corn Laws and the price of corn progressively decreased, thereby improving the lot of the common man. The incentive behind smuggling then started to decrease.

In 1856 control of the Coastguard was transferred to the Admiralty, following the Crimean War when the Coastguard had successfully functioned as a reserve for the Royal Navy. After that they progressively took over responsibility for assisting vessels in distress, taking charge of wrecks and participating in the lifeboat service. The anonymous pleas of Numa as revealed in this book therefore were finally answered.

Eventually, in 1860 volunteer pulling lifeboats were established at Brighstone and Brook, and thirty years later a third at Atherfield. These were crewed by local fishermen and longshoremen, and saved many lives until the last of them, at Brook, finally closed in 1937. However, wrecks still occur on the Back of the Wight.